Run, Alex, Run

Exploits of a Passionate Man

By

Alberto Arcia

KDP

This book is a work of fiction. The characters are fictional. The storyline is strictly a product of the author's vivid imagination. Any resemblance to actual persons, living or dead is entirely coincidental.

Copyright May 2020 - Alberto Arcia
Published by KDP
www.albertoarcia.com

I dedicate this novel to my kid sister, Monica, who chose to remain in Panama. You have Dad's looks, and inherited Mom's unique sense of opinion. Like her, you wear your heart on your sleeve. You both like to quarrel.

You have your sister's inner strength; an enviable trait which serves you well. I do love you, please know that. And in my own peculiar manner I have decided to test the limits of your precarious sense of humor. This amusing, and socially incorrect story, "Run, Alex, Run..." is not about you. I wrote it *for* you.

ALBERTO ARCIA
Acknowledgments

A Hearty thanks to my friend, Paul Bussard for his editorial help, and storyline counsel.

A Special thanks to my good friend and neighbor, Kenneth Hooper, for planting in me (years ago) the idea for the story. But more important, his incessant request that I create and give Alex Perez a feisty kid sister, worked out very well. The banter between the two siblings is wonderful. Deni's unique character provided the momentum necessary to take this long, humorous, socially incorrect series into a final resting place. It also allowed me to set Deni up to take over Alex's leading role.

With Love to my beautiful wife of twenty-seven years, Betsy Burton-Taylor Arcia. Your beauty keeps me home, and your steadfast support keeps me writing.

Thanks to my friend, Philip Mintz. Your ability to laugh out loud at my Alex novels gave my comedic effort the confidence necessary to keep the madness going. You are my biggest Alex fan, and I love you for it.

Thanks again to Robyn Elaine for her creative work on the Alex Perez covers. Your insight and artwork always impresses me.

In Memory of Mike Wells

Your smiling face, laughter, and happy-go-lucky attitude will be missed. I'm sorry you left us so early. We will keep an eye on Sheila for you.

From the Author

Run Alex, Run is my thirteenth book. It's the sixth in the series about the life and times of Alex Perez – a man burdened with a desire for the female form.

Even though I wrote it in 2020, it's the sequel to the hilarious, **"An Ill Wind that blows no Good."** For those of you who have not yet read **An Ill Wind**, I'm including a few pertinent chapters to bring you up to speed. If you already read it, go on to chapter one.

NOTE: I hope you have enjoyed reading these stories as much as I have relished writing them. But in life, all things, good or bad, must eventually come to a conclusion. At the end of this story, the Grim Reaper finally catches up to Alex, and removes him from a place where he has caused more bad than good. Alex is taken to the afterlife where God, not happy to see him show up at the Pearly Gates Brothel and Rum Bar, orders Saint Peter to send him to walk the long road to nowhere, in the company of an unpleasant fellow. A suitable punishment for a man who spent his life having fun at the expense of others.

The manuscript I gave to my cover artist, Robyn Elaine, was the last one of the series. Her cover captured the finality of a Panamanian scoundrel who spent most of his life on the road, running.

Fortunately, sober heads prevailed. My writing buds, Paul and Philip talked me out of killing the scoundrel. Their reasoning was: as long as you can keep the laughs going, why stop the series. I relented, and rewrote the final chapter.

An Ill Wind that Blows no Good

(Revisited)

Chapter Thirty One

Vehicle to Pleasure

I awoke and found myself in a hospital. My right leg was in a cast, and bandages covered half my body. A good looking nurse walked over to me.

"*Buenos Dias, Señor Pérez. Cómo te sientes?*"

"*Mucho mejor, gracias*. How did I get here?"

She smiled and whispered. "A rough looking man dropped you off. He said you had been in an airplane accident."

A person that looked like a doctor came over and dismissed the nurse. He looked at me with a critical eye.

"Are you feeling better?"

"Yes, thank you for asking. Tell me, Doc, how bad am I hurt?"

"You have scratches and cuts covering most of your body. You lost a measure of blood, and your right leg is broken. A man claiming to be a fisherman from the U.S. brought you to us. Before he left, he said you were in an airplane accident. Is that true?"

"Are you a policeman or a doctor?"

"You are in a hospital in Nuevo Padilla. My name is Hankamon Switzer. I'm the doctor here. Tell me, were you in an airplane accident?"

"If you must know, yes, I was."

"Are you an American?"

"Do I sound like an American?"

He frowned. "Your stay here will be better if you can show some cooperation, respect, and gratitude."

"You have a slight accent, doc. Where are you from?"

"Where I'm from is not important. I'm a Mennonite. This is our hospital."

"No shit. I've never met a cultist before. Are you a friend or a foe?"

He looked at me with intensively curious eyes. "Don't play with me, Mister Pérez. Tell me, how many were on the plane that dove into Lake Guerrero?"

"Please call me Alex. No need for formalities. There were four of us. We are hunters returning from a trip in the mountains of Puebla. We were headed for home, but an electrical fire brought us down. Did any of my mates survive?"

"Were you transporting drugs?"

"No way! Don't insult me, Doc. I can't believe you

9

think I'm a drug runner. We were coming back from a hunting trip. Honest."

Without showing any facial expression, the medicine man placed his hand on my forehead, then on the side of my throat. "The fever broke. That's a good sign."

"Thanks, Doc, I appreciate you and your hospital for all you have done. How long have I been here?"

"Ten hours, but who's counting?"

"Do you have a telephone, Doc? I need to call a friend and tell her I'm okay."

"Yes, but it's out of order at the moment. Witnesses fishing in the lake said four parachutes left the plane before it crashed. The police found only three of them. The owners were nowhere around. If you were not involved in anything illicit, why have your mates disappeared?"

"Do the *federales* know I'm here?"

"Not yet, but I expect them soon. Are you concerned?"

I glared at him. "Listen, Doc, I'm an American, and this is Mexico. Yes, you can say I'm concerned. Getting involved with the judicial system of this country is no walk in the park. It can be a costly affair, especially for foreigners."

The doctor called the nurse back, "*Maria, dale un baño y cámbiale las gazas.*"

She looked me over, smiled, and they both left.

Do I escape now or after she gives me a bath and changes the bandages? Then I looked at the cast on my leg. *Oh, no. I'm stuck here. What do I tell the cops when they come?*

The nurse returned with a sponge, soap, towel, and a wash basin. John Henry started to give me a tingle. *Good*

10

boy, you're not hurt.

"*Date la vuelta,*" she said. "*Voy a comenzar con las nalgas.*"

She helped me turn on my stomach, unlaced the back of my gown and began to wash my buttocks.

"*Señora—*"

"I speak English. You don't have to talk to me in Spanish. I am not *a señora.* I'm a *señorita.*"

"And a beautiful one too," I said.

"Gracias, you are a handsome man yourself. Tell me, Señor Pérez, besides being a hunter, what else do you do for a living?"

"Your soft hands are touching my bare ass. Please no formality. Call me Alex. I'm a writer."

"It's a nice ass too," she said, as she scrubbed me with a wash cloth. "What kind of a writer?"

"I specialize in fictional memoirs."

She laughed. "Can you explain what that is?"

"I tell true stories with a lot of lies in them."

She laughed again. "You are published, yes?"

"Yes, Maria, a publishing company from Houston called Arte Publico Press published my first novel."

"Do you have more than one out?"

"Yes I do. Three as a matter of fact."

She stopped talking and concentrated on her task. The cloth bath felt good. The way she scrubbed me, slow and easy, gave rise to the notion that here was a person that might be willing to help me escape from the law. *She seems to like writers. Maybe I can work that angle.*

"Maria, if I turn on my back, will you wash my dirty penis or are you too shy for such labor?"

11

She laughed and slapped by buttocks. "No, I'm not shy, but this is not the place to play fun games. I will wash your back, your nice looking ass, your good leg, chest, shoulders, stomach, neck, and arms. You must wash your manhood yourself."

Bummer. "What is your full name?"

"Maria Contreras. I'm from Mexico City."

"Where is the doctor from? He seems to have an accent. And, what on earth is a Mennonite, exactly?"

"He's from Corazal. That's in Belize. You can ask him that yourself. He'll tell you. He loves to talk about Mennonites. Your driver's license says you're from Texas. I had a boyfriend from Texas once."

"Well, Maria Contreras, your beauty forces me to confess something."

She raised an eyebrow, but never missed a beat from her scrubbing. I realized the woman was not washing me, she was feeling me up. *Okay, she's a good mark. This is it. Don't blow it.* I took in a breath, yet before I could hit her with a good line, she jumped into the frying pan all by herself.

"What kind of secret does a handsome man from Texas carry? Will I like it? Will it pleasure me? Or, will the knowledge of it harm me?"

She slipped the wash cloth between my buttocks, and I gasped. Then a boner developed. *Man, I have to turn over otherwise John Henry is going to injure himself.* "No, the secret will not harm you, yet if handled correctly, it can please and pleasure you."

"I'm all ears. Please tell me your secret."

"First you must turn me over. I'm in some discomfort."

Maria helped me lay on my back. Startled, she inhaled and stood there mesmerized.

"Is that the secret?" she said, pointing at John Henry.

"No," I replied. "He's but a vehicle to pleasure. The secret has to do with the man that dropped me off here. He will come back and take me away. He's a Texas Ranger. I'm an outlaw, just like Jesse James. But instead of robbing banks, I write exposes about prominent politicians. The other two guys on the plane were also policemen. They were taking me to an American jail. I don't want to leave Mexico. Do you have a jail in this town? I'd rather stay here. If I do, maybe you can come visit me on Sundays."

Maria nodded but would not take her eyes off John Henry. He was doing me proud. Pretty soon two other nurses came by and joined in the admiration ritual.

"*Dame el trapo*," said one of the new nurses to Maria. "*Quiero limpiar ese pingón.*"

"*No*," said the other one. "*Dámelo a mí, yo quiero tocar ese tronco.*"

In the middle of the tug of war for the washing cloth, the doctor returned. He had a pair of crutches with him.

"Well, I see you're feeling much better. Let's see if we can change the direction of the blood flow and get you walking."

Damn the bad luck. So close yet so far. I was hoping the admiration of my manhood by the other two nurses would be enticing enough to make Maria territorial, but that didn't happen. What did happen was a male nurse assistant named Mauricio showed up. He grabbed me, put his arms around my chest, pulled me off the bed, and forced me to walk.

13

ALBERTO ARCIA

"Therapy," said the doctor. "Four times a day, for the next three days."

As I walked away in the embrace of the therapy guy, I heard Maria say, "Doctor Switzer, can I have a word with you, in private?"

"Can it wait?"

"No. It's important we talk now."

Chapter Thirty Two

A Mennonite

The following day, Doctor Hankamon Switzer came to see me. I was hoping Maria had put in a good word and seeded the notion of keeping me away from the federales. I needed the white Belizean man to be willing to help me avoid Mexican police trouble. Truth be told, I was up to my ass in concerns. The fate of Ronson and Paco was still unknown to me. I heard the radio in the hall talk about the massacre of guards in charge of a chain gang of prisoners in the state of Guadalajara by unknown assailants. Some of the prisoners had been recaptured, but the reason and the whereabouts of the murderers were not clear yet. Clearly the local cops were not sure who the people on the plane that fell into the lake were, and when told one made it to the hospital they decided to err in favor of caution by setting up a contingency of police to guard me, the patient. That was the main reason Captain Luther Franklin hadn't raised his ugly head, too many cops around. It's been two days since the plane crash, and Lor and Marco were still on the run.

"Alex," said the doctor. "Detectives from Ciudad Victoria are scheduled to be here at two today. There is strong speculation that you could be involved in the shooting of the prison guards in Guadalajara. Were you involved?"

"I've done many bad things in my life, Doctor Switzer, but murder is not one of them. I wrote a bunch of lies about the Mayor of Houston, perjured myself in court, fled to Mexico City, and was captured by a Texas Ranger named Captain Luther Franklin. I'm sorry about the hunting trip lie, but I don't want to go to a Texas jail. Can you help me stay in Mexico?"

He looked me over. "Maria believes you, and so do I. The man who brought you here approached me on my way home last night. He told me he was a Texas lawman and you were wanted in Houston. He wants to take you back, but he wants to avoid dealing with the Mexican police. He offered to donate money to the hospital if I would help him. You don't seem to be the criminal type; he does. So, I'm not going to help him. Maybe I'll help you. Maria tells me you're a writer."

What do you know? Cap corroborated my lies. Feeling lucky, I replied, "Yes, I write memoirs, political leaflets, and revolutionary manifestos."

"Good. I'll make a deal with you, but it will cost you your freedom."

My heart dropped. "Are you turning me over to the Federal police or to the local yokels?"

"Neither. What do you know about Mennonites?"

"I thought you guys were a cult."

"No, we are not a cult. We split up with the Amish and the Quakers. Maybe that is why you think we're cultists. We were once an important religious force in the Netherlands and in Germany. We are a Protestant group, direct descendants of the Christian Anabaptist movement.

Our leader and founder was a Swiss teacher named Menno Simons."

"You're holy rollers?"

He frowned. "You try my patience, Alex. We are a simple modest people, pacifists, conservative, and benevolent in nature."

"If your group was founded in Europe, how in hell did you guys end up in the Americas?

"Don't be an idiot, Alex. We have large gatherings all over the world. The biggest ones are in India, Canada, and the United States. But we are also in Belize, Mexico, and Argentina, to name but a few."

"How did you get here?"

"I was born in Germany, moved to Belize as a young man, and came here to help open this hospital."

"Okay, sorry for calling you a cultist. I'm a Catholic, and we're not too hip on other religions. So, how can you help me?"

He looked around, making sure no one could hear him. "I will help you escape, but for a price."

"I have a broken leg and don't have that kind of money," I said, rather put out at the suggestion.

"No money is required. The leg will not be a problem unless you have an interest in dancing soon. Your writing talents will suffice as payback. There's a man who has a story to tell, someone dear to me and Maria. I will help you escape incarceration, but only if you promise to give up one year of your life for a cause. Will you do it?"

Does a bear shit in the woods? "You can bet your bottom dollar I'll do it. What cause am I going to support?"

"The Mennonite cause; it's in danger here in Mexico."

17

ALBERTO ARCIA

"All I have to do to be saved from the Mexican cops is promise to support your cause for one year. Is that all?"

"Yes."

"No ankle bracelet or guard to shadow me?"

"No, your word is good enough for me. Maria will accompany you to your destination, but she will not remain. Where you are going you don't need a woman. The beauty of the place will capture your heart. You may never want to leave it."

I raised an eyebrow. "Listen, Doc, I've never seen a place that could surpass the beauty of the naked female form."

He laughed. "Well, you are in for a treat. So, we have a deal then?"

"Yes, I already said so. When and how do I escape?"

"Escaping will be easy, but you must do it before the detectives arrive. I will tell them that somehow you produced a gun and got away. I will tell them that before you escaped you were delirious, and you talked about the massacre in Guadalajara. Where Maria is going to take you, a *guero* like you will stand out. There will be no need to guard you because white men are few there. You will be in an indigenous community. It would be prudent for you to remain within our compound."

What do you know? Sanctuary in an Indian religious compound. I hope I don't have to kneel and pray every day.
"Where am I going?"

"To a village called San Nicolas, in the Sierra Chiquita Mountains."

"When are we leaving?"

"As soon as Mauricio shows up with the ropes and you tie us up."

18

"Maria told me there are cops outside. How am I going to get by them?"

At noon there will be fewer. Here is a gun; I hope you don't have to use it. Maria will show you out via a secret tunnel. When we built this place, it felt prudent to design two safe ways out. For your sake, we will have to divulge one. If you fail to reach San Nicolas safely, Maria will accuse you of kidnapping her."

Oh, God, this is getting worse by the minute. "If I get caught, the Mexican judges are going to throw me in jail for life!"

"Yes, they will, but only after the police have given you a good beating. They don't take the murdering of their own by foreigners too kindly. Good fortune and God's speed."

What an asshole. Why do these things happen to me?

Chapter Thirty Three

John Henry

The escape worked as planned. The guards never caught on, and it was easy to imagine how furious the detectives were going to be with Dr. Switzer when he told them about the hidden passage within the hospital walls.

The tunnel came out under a livery stable a half-block away. An old Ford flatbed truck with a load of manure was waiting for us. There were also clothes for me, a bottle of rum, and a sombrero. Maria helped me get my cast into a large pair of pants. I complained about it being too hot for a long sleeved shirt, but she insisted I wear it.

"It will help hide your cuts. Roll the sleeves a little if you like, but not too much."

She helped me climb into the truck, slid behind the wheel, and we took off.

"You better start drinking," she said. "Women don't drive men around in Mexico unless they are drunk."

I laughed. "Here's to my new-found friend," I said, and chugged a couple of swallows. "Tell me, Maria, how much of a *señorita* are you?"

She laughed. "You want to know if I'm a virgin."

"Yes, my curiosity and sexual appetite demands it."

She kept her eyes on the road, yet the smile on her face gave the answer away. Still, I needed to hear it, so I sat closer.

"Tell me. Maria, will you be nervous when I touch you?"

She veered off the road we were traveling and made a right turn onto a dirt road; then she stopped the truck and turned. I didn't know what to expect. *Is she mad at me?*

Her intentions soon surfaced, she came to me and pressed her mouth on mine. Her lips were moist and her tongue hungry.

Oh, my, a horny female. Thank you, God. Yet before I could plan a move, Maria began to unbuckle my trousers. She reached inside, grabbed John Henry, and brought him out. She continued to swab my tonsils with a frantic tongue, and to my delight, started moving Johnny up and down. Then, as quickly, before the moment came, she stopped kissing me, abandoned Johnny boy, and grabbed the steering wheel.

"What happened? I said, bewildered. "I thought we were going to do it? Why in heavens did you stop?"

"I just wanted to touch 'His Magnificence,'" she said, breathless. "You must be a proud man, but we cannot make love here."

"Are you heaping praise on John Henry?"

She was still flushed but managed a laugh anyway. "That is much too common a name for such a beautiful meat bone. Is there anything behind him, or are you just a pretty face?"

ALBERTO ARCIA

I grabbed her and pulled her to me.

She fought me. "Alex, *por favor,* I told you we cannot do it here. But I know a place. Drink some more; there's a police check point up ahead."

"Will they be trouble?"

"No, I know them," she said, and started the engine. We made it back to the main road and drove off. I had to control John Henry; he wanted action, bad. It took a few moments for my mental powers to overpower the physical attraction. With the 'Glorious One' under control, I drank more rum.

The road block appeared; it consisted of three cops, one car, and a stick between two five gallon gas cans. Maria eased off the gas and came to a stop. She unbuttoned the three top buttons of her blouse, messed up her hair, and placed her hand on my crotch. She removed it when one of the cops came to her window.

"*Buenos días, María.*"

"*Hola, Jorge,*" she replied. "*Como está Diana?*"

He looked at her open shirt and smiled. Her face was flushed with desire.

"*Diana está muy bien, gracias,*" said the cop. "*Quien es el tipo?*"

"*Un novio nuevo. Se llama Rory. Vamos a dejar esta mierda que cargo en la granja del viejo Bernardo.*"

Another cop came to my window. He stuck his head inside and looked around. Then he looked me over and grinned. Needing to know the reason for the amusement, I looked down. *Shit my pants are unbuttoned and the fly is open.*

"*Tenga cuidado, Maria,*" said the cop by my side, "*y pórtese bien.*"

22

"Gracias, Manuel. Saludos a tu mujer."

The cop named Jorge made a hand signal and the stick was removed. Breathing a sigh of relief, we continue on our way.

I slid closer and nuzzled her neck. "Maria, I see something big coming your way."

She turned off the roadway again and onto another dirt road. And, just as before, she grabbed me and swabbed my tonsils. Her hand plunged into my open fly. She caught John Henry before he could gather any height.

"What's the matter, pretty boy? You lose your desire for Maria?"

I unbuttoned her shirt the rest of the way, pulled those two small but delicious looking puppies out of their harness and tried to divert my kisses from her mouth to her breasts, but she stopped me.

"No, don't kiss them. It will make me hot and we can't do it here either. Let's go somewhere else."

"You mean to tell me you can't drive with one hand?"

She ignored my sarcasm and succeeded in bringing John Henry out. He had regained his posture. She groaned at the sight and buried her mouth on him.

Before I was able to lay my head back and enjoy the slurping, she quit, shoved him back inside, grabbed the steering wheel and started the engine.

"We need to leave," she said, panting.

"Why?" I said, pissed.

Maria didn't answer, instead, she turned the truck around, and we drove off.

Now, let me say that it is difficult for a man to think straight with no blood in his brain, but I could tell this female had a major issue. The notion there would be no sexual activity in the cards for me, crossed my mind.

Upset with her erratic behavior, I patted 'His Prominence' a couple of times, zipped up, crossed my arms and stared out the window.

"What's the matter, pretty boy, you mad at me?"

I refused to answer.

She reached out with her hand and touched my shoulder.

"Come on, Alex, don't be this way. You know I want you."

I looked at her. "No, I do not know any such thing. All I know is you like to tease, and that's not a good quality in a woman. Are you going to give me some or not?"

"I want to, but not in the truck."

I continued to stare out the window,

"Come on, Alex, pull 'His Greatness' out and let me look at it one more time. Maybe the sight will inspire me, and we can do it in Bernardo's barn."

This was a dilemma. The young woman was playing with me. *Do I follow along like an eager school boy, or do I hold fast and make her come to me.* It took me but a minute to come up with a course of action. I unzipped and brought John Henry out. He loved admiration.

She looked at him, groaned, and reached out for him. I became apprehensive, the speedometer had passed forty and Maria was driving with one eye on the road and the other one on Johnny.

A mischievous look appeared in both her eyes. The daringness caught my attention. Before I could react, she came down and lipped John Henry. I began to panic, the driver of the speeding truck had one hand on the steering wheel, and her mouth was trying to swallow John Henry.

I cringed and yelled, as she crashed the truck.

Chapter Thirty Four

Gonzo Brynn

I woke up inside a barn, lying on top of a pile of hay on a scratchy blanket, naked below the waist. There was a knot the size of a baseball on my forehead, and my broken leg hurt something awful. The memory of the accident came to me; in alarm, my hand reached down and grabbed Jonny Boy. He was okay. I thanked God that Maria didn't cut him in half with her teeth. Once the manhood passed inspection, my eyes went round checking the rest of the body. The leg was still in a cast, but nothing else seemed broken. I wondered where Maria had gone to and what had happened to the baggy pants I'd been wearing. They were great for concealing the bulky cast. *Why am I naked below the waist? Did María help herself to Johnny while I was unconscious?*

"How are you feeling?" said an unrecognizable voice coming from behind.

I turned my head and saw a middle-age, stocky man with shoulder length black hair and dark eyes staring at me.

"Where is Maria?" I wanted to know.

26

He spat on the ground. "The accident changed the plan. She will not be traveling with you anymore. Maria and Bernardo have gone to retrieve the truck. Hopefully they can get it back here before the police get involved. When word of the accident reached me, I came as soon as possible. It was a good thing I was in the vicinity. We need to leave now. Can I help you get up? You need to get on my ox cart."

"What happened to my pants?"

"Maria took them. She left a note telling me you look better without them. I fail to see what she meant by that comment. You look average."

"Hey, don't be throwing stones at me unless you have measured yourself. I certainly have."

"No doubt," said the stranger. "Let me see what I can do to help you."

He unbuckled his pants. I looked for a stick to strike the brazen man.

"By the way, my name is Gonzalez Brynn. Please call me Gonzo. I'm the man whose story you're supposed to write."

He removed his pants and threw them at me. "Put them on, we have to get going."

"If I wear your pants, what are you going to wear?"

"My boxer shorts will do fine for the moment. Let me help you up. You need to get them on. We have to get going; the road ahead is long for us."

He wasn't kidding. The getaway vehicle was a double-ox cart carrying a load of onions. It moved at a snail's pace. Oxen are known for their strength, not their speed. The only good thing about this slow moving cart was its ability to go cross-country. The chance of us running into cops while traversing these homemade dirt roads was not good. I looked at the dude. *Man, I can't believe this. I've been in some tight spots before, but this one takes the cake. I'm running from the law in an ox cart, wearing the driver's pants. This story will not have a good ending.*

I decided to engage the weirdo manning the reigns. "Where is my gun?"

He reached underneath the bench seat, pulled it out, and gave it to me. "Where you are going a gun is not needed."

"That may be so, but I'm not going to travel anywhere with a man wearing underpants. People may think I'm a *maricón.*"

He smiled. "Are you a *maricón*?"

"No, I'm no faggot. Are you?"

He smiled and spat. "No, I'm not. So it appears that we are safe from each other."

"That may be so, but I'm using this pistol to get you a proper pair of pants."

"Why don't you get yourself a pair and give me back mine?"

It didn't take long to come across a pair of pants. Up the road was a man who appeared to be my size walking next to a small horse which was carrying a load of plantains. The pace of the oxen was slow so it took a while to catch up to him.

He saw us coming and stopped, giving us the right of way. When we reached him he took off his sombrero and said, "*Buenas tardes, amigos.*"

I stood, pointed my gun, and said, "*Manos arriba. "Esto es un asalto. Dame tus pantalones.*"

The man dropped the horse's rope and raised his hands, but he seemed unsure as to my intentions.

"*Me vas a robar mis plátanos?*" he said, confused.

"This is going to be interesting," said Brynn, as he spat. "He thinks you want to rob him of his crop."

"Well, let's test his sense of humor.

"*No, yo no quiero tus pinche plátanos,*" I said, indignant at the assumption. "*Yo quiero tus pantalones.*"

He looked at me with disdain. "*Pero señor, usted ya tiene pantalones, porque quiere los míos?*"

"The man has a point," said Brynn. "He doesn't understand why you need his pants. You already have some."

I looked at the befuddled man and unbuckled the belt holding my pants, letting them fall to my ankles.

"*Los pantalones que tengo son de mi amigo, yo quiero los tuyos,*" I said.

Brynn stood up, showing his underpants. The man looked at my manhood with a wary eye. Grudgingly he removed his pants and threw them at me.

I could tell from the look in his eyes that he wasn't sure of our intentions. To my surprise, he was not wearing any underwear either.

With discomfort in his voice, he began to plead. "*No me pueden dejar aquí con la pinga al aire libre. Si me encuentra un maricón en camino, en esta condición me va a perjudicar.*"

"He is right, Gonzo," I said. "We can't leave him here with his willy hanging out. He may run into a pack of homos, and then he's done for. Give him your boxer shorts."

Brynn scowled at the suggestion, but understood my rationale. When he took off his shorts, the man screamed and ran away.

I yelled at him, *"Oye, no te vallas, se te olvidó tu pinche caballo!"*

The man didn't respond; he just kept on running. In no time at all he was out of sight. Brynn said something unintelligible, spat, and put his shorts and pants back on.

Carefully I climbed off and tied the horse to the back of the cart. Brynn gave me a disapproving look.

"You are stealing the man's horse."

"The hell I am. He left the plantains and horse behind. Therefore, they are fair game."

A kilometer or two up the road, I decided it was time to address the snake inside Brynn's shorts.

"What did you do to make your dick that big, put a graft on it?"

He laughed. "No, I'm part Irish and Mexican. Pepe comes from the Spanish side of the family tree. Envious, aren't you?"

There was nothing I could say that wouldn't show my resentfulness, so I kept quiet.

We trudged along, crossing fields and streams. Along the way, my thoughts turned to the task I was supposed to do to earn my freedom. Inquiries became necessary.

"Hey, Gonzo, what exactly is it you're trying to do that requires a writer?"

He spat. "I'm trying to make a name for myself by proposing some changes in my community and in the Catholic Church as well. Your job is to make me look good, and to make my message an endearing one. Are you up to the task?"

"I'm a writer, Gonz. I can turn you into a venerable person and make your cause sound like orders from God. But before I start, I need to know something about you. Who are you, really?"

"I'm an ex-communicated Catholic priest."

Oh, bite me, not another one. "Why were you thrown out? Was it because you don't like men?"

"Don't be a homophobe, Alex. Show the church some respect. My problem was I liked women…too much I'm afraid."

Don't we all? Listen, Gonz, I knew another ex-priest, his name was Humberto. He suffered from the same malady. I know about his fall from grace. Please explain yours."

"I had a church once. When the bishop found out I was fornicating with half the women in my congregation, he forced me out."

"Is that why you're holed-up in a place that has no women? Is this your penance?"

He spat again. "You been reading my mail, haven't you?"

"No, Doctor Switzer told me there were no women where I was going. Why is that?"

"Because I fornicate with every woman around me. I can't help myself, and neither can they. That obsession and ability is not good for the harmony of the community."

I looked at the guy with a new found admiration. *How about that? Brynn is a bird of a feather.* I couldn't wait to engage him in a womanizing competition. Even though Pepe was a tad bigger than John Henry, I had style and could hold my own very well.

ALBERTO ARCIA

"Tell me, Gonz, why is it that there are only men in the village of San Nicolas?"

"Because that is where I have my ministry. The women were relocated to the town of San Marcos, a few miles up the road. The married men come to San Nicolas to work the fields during the day, and they go home at night. The bachelors stay."

"How long has it been since you got some?" I wanted to know.

"Two days ago."

"I'm not talking about whacking off, Gonz."

"Neither am I, Alex. There's a nunnery in a nearby town called Santa Lucia. I deliver food to it on a regular basis."

I beamed with admiration. "Can I go with you on your next rounds?"

"No, once you have entered San Nicolas, you can never leave it. You have to remain there for one year. That is the agreement you made with Hankamon."

We finally reached the foothills of the Sierras, the ox cart began to slow down. Hell, broken leg and all, I could get off and walk faster. Being tired, I decided to take a nap.

I hadn't dozed off for very long when a shot rang out. Brynn pulled the cart to a stop, and a half-dozen men brandishing rifles came out of the bushes.

One of them yelled, "*Alto. Pongan las manos arriba.*"

"*Qué pasa aquí?*" asked Brynn. "*Somos Menonitas.*"

At first this situation didn't bother me too much. I figured Brynn, being a local Mennonite would be able to talk his way out of whatever these guys were after. Then my heart dropped. I noticed that one of the men in the group was the man whose pants I stole.

"*Ese es el hombre que me robo mis pantalones, mis plátanos, y mi caballo,*" he said, pointing at me.

"*Señor,*" said the main man. "*Bájese y venga con nosotros.*"

"*Quién diablos eres tú?*" I asked.

He smiled, showing a front tooth missing. "*Yo soy la ley.*"

Oh, God, the local sheriff is charging me with thievery. Now I'm done for.

Run, Alex, Run

Chapter One

María Contreras

The judge in a small out of the way town named La Esperanza gave me a one year sentence for my work as a bandit. I was lucky, it could have been worse, the man had been scandalized when he realized I had stolen another man's pants. He accused me of being a *maricón*, and told me they didn't care for that type of behavior round his neck of the woods. I felt a beating coming.

I was thrown into a small jailhouse. The walls were made out of stone, which told me there had to be a quarry around. The roof was made out of thatch. This told me they were not worried about an inmate escaping. The place couldn't have been bigger than seven hundred square feet. There were two cells at different ends of the building, a small office, and an inside bathroom. On the outside, there stood an outhouse painted in bright colors. Probably the guest's bathroom.

I had one of the cells, and my jailer named Manolo, a small, burly man with receding hair, slept in the other one. There was also a dog—a sort of mixed-breed bloodhound that seemed to be in the twilight of his life. I say this because the animal slept constantly. Yet when I questioned the dog's ability to chase and catch a one-legged fat man, Manolo insisted his hound, Cucho, could track better than any other jailhouse dog in the area.

Several days after my incarceration, Dr. Hankamon Switzer showed up. He vouched for my masculinity and asked the judge if it would be okay for him to bring me a woman for company when he made his rounds in the area. The judge agreed, feeling elated that I was just a bandit, not a faggot. The expected beating never came.

My new friend, Gonzalez Brynn, also came to vouch for me. He placed his team of oxen and his cart as collateral from me trying to escape. This being settled, I began to do my time in a simple but cozy jail.

Being in a foreign jailhouse was more common of an occurrence than I cared to admit. If my brain cells did not betray me, there was a short stint in Germany, a long one in Guatemala, one in Panama, a couple in Texas, and counting this one, three in Mexico.

One day, Hankamon arrived with María and a short legged woman with small breasts for my monthly comfort.

Disappointed, I whispered in his ear, "I don't want to sound ungrateful, Doc, but I'm not fond of short legged women with small tits. Next time please bring me one with long legs and big breasts."

ALBERTO ARCIA

Hankamon fixed his eyes on mine. "Alex, would you rather I bring you a blonde with blue eyes, or would one with dark hair and brown eyes suffice?"

I felt the sarcasm and decided to not push the envelope. "Yes, I'm good with the local color."

"How about her?" He pointed at María. "She seems to be interested."

I whispered in his ear. "If it's all the same to you, Doc, not María. She's not good for me."

He gave me a puzzled look. "Alex, she's a very good looking woman, and her body makes a happily married man like me look and want her."

"No doubt, Doc, you and half the valley. But I have my reasons. If it's all the same to you, no María for me."

He rolled his eyes. "As you wish."

Dr. Switzer told me and the jailer that the woman he brought was clean, but he wasn't sure about us. We had to go through an intrusive body examination. We were both pronounced healthy.

Afterwards, Hankamon left to do his rounds. María remained behind with my consort. The jailer came to me.

"Hey, Alex. Can I get a turn on her?"

"Before or after me?"

He was taken aback by my response. Not knowing what to say, and suspicious it may be a trick question, he remained tongue-tied.

"Listen, Manolo, if you bring me a bottle of rum and a pack of cigarettes, you can have her first."

"You want the rum and smokes before or after I have her?" He felt good about the repartee and grinned.

"After will be good. Now take her and enjoy yourself. I want to talk with María."

36

He grinned some more. "You want me to put her in the cell with you?"

"No, please don't let her in. I'd rather she stayed outside."

Manolo's facial expression changed. "You *are* a *maricón*, aren't you?"

María, who was listening, interjected. "No Manolo, he is not. What he is, is a *pendejo.*"

He laughed. "Yes, that is what he is for sure. No one has ever robbed a farmer round here. They have no money."

I shot him the finger. He laughed and left with the woman. María, swinging her hips seductively, approached my cell.

"Hola, Alex, you want to make love to me?"

I chuckled at the question. "María, you're outside and I'm inside. Regardless of our wants, the reality is cruel but obvious."

She gave me a mischievous smile. "Not necessarily, Alex. When there is a will, there is a way."

Feeling safe inside the cell, I dared her. "Well, show me a way."

She came closer, turned around and pulled her blue jeans down to her ankles, exposing an uncovered and enchanting derriere. When she squeezed her butt cheeks my heart skipped a beat. Now I was sorry I didn't allow Manolo to let her inside.

"Baby, bring that lovely ass closer. Let me give it proper appreciation."

She laughed and pressed it against the cell bars. I dropped to my knees and showered her buttocks with kisses.

ALBERTO ARCIA

First she giggled, then she moaned. "Alex, you
tantalize me. How bad do you want me?"

Forgetting who she was, I climbed into the stupid
bucket. "María, I want you more than anything else in this
world. Baby, give me some."

She giggled again, and continued to press her lovely
butt against the bars. I kept savoring it with my tongue and
lips, bringing my fever to a pitch.

"María," I said panting. "Since we have these bars
between us, how about if you let me take you from behind?"

"Oh, so you are a back door man, uh?"

"Back door, front door, side door. I'm your man.
Don't move that beautiful behind, I'm coming in."

She giggled some more and wiggled her ass in a
playful manner.

I removed my prison garb, which consisted of white
pajama pants, a t-shirt, and hollered, "Ready or not, here I
come."

I rushed John Henry in the direction required, but
before I could plunge him in, she moved her butt away just
enough to be out of my reach.

"Augh!" I screamed. "María, why do you treat me this
way?"

She turned around, pulled her pants up and gave me a
spiteful smirk. "Pepe would have reached my sweet *culo,* he
has the distance. Your Johnny boy is not long enough."

She laughed and gave me a wicked smirk. "Because
yours is smaller, you will have to work harder if you want
me."

With that hurtful statement, she left me feeling
flustered.

Manolo returned, He was sweaty and smelled bad.

"You can have your turn now. I'm done with her."

"No thanks. I'll pass on her."

He scowled. "I knew you were a *maricón*, Alex."

I shot him the bird. "Up yours, Manolo."

Disheartened, I sat on my bunk and wondered when Hankamon would return with another woman.

Several hours later, Gonzalez Brynn walked into the jailhouse and asked to see me. Manolo brought him over.

"Hola, Alex, how have you been?"

"Hey, Gonz, not doing so well. Can't seem to get laid."

"But I was told by Doctor Switzer that he brought you a girl?"

I gave him a rueful look and turned my back on him.

"Did he not bring you one?"

I turned his way. "Theoretically he brought me two. One was María, but she and I don't get along too well. The other Manolo took. I was not about to get his sloppy seconds. So, no, I did not get laid."

"Maybe I can do something about that. I'm going to visit a nunnery tomorrow morning, The Mother Superior is going to allow me to take several of her nuns to my farm so they can help me with a task. I can drop one off here for you. I'll wait until you're done with her."

I stared at the man. He either had gall or was pulling my leg. "Listen, Gonzo, I already told you I'm a catholic. I can't go around screwing nuns. It's a sin. Can you get me a protestant nun?"

It was his turn to stare at me. "Listen, Alex. The reason you are not getting laid is because you have too many rules, plus a bad handle on style. María has a thing for you. I know that because she has told me so. The trouble is you don't know how to handle her."

"Well, Gonz, let me take a seat on my bunk and you can give me some pointers."

He smiled and asked Manolo to bring him a stool. Once that had been done, he began to lecture me on how to bed women in general. I was galled at the notion he thought I couldn't score on my own.

"First, when Hankamon brings you a woman, you go in first. Let Manolo have seconds. Second, it's not a sin to screw a nun. They are God's brides. Unfortunately, they are human, and God is a spirit. He can't do it, and his priests do a poor job standing in for him. That is where I come in. I gratify them, they go back to the nunnery smiling and feeling refreshed. Then they do good work for another month or two. By satisfying them, you are giving God a helping hand."

I stared at him. The man had no shame.

"Alex, I did tell you I was an ex-catholic priest, didn't I?"

"Yes. You told me you were fired for bedding all the women in your congregation."

He gave out a loud sigh. "Alex, listening is not your thing, is it?"

I stared at him.

"Not all the women, only the ones needing tending too. It's our job as the Lord's Shepherds to tend to the needs of our flock."

I frowned.

He stopped speaking and looked at me. "You do know what I'm getting at, don't you?"

"Yes, you're telling me there are no protestant nuns around."

He smiled again. "Not close by. Want me to bring you a catholic one?"

He had me considering the offer, but more prodding was needed if I was going to cross a new line and screw one of God's brides. Needing to buy time, I changed the subject.

"Gonz, talk to me about María. She speaks in terms of being very familiar with Pepe. What's that about?"

"We are familiar with each other, but that flame has been dead for a long time. The trick with her is to show no interest. Everyone wants to enjoy her physical charms, so she plays hard to get. I didn't want her, so she came to me."

I glared at the cheeky man.

"Listen, Gonz, it's hard to be nonchalant when John Henry is popping out of my pants. He has a mind of his own. Telling him 'down boy, not yet,' does not work."

He laughed. "I believe you. María told me there were two things that she loved about you."

I grumbled, "I'm all ears."

"She said you were an intellectual, easy to talk with. And she said the prowess and independence of Johnny boy was impressive."

"What prowess? The woman has never experienced Johnny's abilities."

He stared at me. I waited for the shoe to drop.

"Don't you remember when I found you in Bernardo's barn you had no pants?"

"Are you telling me she helped herself?"

"Yes, she did. She said you were totally unconscious but Johnny boy was alive and well. She said any man whose joy stick worked independently from the mind was worth his weight in gold. You captivated her."

So, she did help herself. Did I enjoy it? Pissed, I changed the subject. "Are we going to work on your propaganda or talk about my sexual deprivation?"

Gonzo sighed again. "It's not propaganda, Alex, you are helping me prepare a revolutionary and religious manifesto. I want to change the status quo – give the women in the catholic corporate male culture more rights. I want to challenge the male dominance."

I winced at his statement. He was right, the male authority was hard to accept; women in the Church are not treated as equals. *Still, right or not, Gonz is a sassy fellow. Anyone who screws nuns should not be allowed to carry and wave a banner of liberation. So, why am I helping him?* The answer was clear. I was paying out a debt. Doctor Switzer helped me escape due to my promise to elevate Gonzo's cause. I was stuck.

While I was pondering the issue, a bolt of lightning hit me. Since I was obligated to do Gonz and Hankamon's bidding, God could not blame me if I joined in the sexual orgy at the local nunnery.

"I'm ready if you are, Alex."

"Yes, sorry for the delay, Gonz. Please bring me a nun."

He stared at me. I gave him an ear-to-ear smile.

"Alex, I was talking about our work on my manifesto."

I gulped. "Yeah, I'm on it, but if it's all the same to you, bring me one that is not wearing holy garb."

He sighed one more time. "Alex, they are all the same under the long dark skirt. Sweaty and bushy.

Chapter Two

Sister Amalia

Two days later, Gonzo appeared again. He brought me a pack of smokes, a watermelon, and a homely but nice-mannered woman. Her hair was short and her breast size was hard to discern in the baggy shirt. I did however appreciated the fact she was not wearing holy garb.

Manolo became excited, but I told him no, not this time around. Diffidently he let her into my cell.

The middle aged woman seemed nervous. I asked her to sit on the bed and she obliged, but remained quiet. Apparently conversation was needed to break the ice.

I grabbed her hand and gently gave it a loving squeeze. *"Cómo te llamas?"*

She smiled. *"Mi nombre es Amalia. Qué hiciste para quedar aquí?"*

Oh great, a game of twenty questions. "Nada malo. Tengo mala suerte."

Telling her I was not a bad man, just one short of luck seemed to do the trick. She stopped the inquisition and began to unbutton her loose blouse. To my surprise, her puppies were bigger than expected.

43

ALBERTO ARCIA

I looked in her eyes and asked her, *"Soy tu primer hombre?"*

She gave out a muffled laugh. *"No, tengo al padre Macías, al sacristán Olivo, y a Gonzalez. Él es mi favorito."*

I wanted some love badly, but became bothered over the fact my nun was promiscuous. My whole impression of who the nuns were took a hit. I was disappointed.

As a young boy living in Colon city, whenever I or my siblings became sick, the local nunnery would send one or two nuns over, and they would nurse us back to health. Had I known they loved to party, I might have tried to score.

"Tu nombre?" she asked.

"Soy Alex Perez"

I was about to ask something else when she laid on the bed and lifted her skirt, exposing the target.

I shivered at the prospect of finally getting laid. *"Puedo tocarte?"*

"Sí, por favor."

I reached down and touched it. *Yep, Gonz was right. It's bushy and sweaty.*

Sister Amalia closed her eyes and lifted her legs. She was ready to receive me. Her eagerness required attention. I crossed myself, and John Henry dove in.

 The love making made me a believer in the fact that these nuns suffered from the same itch as regular women. I felt vindicated. Someone had to scratch them, so I might as well join in the ritual.

From that day on, I looked forward to the nuns Gonz would drop off. It became a sort of religious quest. How many could I satisfy? Yet he brought me the same one every time. It appeared that Amalia had become enamored with me.

One day, Manolo, grim-faced, came to fetch me. "You are in big trouble, Alex." He opened the cell and we walked towards the office.

Inside was Doctor Hankamon Switzer; he had a serious look. Next to him was a priest who introduced himself as Padre Correa. By his side was the judge that gave me jail time. Behind him was María. She was teary eyed.

Oh, no, this is not going to be good. I tried to show the inquisition a good face. "Hey, the gang is all here." I said.

Maria came forth. She gave me a guileful smile, and rubbed a protruding belly. "Guess what Alex, we're going to be parents."

I glared at her. "No damn way. That baby can't be mine. I never touched you."

"That statement is not going to fly, Alex," said Hankamon. "Gonzalez Brynn told me that you and María had a sexual tryst in Bernardo's barn. Do you deny it?"

Oh, no. Now I'm doomed for sure. I knew bedding that nun was going to bring me trouble. God is upset and fixing to rain on my parade.

The priest and the judge had scowls on their faces. My next words had to be brilliant, otherwise I was screwed. *Here goes nothing.* "I didn't make love to her. She helped herself to me while I was unconscious."

"That's impossible," said Doctor Switzer. "In a state of total unconsciousness, there can be no erection."

"I'm not buying that statement, Doctor Hankamon. You need to believe me when I tell you that she took advantage of me while I was unconscious. I'm not responsible for her condition."

María started to cry. "You use me, and now you don't want me."

She turned towards the priest, "What am I to do now? I will have a baby out of wedlock. God will not bless him."

"I may have a solution," said the judge. He took the priest and the doctor to the side and had a conference.

Great, my welfare is being discussed by a hanging judge and his cohorts.

After the parley he approached me with a proposition. I waited for the other shoe to drop.

"Alex, you have five months left of your sentence. If you agree to marry María, I will let you out now."

I was about to tell the judge to stick that offer where the sun don't shine, when Hankamon closed the marriage deal.

"Alex, if you don't do the right thing, I will feel obligated to talk to the detectives from Ciudad Victoria."

That was it, I was going to be a husband and a father. "Okay, I'll marry María, but I need a dowry. I have no money or property, and both are needed to support a family."

"That's not an issue," said Doctor Switzer. "I will give you both, as a wedding present, a large plot of land so you can raise food for your family. It has a three room cement block cabin on it. "

I was about to complain that the offer fell short when María jumped in and offered me her life savings.

"Alex, I will give you ten thousand pesos. It's all I have. Will it be enough for you to marry me?"

I thought the offer over. Hell, I'm already married to Julia. If I tell them that, the marriage would not take place. Certainly the priest would not perform the ceremony, and the hanging judge would not commute my sentence. *Would Hankamon carry out his threat? Can I risk it? Domesticity and fatherhood versus a beating by the federales and a life in prison. How difficult can this decision be?*

"Okay, let's have a wedding, but I have a condition."

The scowl returned to all their faces.

"Hankamon, when the child is born, I need you to perform a paternity test to make sure it's mine. If it is not, then I want Padre Correa and the judge to dissolve the marriage. Deal?"

They looked at María, she nodded yes. They all agreed, and a wedding date was set. But I would not be released from jail until after the ceremony, which was okay with me, since Gonz had promised me he'd bring Sister Amalia over in the morning.

The holy woman liked me. It appeared that during our third lovemaking session, I had managed to unleash the tiger in her tank. She became insatiable, and to a horny man, it was a good match.

After the marriage contract, everyone left. Manolo, grinning from ear to ear escorted me to my cell.

"You did the right thing, Mister Alex. María will make you a good wife."

I nodded and sat on my bunk pondering things. Reluctantly I had to accept the fact that I was not only an immoral person, but also not a smart one. Due to those two things, plus a few others, I pondered my future. *How can I possibly be a good husband to María and a benefit to my incoming child?* It didn't take long for me to come to the obvious conclusion. I couldn't or wouldn't. It didn't matter.

ALBERTO ARCIA

They both would be better off without me in their lives. So, with that notion in mind, I began to plan my escape.

Chapter Three

The Old Gumshoe

Things being what they were, I decided to put off escaping for a while. There's no need to rush it; the plan had to be solid. If I blew it, there would surely be dire consequences.

My marriage to María turned out to be better than expected. Our three day honeymoon in a fishing cabin by Lake Guerrero went well.

Baby growing inside and all that that applied, she showed an appealing carnal hunger. We bounced the mattress every moment we were not fishing or eating. Her behavior emphasized my life's luck—most girls bang your brain off before they marry you. María was different, she screwed you afterwards.

After the banging and fishing fest, she returned to work at the hospital, and I proceeded to learn how to become a farmer. Truth be told, I was a happy camper.

Gonzo Brynn, realizing I knew nothing about husbandry, loaned me a young man named Mateo. He would come over on Tuesdays and Thursdays to give me a hand with chores, and that included erecting a fence, working the land, and planting a crop. Things I cared nothing about,

49

which was okay. Mateo did, and he worked his ass off for me.

One day, Gonzo arrived, driving his two-ox cart team. He had come to bring me half a dozen avocado saplings and wanted to read some more of the manifesto I was penning for him.

"How long will it take these trees to give fruit?" I wanted to know.

"In seven years you and María will be up to your necks in *aguacates*. There's a good market for them in Texas."

The answer floored me. *Seven years?* He must be sold on the idea I will be living here that long. *Geez, I must be looking comfortable.*

Since it was Mateo's day off, Gonz helped me plant them. Twenty feet apart so they could extend their branches.

One evening, while lying in bed with my wife, talking about things, she grabbed my hand and placed it on her growing belly. I became startled; the baby moved. Up to that point, the kid was just a growth in her belly. The movement made me have a 'come to Jesus' meeting with myself. The prospect of fatherhood both pleased and scared me. *Would I be a hands on father or an absent one?*

The more I thought about my present situation, the more conscious I became of the need to decide which way I would go. Certainly before the kid came out.

If my calculations were correct, he'd be out and crying in nine weeks. Would I run or stay? Regardless, it felt prudent to fine tune my escape plan. Just in case I decided to run.

The following week, two things happened that forced my hand. While out shopping in town with María, an unexpected, old friend showed up.

"Hello, Alex, you don't know how glad I am to see you."

"Kermit, what are you doing here?"

He smiled, removed his fedora, and wiped the sweat from his brow using a kerchief. "Your father-in-law hired me to locate you."

"Blanton? Why?"

"Your wife loves you and misses you."

"How did you find me? This is Nowhere-ville."

He sighed. "You forget that finding people is my business."

At that very moment, I knew my idyllic life here had come to an end. If he could find me, so could Captain Luther Franklyn or any astute Mexican detective.

I needed time to figure out how and when to leave, but first I had to ditch the old gumshoe, and certainly before my wife showed up and told him I had married again. I didn't want Kermit's opinion of me to suffer, and it would if he learned I had added bigamy to my list of misdeeds.

As I was pondering how to do it, María showed up. *Shit, this is going to be embarrassing. I hope Kermit has the sense to play along.*

"*Hola,* Alex, who is your American friend?"

He removed his hat and extended his hand. "Hello, I'm Kermit Laarssen, owner of a company in Houston called "Private Eyes for You.""

Maria showed a lack of understanding, so I opened my mouth and inserted my boot in it.

ALBERTO ARCIA

"He's a sleuth, María. A detective."

Sensing something was not right, she grabbed my arm. Then, with a defiant tone, she let the cat-out-of-the-bag. "I'm his wife. What are you doing here? What do you want with him?"

Before Kermit opened his mouth and sold me out, I interfered. "Listen Maria, go on home. I need to talk with him for a few minutes, alone."

She started to buck me, but I insisted. "Be a good wife and go home. Preparer a good supper, Kermit will join us for dinner."

She looked at the investigator with concern, but I assured her all was well. She gave me a kiss and rubbed her belly so Kermit would take notice.

"The baby and I will be waiting for both of you. I'm cooking *fajitas de res, yucca, arroz, frijoles, y plátanos.* We will have homemade corn *tortillas too,* and drink good Mexican *cerveza* with our dinner."

Kermit's stomach growled, giving her a sense there would be no trouble. She left us.

The old gumshoe looked at me with those disapproving eyes of his. "Does she know you are married already?"

"Of course not. And before you start in on me about my lack of moral behavior, let's go have a tequila at the cantina. We need to chat about things."

Kermit placed his hat back on his head. "I don't drink tequila, but I could use a cold beer."

We walked to Las Palmas cantina, sat at a corner table, and ordered a beer and two tequila shots. When they came, Kermit raised his beer.

"Here's to you Alex."

I raised my shot glass. "Here's to you, Kermit."

Once the formalities were dispensed with, he gave me his annoying serious look again and leaned my way. "Listen Alex, Blanton has offered me a large bonus if I bring you back in one piece."

I was about to interject, but he raised his hand, stopping me. "I don't know if you realize what kind of trouble you're in, but I'm thinking you do, which is why you have married again and live in these backwoods."

I gulped.

"I thought so. Now drink the other tequila because you're going to need it."

I drank it and waited for the bad news.

Kermit leaned my way again. "Please listen to me. Ronson is in jail."

That statement floored me. "What?"

"That asshole, Franklyn, shot him and left him behind. He's been charged with the murder of the prison guards the man-hunter shot."

I was too dumbfounded to speak. Now my troubles seemed trivial. I leaned his way. "Is he all right?"

"No. I went to see him and you wouldn't recognize him. He's lost a lot of weight, and his body shows signs of constant beatings."

"So, what's the plan? What are we going to do about it?"

Kermit leaned back on his chair and wiped the sweat off his brow with the kerchief.

"I'm relieved your sense of loyalty is still strong, Alex, because it's going to be tested. Breaking him out will be extremely difficult, the Mexican authorities have him sequestered in a maximum security prison."

I whispered, "Kermit, I'm going to be a father."

He gave me an acrimonious look. "Is that going to be a problem?"

I swallowed hard. Ronson was my mate. A choice had to be made: stay here and raise a kid, or go and recue my Swiss friend. *What to do?*

"Listen, Kermit, María can raise the boy without me. You have any money?"

Kermit's eyes bugged out. He hated to part with money. It took him a minute to answer, but when he did, my fate was sealed.

"Blanton gave me a working budget, but we need every penny to ransom Ronson."

I became upset. "No way can I leave my wife alone with a baby and no money."

Kermit buried his steely eyes on mine. "Listen to me, Alex. Blanton gave me twenty-five thousand dollars to find you, with a stipend of another ten thousand when I brought you back, and a bonus of an additional ten if you came back before the year ended. It's mid-September."

"How much do you think it's going to cost us to bribe Ronson's keepers?"

"Probably around one hundred thousand, and only if we give them another prisoner in exchange."

The bottle came, I poured a shot, and drank it down.

"Kermit, you're joshing me, aren't you?"

He stared at me, but remained quiet.

Downhearted, I ask him a necessary but worrisome question. "Who are we going to feed to the Federales? Not me, I hope."

"No, not you, but thanks for considering it. We're giving them the actual shooter. They will release Ronson for money and the man who gunned down their cops. I was able to convince the man in charge that Ronson was an accomplice but did not kill anyone."

"When do we leave?"

"Right now."

When Paco entered the cantina, I knew María was going to raise my son alone and with no money.

Paco came to the table, said hello, sat, and grabbed the bottle of tequila. "We need to leave guys, the jeep is outside."

Angry, I complained. "But I want to say goodbye to María."

Kermit paid the bill, reached into his back pocket, and brought out a crumpled note pad. He gave me his pen. "Write a short note and give it to the bar boy. We need to leave."

I wrote that I loved her and was sorry I wouldn't be there to help her with the baby. I don't know why I penned the 'I love you' part because I didn't really love her. Mostly, I liked her. It just felt necessary to write it.

We walked outside, and there was Miguel manning the wheel. He kept revving the engine, signaling it was time to go.

"Hello, Alex," he said. "Long time no see."

I shot him the finger and climbed in the back seat with Paco. As we were pulling out of Nuevo Padilla, I saw Mateo, the boy who helped me work the farm. He was standing outside a feed store. He waved at me. I did not wave back.

"Okay, Alex," said Kermit, "hear me out. I don't want any misunderstanding between us. We are all doing pro-bono work, and that includes you."

"How are you planning to capture Captain Luther Franklyn? Do you know where he is?"

"Yes, and here how this is going to go down. We will deliver the shooters, plus one hundred thousand dollars to a man in Mexico City. He will arrange Ronson's release."

"Shooters? As in two?"

"Yes. We already have Lor and know where to grab Franklyn."

"Yeah, right," I said with a smirk. "Like the captain will fall for a ruse."

"Don't be a jerk, Alex," said Paco. "It's a good plan."

"Right, Paco, and how do we capture the captain?"

"We put out the right bait," said Miguel.

Oh, God, so that's why they brought me along. "No way. I'm not going to be the bait. You can't do that to me. I'm going to be a father. My kid needs me."

"You need to cooperate, Alex," said Kermit. "The plan will work."

"Where is the captain?"

"He's with Gloria and Julia. They're holed up in a hacienda outside Merida."

"Kermit, are you telling me he's screwing my girlfriend and my wife?"

"No, Alex, he has kidnapped them. He sent word to my office; told me where you were, and wants to exchange you for them. That is the reason Blanton is funding the operation. He doesn't give a shit about you or Gloria, but wants his daughter back."

"Where does Ronson's deal fit in?"

"Ronson's operation is side work." said Miguel. "Remember the slogan, 'We don't leave anyone behind.'"

"We're not the damn marines, Miguel."

That was the end of the conversation. We drove through the countryside in silence. I was seething. My new wife will feel abandoned. Sister Amalia will wonder why I left without saying *adios*. Gonz will think me to be a bad friend, and Hankamon will think I welched out on his deal. My only chance at not losing face was the kid, Mateo, and the bar note I left on the table. Maybe Mateo would tell everyone I had been taken away under duress.

We pulled into a side road and drove to a makeshift airport. There was a vintage two-engine airplane waiting. In front of it was a uniformed guard with an automatic weapon. *Oh, Jesus, not another plane ride.*

We drove next to the plane and climbed out of the jeep. The guard drove the jeep away. We climbed inside, and there, strapped to a seat, was the crazy Swiss-Italian *pistolero*, Lor Boselli. His countenance showed an angry disposition. Obviously he was not pleased to take another plane ride either.

Kermit climbed into the pilot's seat. Paco took the copilot seat. Miguel and I strapped ourselves in. The engine started, and we took off. When we became airborne, I silently cursed my friends.

"Señora María, " yelled Mateo. *"Se llevaron a tu marido!"*

"Take a breath, Mateo, and slow down. Tell me, who took my husband and when?"

ALBERTO ARCIA

"The strangers who came into town, they took him, just now."

"Mateo, *dime*, how many gringos were there, and which way did they go?"

"María, there were three. They left town in a jeep going towards Ciudad Victoria."

"Mateo, please listen to me, this next question is important. Did he leave willingly or did they force him?"

"He handed her a note. "The boy working the bar gave it to me. He said Alex did not look happy, María. I saw them. They took him."

"Gracias por la información, Mateo. Now go and get Gonzalez Brynn. Tell him to leave the *bueyes* behind and drive his tractor. He needs to come to the hospital, *pronto.* Go now."

Maria Contreras tapped her belly. "Don't you worry, little one, I will bring your father back."

At dusk, a meeting in Doctor Hankamon Switzer's hospital office was in progress. He drew on a chalkboard, explaining the options available to them.

"It appears to me that if they went towards Ciudad Victoria, they are going to an airport, yet you can't get someone to board a plane if he's being kidnapped. Therefore we must assume they are getting on a private plane at an airstrip outside of the city." He made a circle to designate Ciudad Victoria and drew an airplane.

"The other choice is driving a reluctant man towards Texas." He drew a car and a straight line to the border. He drew an *X* and spelled Laredo. "Crossing here is not a good idea since there are many border guards to deal with." He drew a large *X* over the car. "They will not risk it."

"What do you suggest our next step of action should be, Doctor?" asked Gonzalez Brynn.

"Yes, how do I get my husband back?"

Hankamon drew a line from where they were to Houston and circled it. "When Alex first came here, wounded, I removed his wallet and wrote down his driver's license number and his address. I suggest you, María, and you Gonzo, if you can spare the time, go there and knock on the door of his house and ask questions. His neighbors might know something. Find relatives, they might be of help. Go to the police if necessary. Take your marriage license with you, María, it will give you legal reason to ask questions. Tell them he has been kidnapped."

On their way out of the hospital, María cornered Gonzo. "Do you think there might be a chance, in spite of Mateo's assurances, that Alex has left me willingly?"

Gonzo placed his arm over her shoulders. "Listen to me, María. If I thought there was such a chance, I never would have volunteered to go with you. Alex is now a husband, and he will be a father soon, No one leaves before the child is born. Afterwards is anyone's guess."

He removed his arm and questioned her. "Are you pleasing him?"

"I'm feeding him two meals a day, bathing him, and washing, drying, and ironing his clothes."

"That's not what I meant, María."

She gave him a smirk. "I know what you mean, Gonzo. Men are all alike. It's about sex. Let me say to you that I'm screwing his brains out."

Gonzo smiled. "No man leaves a woman like you behind."

"You left me."

"No, I did not. If I remember correctly, we both decided that we were not suited for each other. Amiable is a word I can use to describe our breakup."

She placed her hand through his arm, and they talked as they walked. "I have always admired you, Gonzo, and our breakup was painful."

"You never showed any visible pain, María. I thought you were okay with it."

"I'm a woman that does not wear her heart on the sleeve of her shirt."

Gonzo laughed. "Maybe not your heart, but your daringness and sexual appetite were obvious and admired."

She tip-toed up and kissed him on the cheek. "Thanks for being a good man. Mama didn't have one, and she deserved better. I need one and fear Alex may not turn out to be a good one."

"And you say that because?"

"Just intuition, Gonzo. Nothing more. I walk around with my fingers crossed all the time, hoping there's a good man under all that restless machismo."

The following week, María and Gonzo left on a bus to Ciudad Victoria. They needed to visit the American consulate to get their crossing papers. Once that was done, they were to take a bus to Houston.

Chapter Four

The Trap

The house had a Humvee parked about ten yards to the side and a plethora of windows—not the kind you would expect a kidnapper to have. The immediate area had no trees nor bushes around, and the building commanded the hill, affording an attacking force little cover. Not that we were going to launch an assault; the original plan consisted of sneaking in at night, yet the many lights illuminating the approach made even that move dangerous. *So what then?*

When we arrived, a local man and a recent employee of Kermit, a burly man named Amado, met us. He had been keeping an eye on the house.

Once in position, we had a meeting to decide how to achieve the goal of capturing Captain Luther Franklyn without getting me or the women killed.

He had made his demands clear—me and a clean getaway in exchange for both women. One female would be released during the swap, the other would be dropped off at the side of the road once he understood no one was after him.

ALBERTO ARCIA

Frankly I had no issue with the request. I was ready to be traded. Apparently the captain wanted to turn me in to Blanton Murray and collect his reward. No harm would come to me. Not then. It would be during the attempted capture of the man-hunter, which would come right after he dropped off the last woman.

The plan and the trap were set. Now all we needed to do was execute it. Miguel Hargoza and Paco Williams would be waiting a ways down the only road. Miguel would place a board with large nails, designed to blow the tires. If that didn't stop the vehicle, Paco would spray the radiator with bullets. That would eliminate the chance of using the car to escape. The trick would be not to hit any of the occupants.

Miguel, coming from behind, would let a burst from his Uzi into the air with Paco doing the same from the front right after shooting the radiator. This action, we hoped, would make the captain realize the jig was up and surrender.

He could try to use me as a shield, but we doubted he'd do that. Especially since I would have promised him we'd let him go. All we wanted was the girls.

I made the sign of the cross and kissed my Virgin of Guadalupe medal, then walked into the open with my hands up. Halfway there, the door opened and Gloria walked out. We passed each other and traded a few words. She extended her hand and I did the same. We touched and she dropped a bomb at my feet.

"Alex, I'm so sorry, but things being what they were, I had to tell her."

The hairs on back on my head stood up. "Tell her what?"

She didn't reply, just kept on walking. I turned towards her and shouted, "Tell me you didn't?"

She waved her hand in a motion that increased my already high state of anxiety. Then she stopped and turned. "I told her we have been lovers for a long time."

"Augh! How could you. How long did you specify?"

She didn't respond, just walked away.

I was incensed. *Why in hell does a woman feel the need to cleanse her soul by throwing a man under the bus?* Needing to regain my composure, I stopped for a moment of reflection. Then, knowing there was no turning back, I swallowed hard and arrived at the open door.

The captain was waiting for me. "Come on in, Alex. It's good to see you again. For a peckerwood, you're a hard man to catch."

I walked in, and there stood my sweet wife, Julia, untied and with a non-friendly demeanor.

I took in a deep breath. "Hello, Baby. It's so good to see you,"

She did not respond—just stood there, simmering.

Captain Franklyn pointed me to a chair. I sat on it. He tied me while Julia looked on. The damned woman could have made a dash out the open door but she didn't. The look in her eyes scared me. It was a cold, mad-as-hell stare.

A feeling of despair came over me. There is nothing a guy can do while sitting with his feet and hands tied to the legs of a chair. I was a doomed man awaiting the executioner. And she came soon enough.

The need to warm up the cold atmosphere in the room became necessary. I made the effort. "Julia, sweetheart, I want you to know that I categorially deny anything Gloria might have said to you about me being unfaithful."

Julia turned towards the captain. "Luther, can I do it now?"

Luther? Did she called him Luther?

He nodded, and she walked to the corner and grabbed a baseball bat. My eyes grew in size. "Baby, please don't hurt me. Nothing Gloria said was true. You know I love you."

Julia approached me, then with a defiant tone, judged me to be guilty. "Alex, you are the liar, not Gloria."

She waved the bat over her head a couple of times, which I concluded to be nothing more than theatrics. *Maybe she just wants to scare me.*

"Now, let me see, where do I strike a cheating husband to extricate the most pain? Do I hit him on the forehead or do I land the blows on his legs?"

I looked at Captain Franklyn. Maybe he would interfere. After all, I was his hostage. His eyes met mine. He walked to the table and poured tequila into two tall shot glasses.

Oh, great, he's not going to intervene, but at least I'm getting a drink to help with the upcoming blow.

Captain Franklyn came my way and gave one shot glass to Julia. They clinked the glasses and she shot hers down. *Oh, God, there will be no mercy for a condemned man today.*

She gave him the shot glass back and raised the bat. I cringed, waiting for the blow. Yet the blow did not come. She lowered the wood.

Ah, what luck, she's not going to hurt me. She still loves me. Thank you, God.

Julia placed her face close to mine. The devilish look brought fear into my heart. *Oh, God, she* is *going to hurt me.*

She grabbed the bat and, bayonet style, shoved the bottom of the wood into my groin. The pain was so intense, no scream came out. I fell to the ground and tried to squirm but couldn't. I was tied to the chair. Yet I flopped around like a fish out of water gasping for air.

Let me say this, I have experienced pain before, but nothing ever hurt as bad as this unwarranted blow given to John Henry and the family jewels.

In the midst of this arduous pain, the notion that my marriage to Julia was over hit me. The same with my long term relationship with Gloria. *Screw them. Who needs angry and double-crossing women?* Not me. The only female I need now is María.

There's nothing like intense pain to make a man realize he's on a bad road. Hell, I was forty-three and thinking this cloak and dagger life was no longer feasible. I missed my new wife, my plot of land, and my avocado orchard. Keeping my marriage to Julia from María and from the rest of the Mennonites became important.

Captain Franklyn taped my mouth using duct tape. The torture would continue, I had a moustache. My legs were untied but my hands were not. We walked to the armored vehicle, and the captain shoved me into the back seat. Julia sat in front, untied. The woman acted as if on a picnic outing. Little did she know all hell would break lose any minute.

It would have been presumptuous of me to think Captain Luther Franklyn, a renowned man-hunter, would not have a trick or two up his sleeve. A blind man could see the trap ahead. Only one road in and out. When we discussed the plan, I knew it to be a simple one. I didn't complain because surely there had to be another one, more complex in store for a man like Franklyn. I was right on all counts.

The Humvee started down the road and quickly veered away, plunging into the bush. The captain was going to take my associates on a wild, cross-country chase.

The ride was rough. I was thankful they seat belted me, otherwise I would have tumbled every which way.

Julia kept looking back. "Luther, they are not following us."

Luther? Us? Has this brigand bedded my wife? I became upset. She crushes my nuts because I've been unfaithful, and she has been in bed with him. *I wonder if he did Gloria too.*

"Not yet, they aren't, but they will be upon us in a minute. Hang on, Baby, the ride is going to get rougher."

No sooner had he spoken those words, than the sound of an airplane intruded. It made one low swoop and then an explosion detonated a ways out in front of the car. A warning for the captain. If he didn't stop, the next grenade will explode closer. He kept on going.

Another explosion came. This one came close enough to throw dirt on us. Julia lost her bravado and screamed for him to stop.

He told her to shut the hell up and floored the gas pedal. All the jostling made my balls hurt.

Julia began to cry and beg. "Please, Luther, I don't want to die. Stop the car."

"No way, Baby, I'm not the surrendering type. If we can make it to that tree line the plane won't be able to hurt us."

The third grenade blew a hole in the ground in front. The windows and tires were toast, and the Humvee overturned. Julia screamed again.

Behind us came the jeep. A burst of bullets sprayed the area to the side, and Luther Franklyn came out, hands up. We had achieved our goal, we captured the villain.

We tied him, torched the vehicle, and drove to home base where we met Kermit. Franklyn was fit to be tied. He kept cursing us. Julia just stood there and cried.

We moved inside Franklyn's rented house and settled in for the night. I found a pair of scissors and cut off the bottom part of the duct tape, allowing me to speak. The upper part would not come off without giving me pain, so I tried to cut it off piecemeal, hoping to avoid as much pain as possible. The process took time and proved ineffective.

Miguel, tiring of my bitching, gave me a stick for my mouth. Then he yanked the tape off. I yelled. When blood started to ooze out, I fainted.

I awoke and saw Gloria hovering over me. She had shaved the moustache off and had applied Vaseline. When she saw me open my eyes, she apologized for her indiscretion.

"I'm really sorry, Alex. Can you please forgive me?"

"Why did you do it?"

"It was nothing more than a momentary lapse of reason brought on by female bonding. We were experiencing a situation not to our liking."

"Did you screw the captain?"

"No, what kind of a woman do you think I am?"

"The kind that betrays her lover."

"Alex, I said I was sorry. Julia screwed the captain, several times. You should have heard all the noise coming from the bedroom. She really got into it."

"Okay, no need to elaborate. But I'm not sure forgiving is in order. At least not yet."

She whispered in my ear, while placing her hand on John Henry. "You want me to blow you?"

"Augh," I yelled. Don't touch him, He's broken. Julia killed him. Johnny boy is fatally injured."

"Listen, silly man. Your bone is a meat bone, not a bone bone. It can be hurt but not fractured. Let me see the damage."

She removed my pants and underwear and gasped! "Oh, my God, he's bent. How did it happen?"

"Never mind how, Gloria. Is the bend that bad?"

"If you stand before a urinal and take a pee, you'll soak the guy shoes standing next to you."

"Augh!"

Miguel and Paco came into the room. Miguel saw Johnny boy and grinned. "That's quite a bend you have there, Alex."

I shot him the finger.

Paco scratched his face. "You'll never find the honey pot straight on with that curve."

I shot him the finger, too. They both laughed and left.

Gloria tried to sooth my hurt ego. "Don't worry about where it's pointing. I'll put a double splint on it, and Johnny will be back to normal in no time."

Kermit walked in and looked at my dick. He cringed but refrained from making a hurtful remark. Instead, he gave us an order.

"If you two can stop playing doctor, we need to discuss our next step. Please come to the meeting."

Chapter Five

The Exchange

We left Amado behind. He was in charge of the jeep and the women. His instructions were to hang on to them until we returned. We told him to tie them. The rest of us, captives included, took off in the plane Kermit had rented.

On the way, Lor, who had been tied and sitting next to me, asked why I was doing this to him. He reminded me that he helped me when I was in trouble in Munich.

"You no have gud feeling in your heart for Lor?"

I cringed. The remark cut me to the quick. He was right. I owed him, even though the crazy Swiss/Italian gunman killed way more people than was necessary. He was responsible for the trouble blood bath in Munich caused me.

"Your English is getting better," I said.

He leaned my way. "You go and help your friend, but not help your friend's friend. Why is that?"

I looked at him, the man was making a point.

"You help Ronson, and he help me. Why not you help Lor. Ronson will not fight your boss if you help Lor."

That did it. The man, with his broken English made me see the light. Ronson would not leave Mexico without him. That I knew to be a fact. I could not allow Kermit to

70

trade Lor and the captain for Ronson. It made no sense. Lor and Ronson were close friends. He would resent us, and there would be trouble. Why go through all this if the end result will not be pleasing. It was time for me to change sides.

I told Paco, who sat in the co-pilot seat, to go take a walk.

He refused but Kermit told him to leave. "Alex has something on his mind, and it's best to hear him out."

I sat next to the Norwegian.

"What's on your mind, Alex?"

"Ronson and Lor."

He gave me an enigmatic look. "You're going to be a problem, aren't you?"

"Hear me out, Kermit. There is something you haven't considered."

His face turned serious. "You're going to take a dump on our parade, aren't you?"

"You, of all people should know that Ronson and Lor are good friends."

Kermit reached under his seat and pulled out a bottle of Schnapps. He took a swig and placed it back without offering me one.

"Explain yourself, and spare me the sentimentalism."

"When Ronson realizes you traded him for Lor, he will not be happy, and he will not leave Mexico until we spring Lor."

He made a motion with his hand for me to continue with the issue. I looked down at the seat and motioned with a nod of my head for a drink, but he didn't bite.

"No booze for you until this conversation is over. Get on with it."

"I owe both these guys, although I'm not inclined to risk my life for Lor. But I cannot abandon Ronson. I will risk my life for him. I owe him, big time. He has always been there for me."

Kermit gave me a languorous look. "Are you telling me you are not coming back to Texas?"

"Correcto mundo, Kermit. And you will not get paid unless you can deliver me to Blanton."

"I can always tie and gag you. Besides, I have Julia, and he will pay me for bringing her back."

He waited for a moment so I could digest the statement. The smile that crept out of his mouth hit home. He had me by my injured balls. Julia would tell her father that I was a cheat and she was through with me. Blanton would then cancel the reward. I was not worth a plugged nickel to Kermit.

With a smug look, he ended the conversation. "Comprende me?"

I left the cockpit and took my seat. Lor gave me an inquisitive stare. I pointed my index finger at him, and then ran it across my throat. His face turned white. He closed his eyes and slumped in his seat.

We landed on a private airstrip in the outskirts of that vast area of smog-covered land called Mexico City. There, waiting for us, was a man in a black Limo. Before we deplaned, Kermit called a quick meeting.

"Listen guys, we are going to try a different strategy. It's been my experience that when dealing with an exchange of prisoners, an ace in the hole is always necessary."

We stared at him in silence.

72

"Paco and Lor are going to remain in the airplane. If the trade is nothing more than a ruse or if the money-man refuses to honor the deal, we can use Lor to our advantage. These type of people are usually untrustworthy, so we need to hedge our bets. Understood?"

"Aye, Captain," was our reply.

The Limo driver took us on a long drive to a construction warehouse in the center of the city. The place reminded me of an ant colony. People and cars everywhere.

We met a bald, fat man, flanked by two thuggish bodyguards. We gave him custody of Captain Luther Franklyn, and Kermit handed over half the money promised, telling him the other half would be given after he gave us Ronson. The guy was not happy, insisting the deal was for two men.

Kermit took him aside for a private conversation. By the amount of hand waving, the fat man seemed none too happy. Yet in the end they made a deal and shook hands.

To our delight, Ronson came out of a door in the company of a beautiful woman. After a closer inspection, we saw she had a pistol stuck to his side. The exchange was made, and we left the warehouse.

Kermit held us back. He did not want to get into the car yet. He used his cell, called Paco, and told him to move the plane and keep an eye out, just in case the Mexicans were planning on keeping the plane and arresting us all. Yet that precaution was not necessary. Everything went down smooth. The Limo driver took us back and drove away.

Lor beamed when he saw Ronson. His ties were removed, and they hugged. We all rejoiced.

ALBERTO ARCIA

On the way back Paco came by my seat. "The old sleuth wants you."

I climbed into the co-pilot's seat. Not knowing what lay in store for me, I kept quiet. The old gumshoe pulled out the schnapps and offered me a drink.

"Every once in a while you surprise me in a good way."

I smiled and took a swig.

"I will admit that Ronson's friendship with Lor concerned me. Your warning made me address that nagging problem. The Mexican was not happy, but I told him Lor had escaped, and all we had was Franklyn. I mentioned that Franklyn was the sole shooter, and he held the rank of captain in the Texas Rangers. That bit of info, plus more money sealed the deal and allowed us to make a clean getaway."

I was going to take another swig, but he grabbed the bottle. "No more. The exchange cost me extra money. Go back to your seat."

Kermit's gratitude was always short lived, but so what. He had given me a drink and a thumbs up. That suited me fine. I felt like a hero.

We landed on a strip of land close to the house on the hill. Amado was there with both women. Ronson, although pale and skinny, was glad to see Gloria. She was ecstatic.

We had a party that night, and Gloria spent the night with Ronson. Julia kept to herself. She had no festive bone in her body. Obviously she pined for the man-hunter.

The whole situation felt bad. My girlfriend is screwing Ronson, and my wife wanted to ball a rough man. My life needed a different direction. So did my demeanor. I had to change, or nothing would change.

74

In the morning we had another one of Kermit's meetings. He proposed we split up when we arrived in Texas, and meet again in his office on Monday. It was Friday, so the long weekend suited me.

The old private eye phoned Blanton and set a meeting to hand me and Julia over. Amado drove us to the plane, Kermit paid him, and he left with the jeep.

We landed at Hooks airport in Tomball. Kermit had a broad smile—he loved money, and he would soon get plenty from my father-in-law for our return.

Kermit explained to Julia that all of us had worked hard for her and my return, and it would be a shame if she told her father that Alex was no longer welcome. That would affect the money promised, and he had to pay out of his own pocket to get Ronson out.

She looked at him without sympathy. His plea fell on deaf ears. Julia didn't seem to care. Yet Kermit did not relent.

"Alex promised me he would not mention to your father the affair you had with a bounty hunter like Luther Franklyn. There is no need for you to mention Alex's disloyalty either. Your father spent a lot of money for both of you to be rescued. He ought to feel good about his efforts."

She gave him a crocodile smile. "Do not worry. Mister Laarssen, I will keep my mouth shut. You will get the money promised. I will behave, but only until such time as I can file for divorce."

Blanton was waiting at the airport. So was Bernie, Kermit's private secretary. A woman whose body made men cry.

ALBERTO ARCIA

Blanton hugged Julia, shook my hand, and handed Kermit an envelope. The deal had been concluded.

We left in Blanton's Lincoln Continental. I had to ride in the front next to the chauffer. My associates climbed into a Chevrolet Excursion driven by Bernie.

The next day I received a call from Bernie. She wanted me to come by the office. I wondered why? We were supposed to stay away from the office for a few days. I dressed and took the Honda Accord out.

Julia and I had slept in separated bedrooms. The woman turned cold on me. It became obvious our marriage would not survive this escapade. I could not forgive her for screwing the captain.

I walked into the office, and Bernie greeted me with her sparkling eyes and a big smile. I swear that woman wanted me. I stretched my hand out.

"Kermit is not here," she said, "you can hug me if you like."

I opened my arms and received that gorgeous ample bosom into my chest. I squeezed her waist and she giggled and whispered, "Not too many liberties, my friend, Kermit is a jealous man."

I let go. "Bernie, if the old guy ever leaves you, don't forget my number."

She giggled and adjusted her bosom. "You're first on my list, handsome man."

"You have any booze, Sweet Thing?"

"Yes, but we can't drink now. You have someone in the meeting room waiting for you."

"Man or woman?"

"Female, of the family kind."

RUN, ALEX, RUN

I approached the room, and with trepidation turned the knob. I walked inside and the hairs on back of my neck stood up.

"Hello, Bro, long time no see."

Chapter Six

Lil' Sister

It could be said that I was ill-prepared to see my kid sister. My reaction could have been better, but her appearance threw me into a state of anxiety. Deni, as she is known, had a reputation in our family for being opinionated, quarrelsome, and just plain contrary. A different drummer to say the least, certainly from the rest of us. My main reason for concern had to do with why would a person who has made it her life plan to stay away from me, show up in Houston looking for me? Trouble had to be the reason.

She hadn't changed much in looks. Deni had discovered the fountain of youth. For someone in her early thirties, she still looked like a kid. I bet she gets carded when buying liquor. I opened my arms to give her a hug, but she extended her hand out for a shake. Fair enough. I shook it.

"Surprised to see me, aren't you?"

"Yes. What brings you to Texas? Did mother pass?"

"No, she's still alive and kicking me."

I looked in her pretty brown eyes, trying to figure out a reason for the visit, but no luck. She still had a poker face. Discerning her reason would require more than a casual visual inspection.

"Okay, glad to know mother is well. So, other than being here because you missed your older brother, what brings you here?"

"Trouble."

I knew it.

"I need your help."

I knew that too. "What kind?"

"Someone is trying to steal our family land in Colon."

That's a surprise. What land? I thought we sold everything in the city when Dad passed."

"It's not Dad's land, and it's not in the city."

Oh great, another game of twenty questions. "Whose land, where, and who is the thief?"

"Abuelo's land, and it's in the interior of the province. The thief's name is on a need to know basis."

"Okay, I see this will take some time. Let's blow this place and find us a café so we can discuss what it is you think I can do for you."

I told Bernie that Deni was my little sister, and we were going to La Dolce Vita Café down the street for a conversation. She twinkled her eyes at me.

We left the office and, on our way to the car, Sis began her usual annoying cross-examination. Disapproval was her specialty. She could screw up a wet dream.

"Surely you know, or should know by now that you don't drag your Willy where you work."

"I'm not screwing Bernie, the boss is."

"She wants you to do her."

"You figured that out in the half hour you were in the office?"

She gave me an annoying smirk. "I don't have a Willy, therefore the blood flow stays in the brain where it needs to be. Don't sell me short. I can see the lust in her eyes. She wants you."

"That may be so, but she can't have me, I'm a married man."

She laughed. "What number are you on? Fourth or fifth?"

"Third, Smarty Pants. First was Ramona. Then came Liz, and this one is Julia."

"Well, I can't wait to meet her. Can you put me up? I'd rather not spend my meager funds renting a motel room."

Jesus H. Christ, what bad timing. If I ask Julia to allow my kid sister to stay with us, she'll either say no or she will tell her all about what a lousy husband I've been. Either way, it's more fodder for Deni to abuse me. "I'll phone her and ask."

"You have to ask permission from your wife to give your sister a room? Are you serious?"

Oh, God, please make her leave. "Yes, it's called courtesy. Now, can you please retract the fangs and claws and show me some civility. It's necessary, otherwise you will have to buy your own coffee."

We parked the car and found a table on the sidewalk. The coffee and cream-filled wafers came right away. This place had excellent service.

Deni took a sip and floored me with a story. "Our grandfather left Dad eleven tracts of land designated as farms in the province of Colon, a ways past Sabanita—in the Santa Isabel district. Father passed them on to us."

"Why did we not know this?"

"Because they were working farms when Grandfather died. Dad didn't have a head for business and pretty much left the workers in charge. Also these farms were not worth much in those days, and he did not want to expel the families who worked them. That is why he did not put them up for sale."

"Farms? What kind of farms? If my memory serves me right, he had several milk dairies.

"Yes, those were sold. These farms were covered with coconut trees, which gave the inhabitants a source of a living. Dad didn't want them, so it's part of our inheritance."

"How did you come to know these tracts existed?"

"Going through old boxes that belonged to Dad. I was trying to see what could be kept and what to throw away. The deeds were attached to a hand written will."

I sipped my coffee while trying to figure out why she needed my help. If she thought I would assist her in throwing out poor farmers, she had another think coming. *I'm a bleeding liberal. Helping the needy is my thing.* Here comes the dreaded question.

"Sis, how can I help you?"

She gave me a smug look. "If you think I'm going to ask you to help me throw these people out of land that belongs to us, you're wrong. I know who you are. You're a wuss. I hired a legal firm with muscle to do that for us."

"And you are here to have me pay for my share of the expenses, is that it? Have you asked Salvador and Liliana for their share? Do they even know these farms exist?"

"Not yet. Do you have any money?"

"No, as a matter of fact, I don't."

ALBERTO ARCIA

"How about your wife? Legally she is entitled to our family rewards and should be responsible for the expenses."

Bummer, I'm going to have to let the cat out. "She has money, but she won't pay to play. We're getting a divorce."

She smiled. "So, where are you living, Bro?

"At the moment, with her, but not for long. I'm fixing to get an apartment."

"Tell me, Bro, why do you still live in Texas?"

"If you must know, I love Panama as much as Texas. Well, probably not as much, which is why I still live here. Texas is a place created by foreign heroes; very few that died in the Alamo were native sons. They like foreigners here. Being one, I found a home here."

A car pulled to the curb. Inside were my friends, Ronson and Lor. Ronson stuck his head out the window. "Hey, Alex, who's the good looking woman with you?"

I waved them over. They parked and joined us. I did the introductions. The interruption bought me time to figure out what to do. I had just gotten off a Mexican merry-go-round, and did not want to get on the Panamanian version. At least not this soon. *What to do?*

My cell rang. I looked at the screen. It was Julia. I picked up the call. "What's up, Baby?"

"You need to come here, right now."

"What's up?" I repeated.

"There's a pregnant woman here that claims she's your wife. Father drove her to me."

"Is your dad still there?"

"Oh, yes, and so is a guy named Gonzalez Brynn. They both are looking for you."

"Julia, did you tell her I'm married to you?"

"Oh, yes, I sure did."

"Be there right away." I hung up the phone and looked up. *God, why do you treat me this way? Like it or not, I'm your son. How about a break from time to time?*

"Why the grim look, Bro?"

"Yeah, Alex," said Ronson. You look pale."

Lor butted in. "You need Lor to help you fight somebody?"

"No, thanks for the offer. What I need is to see a man about a horse. Be back in a minute or two."

"What horse?" she asked.

"He's going to the water closet," said Ronson.

I left for the bathroom, snuck out the back, climbed into my car, and quietly left the café. This trouble did not concern anyone but me. My buds will see to my sister's safety and comfort.

As I came closer to Julia's house, the car slowed down. Nothing I could say or do could keep me from hurting María's feelings. The lies would expose me for what I really am, a scoundrel. Gonzo, who became a dear friend, would feel betrayed as well. Julia will call me names, and Blanton will threaten me. Probably bring that mindless aberration called Deputy Tom back into my sorry life.

I could throw myself at the mercy of God, but we were not on good speaking terms at the moment. The entity kept dumping on me. The notion of asking both women to forgive me did cross my mind, but my *por mi culpa* would need an explanation, and there wasn't one worth a plugged nickel.

I parked by the curb, and as I've done many times before, prepared to face the hot poker. Hell, I deserved to get burned. Marrying more than one woman had to be the

ALBERTO ARCIA

dumbest thing I have ever done. Even marrying Ramona twice didn't rate as being this senseless.

Thinking I needed to scout the enemy before walking into their den, I decided to spy from a window. Inside stood Blanton with a glass of whiskey in his hand, next to him was Julia. She had a martini, and so did Gonz. María sat on the coach and had what appeared to be a glass of water. *Good girl, she's not exposing my son to alcohol. That's my job.*

Deciding not to go inside just yet, I sat on one of the two swings out in the side yard. Maybe if I wait a few more minutes, the booze will dampen their anger.

While I sat there waiting, a car pulled next to mine. Ronson came out and walked towards the house. I stood up, and he came my way.

"What's up? I said.

"I came to rescue you. Kermit told me of your problems."

"Are you telling me you want to go inside and take the heat for me? Is that your deal?"

He frowned. "No Alex, I am telling you there is an opportunity in that car," and he pointed to his vehicle, "to get away from here and avoid this mess."

I looked at him but did not speak. If he wanted me to walk away from my troubles, he needed to be more explicit. Running away would only work if I did not do it by being a full blown coward. I needed a good reason.

"Is my savior in the car?"

"If you're talking about your sister, no. She rented a motel room. Lor is with her."

Thank you God for these small favors. Ronson, has she told you what she wants?" *As if I didn't know.*

84

"*Ja*. She has. She needs you to help her with some trouble in Panama. Something to do with squatters on family land."

I found myself facing a crossroad. One way would take me inside a hostile house to face people I cared for but wanted me to admit to my wrongdoing. An admittance that would surely bring tears and words of anger. The other way would take me back home to deal with a situation that required someone with skills I did not possess. *What to do? Which road to take?*

"Listen friend, let's go and rent a furnished apartment. I have my eyes on one called the Barbary Coast in San Felipe Street. It has a nice big pool and is favored by flight attendants."

Chapter Seven

A Team Comes Together

There's not much that a man can say about who or what he is, particularly when he runs from his troubles. Self-respect is the first virtue that falls, usually replaced by shame.

María did not deserve a man like me for a husband. Instead of facing her, I ran. Worse, I left a woman pregnant, and broke in a foreign country.

Sometimes even I can't describe the reasons for my lack of courage. Surely after being shot numerous times and after cheating death on more than one occasion, I should be able to rely on strong legs. But no, here I am again, hitting rock bottom and hanging out with my inner weasel self.

To forget my misery, I took on a task that required me to run. When the conversation began, as to the real purpose for going to Panama, I immediately objected. Deni had misrepresented the danger involved.

"Listen, Sis, no amount of land or money is worth going against a drug cartel. If they have a lab on our land, let them use it. At some point the government or the gringos will shut it down and arrest everyone involved."

She seethed, but remained quiet.

"How much money are they paying you for allowing them to process the coke? Surely it has to be a nice sum."

She broke her silence and attacked my intelligence. "You're dumber than a box of rocks, Alex. The cartel does not pay rent, they take what they want. The gringos will do nothing more than give logistical support to the government, and when the cartel pulls out, the government will confiscate our land due to it being used as a criminal enterprise. We need to remove these drug thugs before the gringos push the government to take action. I do not want to lose our land."

Right after that statement I should have bailed out. Sis was on a suicide mission, and she needed a commando unit. An imbecile could see the impossibility of the undertaking. To challenge the cartel is to sign your own death warrant. They are cruel and have more money and power.

She looked me in the eyes, and then cut me to the quick. "Well, Brother, there is nothing left here for you. You have mentioned to me before that Texas is a land of heroes. It is obvious that you are not one, therefore not fit to live here. So, why not come with me to Panama? Maybe you can become a hero there and save yourself from a life of shame."

What a cheeky bitch. Using my own words against me.

Ronson came to my rescue. "Alex, she's right, there is nothing left for you in Texas. Here you will live inside the box of shame. Go pay a few months' rent on your apartment, and let's go to Panama and at least scout the situation. Maybe we can find a way to rid the drug lord from your family land without losing our lives."

My ears were still stunned from hearing that idiotic comment, when more insanity hit me. Lor, the trigger happy, half Swiss and half Italian joined the conversation.

87

ALBERTO ARCIA

"Deni, I will face danger in the eye. I go help you. Lor is not afraid to keel Panamanians."

She looked at me. "Is he for real?"

I gave her a sly smile. "He's as real as the mole on my big toe. I hired him in Munich years ago to eliminate a Colombian assassin who wanted to kill me, and he gunned down a whole troupe of Mexican Mariachis instead. You turn him lose in the Province of Colon and the population will dwindle. Indiscriminate killing is his forte."

My sister's eyes sparkled. She had met her soul mate. "Lor, you do not kill Panamanians, but you can kill Colombians. Is that okay?"

He gave her a sheepish grin. "Lor loves to keel Colombians."

She beamed again. "Lor, you and me, we will become good friends. You will love it in Panama. We have a mountainous area people call the Switzerland of Central America."

"Liar," I blurted out. "That is what people call Costa Rica. Where he is going is part of the Mosquito Coast."

"Uff!" moaned Ronson. "I hate heat and bugs."

Sis looked at Lor. "How about you? You have climate and bug issues?"

He gave her an endearing smile. "Lor has big balls. He is afraid of nothing."

That was it. Deni found her soldiers of fortune. She looked at me and Ronson. "Okay, so we're a team?"

Before we departed, I emptied my bank account and paid a few months' rent on my new place. My life savings consisted of twelve-thousand dollars. Why not? Couldn't spend it in the grave, and I'd be pushing up daisies in no time.

RUN, ALEX, RUN

When you mess with a cartel, you die quickly, but only if you're lucky. Most of the time you die slowly and painfully. These wild-eyed gunmen were not afraid to die. Neither is Lor, but I am. Likewise for Ronson. So, what is our reasoning for going into the jaws of death? Mine had to do with losing my self-respect and needing to regain it, not sure about Ronson. Yet I figured it probably had to do with paying a debt of gratitude. After all, I did help rescue him from a life in a Mexican prison.

Sis wanted a kamikaze warrior, and Lor volunteered for the position. My only saving grace was that maybe, if I was fortunate, I could die saving someone. That should get me a ticket into the Pearly Gates Brothel and Rum bar. I bet the gate keeper, that insolent Limey, and the obstinate French inspector, Claude Potignon, would be surprised to see me show up. An eternity in a rum-laden whorehouse was my kind of heaven. It's where I belonged.

There were a couple of things I needed to work out before I stepped on Panamanian soil: one being my bud, Ronson. He is not in good shape to deal with an adventure of this nature. He needed to put on some weight, go to a gym, and get laid a few times. I knew the right place, San Jose, Costa Rica. A brothel called Casa Mendez. They had a bunch of nice girls working there. The place came with a restaurant and a bar. It was a one stop whorehouse. You paid a fee and they screwed, fed, brought you drinks, and housed you. For an additional fee you could get a blow job to go with your regular, daily screw. They rented rooms daily, but they were cheaper on a weekly rate. These rooms were nice, upstairs, and came with a balcony that afforded you a nice view.

ALBERTO ARCIA

Since Ronson needed to recuperate, and since I was going to Panama to die, I planned to book two rooms for two weeks, with the additional morning amenity. Having a girl blow you would be the perfect way to start the day. Ronson thought so too.

As luck would have it, there was a gym around the corner called Gimnasio Ramos, so we were good. Everything we wanted and needed was on hand. Life would be sweet for a little while.

Another issue to deal with was entering Panama. I am considered by more than a few immigration officers and government officials to be a *persona non grata*. I had to enter without attracting attention; that eliminated the ports and airports. A car, preferably not registered to me or a bus, hopefully during a rainstorm with the computers not working, would do the trick.

A condemned man ought to be able to ask God for everything, especially if the entity is primarily responsible for the misery afforded his doomed son. God should, for at least a while, become his neglected son's wingman. I made a mental note to complain about his treatment.

Chapter Eight

A Revelation

We arrived in San Jose and took a bus from the airport to the city's square, where the brothel was located. Inside, I asked for *Señora Samovilla,* but she had passed. The new owner and manager introduced herself as Maribel, her eldest daughter.

To my surprise and enjoyment, the young woman remembered me. I was as proud of that as I am of the statement written in the women's bathroom wall of Henrietta's Bar & Hall of Horns, in Plantersville, Texas. The words were flattering, accusing me of doing it twice. Probably written by a bar girl after a night when I felt airy and my wife had gone out of town.

I grinned at being recognized and introduced my companion. Usually, it didn't take much for Ronson to catch a woman's attention. A muscle flex and a smile. He had an endearing one plus the physique of a body builder. He stood well over six feet and projected an air of confidence. Most women found that blend irresistible. But that wasn't what made them loosen the grip on their panties, it was his unexpected shyness and quiet demeanor. Yet he did not impress Maribel.

She notice his dejected countenance and pulled me to the side. *"Qué le pasa a tu amigo?"*

"Nada malo, solamente necesita comer y coger e irse al gimnasio."

She laughed and assigned us two rooms facing the back of the building.

"What was all that about?" he asked.

"She wanted to know what is wrong with you. You look hollow."

"I can't help feeling low. I've gone through some bad times. The Mexican jailers were not kind to me. They kept me in a dark room. Most the time they beat me with rubber hoses, and fed me rotten food. If you guys had not gotten me out, I would have died there."

"Well, friend, you can put those bad memories behind. We have hit the mother lode here. There are no better people, in terms of hospitality, than the Costa Ricans. You will rehabilitate well here."

San Jose is indeed an air-conditioned city. The days were cool and the nights came with a slight chill. We took walks round the square, ate lunch at different spots every day, and worked out at the gym regularly. At night, we either hung out at the whorehouse bar or took in a Hollywood film at the Rex Theater.

Maribel signed us up for the house special, which was offered to all who booked more than an overnight room. If you stayed for three or more nights, she gave you an extra discount on the price of the room. The brothel had a sort of an all-inclusive deal, except that you had to pay for your alcohol. They served only breakfast and dinner.

With the extra time discount included, I paid the equivalent of ninety dollars per night. That rate came with two meals and one screw, either in the morning, afternoon, or night. Your choice. I paid an extra sum of twenty-five dollars daily for the morning blow job.

Usually I'm not this liberal with my money. It's never been easy for me to get my hands on much of it. Salvador had a trade, Liliana married well, and Deni took care of dad and handled all his business affairs.

To my unease, Ronson had foolishly become attached to his regular whore. A gorgeous woman named Mariana. She was tall, and that suited Ronson. She came with long golden brown curly hair and hazel eyes. Her breasts were proportioned, her waist small, and she possessed a delightful round butt. She also spoke English, which helped with the conversation.

At the beginning of the second week, on a Tuesday, it was Mariana's day off. Ronson asked her to spend the day with him. He needed sand time.

We rented a car, and I drove them to Jaco beach on the Pacific side—a must see spot. Blue water, white sand, and coconut trees. We enjoyed a nice outing. I was sorry I didn't bring my favorite whore, but it was not her day off.

During the outing Ronson kept doting on his woman, holding hands and always kissing her neck and shoulders. I had a bad premonition. He seemed to be falling in love with his whore, and we were only there for two weeks.

Let me say something about the whores in Costa Rica. Their guile and enthusiasm is evenly matched with their knockout beauty.

The blow job program at Maribel's whorehouse worked this way: The women were never the same. The blow job girls were usually younger and not experienced enough to handle the love-making sessions. We never knew their age, and sometimes wondered just how young they were.

Maribel, like her deceased mother, knew the importance of developing relationships between the johns and her girls. It created regular customers, and that was good for business. She sent you the same one every day or night, unless you demanded a different one. And that request had to be made before the noon hour. Maribel had a schedule to keep. Ronson was contented with Mariana for all his evening screws.

I know I've mentioned this before, but there's a need to say it again. This guy broke the golden rule and became enamored with his hooker. Nothing good would come out of it. He will end up broken hearted or he would try to steal her. An ill-advised move.

These girls were the property of the Madame. In most cases, money had been paid to her parents, and also spent on their education. This included manners, diction, and style. If one of the girls left without being dismissed, either the police or a man-hunter would be sent to get her back.

One day, late during the second week, we rented another car and took a two day trip to the Caribbean coast. I wanted to visit Puerto Limón and give Ronson a chance to experience what the term Mosquito Coast meant. I also wanted to explore the coastal road that led to the Panamanian border and hopefully score some good shit to smoke. We did not take any women with us.

On the way there, Ronson engaged me in conversation. He expressed his gratitude for my help in securing his freedom and wanted to know why I would not settle down with one woman and grab on to an easier life than this one we called adventuring.

"We're getting older, Alex. The Mexican jailers made me realize it was time to settle down. I had a woman in Winterthur when I left, that I liked very much. If she will still have me when this escapade is over, and if I survive it, I will marry her and begin my family. I'm done with you and Kermit, please don't call me anymore."

I felt bad. He was correct, I'm a trouble magnet. Since very early in life, the ability to be easily drawn into trouble bothered me. I'm not a thug, never was, and will never be. I come from a good family. We were never deprived of things. So what is the reason I'm bent and determined to seek woe and push my luck?

"You know, Ronson, I want to reveal a private thing about me to you, but I'm not sure I should."

He looked at me. "Why is that?"

"Because you will think less of me."

He laughed. "I don't think more of you now. You are a Hispanic man, I'm Germanic. You have noise and disorder in your culture, I have order and quiet. I can never be like you, Alex, so I cannot judge you. You can tell me your dark secrets."

"I have two main phobias in my life. One is the fear of dying and leaving unspent money in a bank account. The other is an anxiety over becoming homeless."

"It appears to me, Alex, that these two concerns balance each other well. You should not fear them. In your case, the phobias are necessary. You spend your money on things you want, but only as long as you have a home."

ALBERTO ARCIA

"Ronson, I don't have a home anymore, and my bank account is empty."

He placed his arm over my shoulder and gave me a slight squeeze. "Alex, all the years that I have known you, you have not shown the slightest effort at being nothing more than an adventurer. It's like you don't have a rudder. Don't know where you are going or should be going, so you move around. Just like the shark, Alex, you move to stay alive."

"But all that moving keeps me from settling down."

"Yes, that is your problem. I'm glad I don't suffer from it."

"I have other secrets, Ronson. You want to know them?"

"No. More secrets from you is not good."

We drove for a spell in silence.

On the outskirts of Puerto Limón, he broke the quietness and approached the unmentioned subject. Ronson couldn't leave it alone. I knew he wouldn't. One of the reason I like him had to do with the fact he is easy to bait.

"Tell me your secrets, Alex. I promise not to think badly of you."

"Okay, here goes: My reason for living is the same as my reason for finding misfortune. I was born with a burning fire down below the belt. My problem was, and still is, women. Especially the ones that are attached. I could never resist bedding a married woman, and that is the main reason I have a problem with being monogamous. I know women can't be trusted."

He laughed, "That don't make no sense. You don't stay married because they can't trust *you*, you *dumkopf.* You have gone through three wives, and you will soon lose the fourth one. And why is that? Please tell me."

"Glad you asked. Let me light up a smoke and I'll tell you all about it."

He rolled his window down and turned the radio off. I lit the fag, took a puff, and began my discourse: "Let me say I learned during my teen years that girls could like more than one boy. That knowledge increased as I became a young man."

I stopped talking, waiting for the question. It came quickly enough.

"What did you learn? Please tell me."

"If nobody could see them, they would give you some of their affection. When I became a man, I exploited that knowledge."

He looked at me. "Alex, I'm not introducing you to my Layna."

"Listen, Ronson, I don't mess with my best friends' wives or girlfriends, I have standards."

"Yes, you do—toilet ones."

"You promised not to be judgmental, Ronson."

"Yes I did. Sorry. Please go on."

"I'm going to tell you just one story to make my point, which is you can't trust them to only be with one man."

"Let me have a cigarette, Alex."

"But you don't smoke."

"This sounds like it's going to be a good story, so I feel like having one."

I passed him a smoke, gave him the lighter, and warned him about inhaling. "Don't do it, just puff the smoke away."

ALBERTO ARCIA

He puffed and coughed several times.

"You do know, Ronson, that for a time I made a living as a traveling salesman."

He nodded his head in agreement.

"It was then that I developed this fear of trust with women. I had honed a daily hotel routine to help me bed a woman. I never went to work early. Checking the free breakfast room or restaurant to see which woman's husband was dressed for work. After that, I waited about half an hour before eyeballing the pool for babes alone. If they had bikinis, the odds increased in my favor. Cautious women don't like to expose their bodies. I put my swim trunks on, joined them, and began a conversation. I'm easy to talk with; and quite good at talking about female subjects. From time to time I would score. Anyway, here is the nut of the story: One day in Lake Charles, Louisiana, at the Howard Johnson Hotel, I met this young woman who had come there from Houston to get married. She wanted to spend a few days alone to contemplate her upcoming nuptials. To make this story short, I made love to her twice that day, but only that day. She told me it was okay because she wasn't married yet, and one last fling appealed. Then, there was the wife of a soldier in San Antonio. He was off fighting in Viet Nam. I met her at a roller rink. She gave me some because she was lonely."

Ronson threw his smoke out the window. "I can't believe you, Alex. The more you make love to forbidden women, the more you do not trust your own. You're a shocking man. I'm not inviting you to my wedding."

"Obviously you missed the point."

"What is the point, exactly?"

"If you don't keep a constant eye on your woman, Sancho will enjoy her."

"Who is Sancho?"

"He's a satisfier of dissatisfied and lonely women. He's probably screwing your Layna right now."

He shot me the finger.

"Have you called her since you got out of prison?"

"No time for romance now. I have this trouble with your family land in Panama. I will call her afterwards."

"Right, right after you remove your face from Mariana's ass?"

A few minutes later he spoke. "I like Mariana, she's special. And I do know about Sancho. We have one too, but his name is Winkel. We call him the Winkelman. When he visits your woman, she is not yours anymore."

"Does he take them away?"

"No, they go with him."

"Well, let me say that our Sancho is not like your Winkelman. Ours comes and goes, leaving her behind. Sancho never takes them with him. That is not his purpose. He just gives them something she is not getting from her man. Usually its sexual attention. I want to meet your Layna."

He shot me the bird again.

Puerto Limón was nothing to talk about. A typical port town, dirty and void of architectural beauty, but loaded with Afro-Caribbean culture. To best enjoy it, we made our way to the beach area, befriended a few Rastafarians, and scored two joints.

ALBERTO ARCIA

During a conversation with an individual who claimed to be a smuggler, we were told that we could drive or take a bus to the Panama border.

"It's not much of a border," he said, "and it can be crossed with minimum trouble."

He smiled, puffed on a reefer, and continued. "If you two want to avoid police trouble, for a sum, I will take you to the Panama side on my boat. I'll put in on the Island of Colon, in Bocas. You can take a bus from there and go anywhere you want."

I thanked him for the offer, but declined. No need to take a chance of that nature with a total stranger. I had already began to work on a plan to cross over.

I gave Ronson the car keys and asked him if he wanted to see the biggest tropical rainforest in the region, He said yes, so he drove north to Tortugero National Park.

He enjoyed the drive there. The area's rustic nature gave him a sense of wellbeing. It turned out we both had a good feel for the Afro-Caribbean culture.

When we arrived, we learned there would be a guided tour going out during the night to see the giant turtles come in and lay their eggs. It was October, the last month this would be possible. We joined the guided tour.

Right about eleven, the first of three came out of the ocean and made their way up the beach. I had seen this ritual before, but Ronson hadn't. He became fascinated with these giant creatures. The process of crawling in, digging the hole and crawling back was mesmerizing.

We returned to the encampment, covered ourselves with Cutter's insect repellent, and spent the night in our net-covered hammocks. The next day we returned to San Jose, making a stop at the highest point in the country, Cerro

Chirripo. The main attraction here is the ability to see both oceans. However, it required a clear day, and like countless other times I've been up there, the clouds prevented it. Bummed, we drove back to the capital. We had already missed one paid-for screw and two blow jobs, we didn't want to lose any more love action. Besides, Ronson missed his woman.

Chapter Nine

The Road to the Border

On the last day of our stay in beautiful San
Jose, my sister showed up. She sent word for us to meet her
at *Arturo's Panadería y Café* at 11:00 in the morning.

We arrived at 10:30 and found her already there. She
sat with Lor. They seemed too comfy for my taste. I hoped
Lor was not boning her. But I was wrong.

"Hello, Alex," said Deni. "Scrub the bad face off, I
can screw whomever I want," and she pointed at Lor, "I'm
doing him."

Lor grinned.

"Time to go fight drug dealers already?" asked
Ronson, showing discontent.

"Well yes, time waits for no man or woman."

She looked him over and touched his arms. "You have
recovered nicely, so it must be the right time to leave."

She looked at me. "Since you both arrived here
without any issues, I suppose your traveling papers are in
order. If so, we can leave tonight. I have arranged a meeting
with the cartel's man in charge of our area. We meet him
four days after tomorrow in the town of *Nombre de Dios* at

2:00 in the afternoon. But we need to be there early to do a proper scouting of the area."

"Do you have any hardware?" I wanted to know.

"Lor and I purchased some, but my money is limited, so we will have to acquire more, later."

She glued her dark piercing eyes on mine. "You sure you're up to this, Bro?"

Here comes the big lie. "I'm ready to die for you, Sis."

"Don't be so melodramatic, Alex, but I do appreciate your commitment. Can you two pack your things?"

"Ronson may be able to, but I can't cross the border."

Deni's eyes narrowed. "You can't or you won't?"

"Can't or won't, it means the same thing."

She looked at Ronson, he shrugged his shoulders. "Don't know why either, but I'm not ready to go neither. I will stay here two more days."

She turned her gaze my way. "You want to tell me why neither one of you is ready to leave? By now I figured you both be tired of screwing and resting."

"Deni, you and Lor can hang in here until Ronson is ready. Give me the directions and I will meet you at the farm in Colon before meeting day. I am leaving today, but alone."

Deni bowed on me. "I'm not leaving here unless you give me a good reason as to why you can't come with us."

"Sis, I have enemies in the government; border crossing are not easy for me. I need to get into the country without alerting anyone who may still harbor a grudge. Computers have a long memory. I will cross into Bocas Del Toro instead of Chiriquí."

ALBERTO ARCIA

That settled the matter. She didn't argue. We walked back to the brothel and I checked out. Maribel reminded me that she did not give refunds.

"No hay problema, Maribel, el Suizo se queda dos noches más. Yo salgo ahora."

I said my goodbyes, and Deni drove me to the bus station. Before she dropped me off, she handed me a cell. "Call if you're going to be late or if you decide not to come at all. If necessary, I may be able to change the meeting date and time. If I can't, I'll deal with this without you. Good luck and don't fail me."

With that, she gunned the engine and left me. *Good riddance.* I purchased a ticket to Coahuita and sat down to wait. Two hours later the bus took off. It was crowded as usual, but I planned to sleep most of the way.

When we stopped at Puerto Viejo, an American woman climbed into the bus. She looked around and sat next to me.

"You an American?" she asked.

"Not really."

"What does that mean? You're either an American or not."

"I'm an American from the center of the continent, not from the north end of it. So, no I'm not an American like you."

She hardened her posture. "Sorry for asking, but you do look like me, and I'm an American."

Oh, God, spare me, please. "Listen, Miss, let's agree that we're both Americans and drop the subject."

"I'm not a miss, I'm a missus. My name is Leslie Duvall. I'm from Lafayette, Louisiana."

I extended my hand, she shook it. "I'm Alex, from Texas. Where is your other half?"

"He's waiting for me in Bocas."

She thought about my answer and frowned. "Wait a moment, I thought you said you came from the center of the continent? If you're from Texas, you're an American."

"I'm from Panama but live in Texas."

"You married?"

"Yes, I'm on wife number four. How about you?"

"First timer. I hope I can hang on to him. He's a handful."

"A high maintenance hubby, uh?"

"You know it."

I turned my head towards the countryside, wanting to end the inane conversation. She picked up on it and left me alone.

I glanced her way from time to time, she kept her back pack on her lap instead of the upper luggage carrier or the floor beneath her feet. She also had a grip on it. Her posture told me something was not right. *Why is she traveling alone on this backwater road?* This area is populated by unemployed Rastas, drug smugglers, and pirates dealing in the human trade. Round here, tourists didn't wander too far from their group guides. Most of them preferred to visit the central valley of the country, where it was safe.

First thing that came to mind was, *she's a mule.* Her husband gave her the stuff and is hoping the silly young woman can cross without being searched. *What an asshole.* She has a beacon of light shining on her, telling everyone she is carrying drugs.

ALBERTO ARCIA

I thought about that scenario but decided against it. No one is stupid enough to carry drugs into Panama. You can buy all you want there. So, what could she be carrying?

The bus made it to Coahuita. I looked at my companion and noticed her face had tightened.

"Listen, Leslie, I'm an old hat when it comes to crossing borders, if you're carrying something illegal in your pack, Sixaola is the wrong border for you. You should try your luck at Pasos Canoas, on the Pacific side."

"Well, what do we have here? Mister don't-bother-me has now decided to mind my business. What is this? All of a sudden you have become my father?"

"I'm too young to be your father, Leslie, I'm just trying to give you sound advice. Take it or leave it. It's no sweat off my ass."

She opened her pack and showed me its visible contents. Camera equipment. "I'm crossing at Sixaola because my boyfriend is at the Angela hotel on the island of Colon in Bocas. The other border puts me too far. Besides, I would need to take a bus to David, and from there to Bocas. I'm told by many that the bus ride over the mountains is too dangerous."

I laughed. "Yes, very much so. I rode that route once and didn't appreciate the driver taking the curves at a speed of seventy kilometers an hour. The damn bus would chug, chug up the mountain and then the driver refused to apply the brakes on the way down."

As I prepared to get off, she quizzed me. "Alex, why are you getting off here, Sixaola is further down the road."

"I need to cross into Panama without exposing my passport. Coahuita is the end of my bus trip."

"How are you going to do that from here?"

"Ever heard of the Bribri people?"

She shook her head.

"They are an aboriginal tribe that lives in the Yorkin Indigenous Reserve. I know one of them. His name is Molo. We met in San Jose a while back. He owes me a favor, and I intend to collect."

She stared at me in silence.

"I intend to cross into Panama from their territory. It's a long hike, followed by a longer canoe ride on the Rio Sixaola. From there I'll make my way onto the Island of Colon from the mainland."

"Is someone waiting for you there?"

"No, I'm heading for trouble, and I'm taking the long way there."

The look in her eyes changed, so did her body posture. Something I said caught her interest, and she touched my arm. "Can I go with you?"

I looked into her eyes. They showed a daringness. But a woman on a dark road could bring me trouble. "No, Leslie, you need to go your own way. I'd rather travel alone."

She grabbed my hand. "Please take me along."

So, she is carrying contraband. "Don't you have a husband waiting for you?"

"Yes, a difficult one. And like you, I'm not in a hurry to get to my destination. I want to see these aborigines. I've never been to an indigenous reservation."

"The road there is not easy, it requires a long hike, and there is always danger around. I'd rather traverse it alone."

She came closer and whispered, "I'll sleep with you if you take me."

ALBERTO ARCIA

The offer tempted me, but I hung on to my guns. "Thanks for the offer, but I'm too old for you."

She moved my hand to her left breast, I felt it swell, and so did John Henry."

"You told me you were too young to be my father. Don't you want me?"

"I'm inclined to accept your offer, Leslie. Your body is tempting, but I don't think interlocking limbs is a good idea."

She placed her hand on John Henry and gave him a squeeze, sealing the deal.

"Okay, but stay close and don't complain. The road ahead is hard."

Chapter Ten

A Porn Star

We entered the reservation and walked to the office cabin to pay for the permit required. I asked the man if Molo was around. He nodded.

"I would like to see him. We're old friends."

We were told to wait outside. An hour later, Molo showed up wearing khaki pants and a red shirt. He must like that combo because that is what he wore the last time I met him in San Jose.

He seemed glad to see me. We shook hands and I explained my needs. He agreed. At that point I introduced Leslie. He removed his hat and extended his hand. They hit it off right from the start. For an aborigine, he had good facial features.

We hiked for a long time, until we came to a small community close to the Sixaola River. The buildings were built on stilts, using thatch for walls and roof.

"Alex, the community has an empty hut reserved for travelers. It costs three hundred *colones* per night, but if I slept there, there's a chance we could get it for free."

ALBERTO ARCIA

Leslie insisted he sleep with us. I felt my carnal pleasure slipping away. She liked him, and vice versa. We agreed to spend the night.

We ate a meal of coconut rice, black beans, and fish before we turned in. I knew Molo would not move in on Leslie unless he felt it was okay with me. After thinking about her willingness to bed road strangers, it was okay. The girl felt too daring.

We started the night in the hut, and at some point I expressed a desire to sleep in the open air. I took my hammock and hung it outside on the grounds. There was a nice evening breeze, and the mosquitos were not yet a problem. As usual, I applied a generous ointment of Cutter's insect repellent and hung up my net. At midnight the wind stopped and the mosquitos swarmed, I was forced to leave the hammock and seek shelter in the hut. Leslie was asleep in her bag, Molo in a *tapete* next to her. I climbed in my bag.

The next morning, I felt Molo's embarrassment. He wouldn't look me in the eyes.

"Don't sweat it my friend, she does not belong to me. She is free to choose any man she wants."

He beamed at the revelation.

We had a morning meal of fish and something mushy made with ground cacao beans and then, set out for the river where a man in a long wooden canoe waited.

The river trip was challenging—too many rapids for my taste. We arrived at a site where the canoe man dropped us off. Molo told me to use my compass and follow a straight south route until I came to a village. From there I could hire a horse and go until I ran into the Caribbean ocean. Across from it would be the island of Colon. I told him *adios*, and looked at Leslie, who seemed reluctant to leave. *What is her deal?*

She whispered something into Molo's ear and he nodded in the affirmative. He removed his hat and approached me. *"Oye, amigo, la mujer se quiere quedar conmigo."*

I gave him my hand and smiled. *"Ten cuidado. Tu problema no es el mío."*

He grinned. *"Esa mujer es un buen problema."*

Hell, I was good with her wanting to remain with him. She probably was going to talk him into crossing with her. She's smuggling something all right. *Good riddance.* I left them holding hands.

On the island of Colon, I took a taxi to the Angela Hotel and inquired if someone with the last name of Duvall had a room. I was told no. From there I took another taxi to the Sue Lynn Hotel and asked the same question. Again the answer was no. I wondered why she lied and hoped Molo would not get into trouble. I decided to check into the Angela Hotel and then made arrangements to fly out the following day.

That evening, I took a walk down the strip. The whole place seemed stuck in a time warp. The town of Bocas reminded me of what Key West must have looked like in Hemingway's time.

I stopped at a place billed as the Library. There was a crowd outside comprised of locals and foreigners. They were chatting and drinking. The smell of *colitas* hung over the air. Music came from the inside. Someone was playing old time tunes. I recognized the singer and the song. Mario Lanza belting out the piece *Drink, Drink, Drink.* Impressed I walked inside. There I met a good looking woman who had to be in her middle to late fifties. She was spinning records. I introduced myself, asked her name, and applauded her taste of music, mentioning that opera was the last thing I expected to hear in this salty, pirate enclave.

She laughed. "I'm not the owner. Miranda is out with her beau. I'm Celeste."

"You have an accent I can't place," I said.

She laughed again and gave me the once over look. "I'm a retired actress. I came here from Sweden. You also have an accent. Where are you from?"

Been here, done this before. If I tell her I was from Panama, specifically from the province of Colon, she'd call me a lair, and the conversation would go south. I smiled. "I'm from Texas. Just arrived."

She thumbed through the old record collection and found one. "Here, handsome, let me play this one for you."

She put it on and left to use the toilet. When it came on, I smiled. It was Marty Robbins singing the *Ballad of the Alamo*.

A guy came in and asked where the sex movie star had gone.

Movie star? I pointed to the toilet.

"Celeste is a porn star?" I said with admiration.

"Yeah buddy. During her youth, she was Sweden's Brigitte Bardot. Now she owns a bed and breakfast place called *"Celeste."* She's a load of fun to be around."

Shit, I'm staying at the wrong place.

She came back and smiled. "You like the record?"

I smiled and reached for her hand, which she gave me. I kissed it. "Love that song. San Antonio is my hometown, and Marty Robbins is my favorite balladeer. Your choice flatters me. Thank you."

Her eyes glimmered. I knew I was almost there. She leaned over and asked me, quietly. "You said you just arrived. Have a place to sleep yet?"

"No, not yet. I left my back pack in a locker at the bus station."

She gave me a smile that I swear, melted my socks. She turned her back to me and reached out for another record. Without looking at me, she spoke. You like Willie Nelson?"

Here it is, my chance. "Yes, but not as much as I like you. Celeste, look at me."

She turned and, like magic, the two top buttons of her blouse had been liberated. The cleavage almost gave me a heart attack.

"Celeste, you are indeed a beautiful woman. I'm enchanted. Do you know where I can find lodging?"

That night, round the midnight hour, I found myself in another rented room, waiting for an aged angel to appear. When she did, Celeste's long curly blond hair seductively spread over her shoulders. She wore a red baby-doll nightie with long black stockings attached to garters. She was braless, and those old puppies were still upright. She had on high heels and she moved towards me with a hip swing that captivated my heart. John Henry had the same appreciation for her as I did. Tonight both of us would enjoy love at its best.

She came to me and removed my shirt. I tried to kiss her but she whispered, "Not yet, Honey. Let me finish setting the mood."

113

ALBERTO ARCIA

She unbuckled my pants and let them drop to my ankles. I removed each leg and kicked them to the corner, then reached for her. Again, the "not yet, Honey," came out. But this time it was accompanied by a "stay here, don't move."

She swayed towards a radio-tape deck combination, placed in a cassette, and turned it on. Edith Piaf, the song bird of France, began to sign. I knew that moment this evening belonged to the ages. My hurriedness surrendered, and I prepared to enjoy this woman's charms.

She walked to the bed and placed her body in the pose of the "Naked Maja," and whispered, "Come to me, Honey bun. It's time to love Celeste."

And that I did. John Henry did me proud that night. All that screwing in San Jose had emptied the sack, giving him no reason to accelerate his enthusiasm. The music, the slow body rhythm of two bodies entangle in an erotic sexual motion, increasing and decreasing in total unification, sent me to the moon.

I woke up looking for more, but she had gone. Celeste left me a personal note attached to the room bill. The note said, *thanks for the great night* written on it. *I'm going fishing with my boyfriend today. Love, Celeste.*

I checked out of both places, phoned Deni, and caught my flight to Panama City. Time for fun and games had come to an end. Now I had to pay the piper.

Chapter Eleven

A Bloodbath

The road to Nombre de Dios had been greatly improved. I remember it as being nothing more than a rudimentary, pot holed, two-lane asphalt road. When I inquired as to why the government spent money on a road in this forgotten part of Panama, I was told it was the cartel. They needed a good highway to the coast.

"You ought to see the improvements done to the airport," said Deni.

"Good. We may need it to escape. Can we afford an airplane?"

Deni had a good laugh over that absurd comment. "You amaze me, Alex. We're not escaping from here. We will make our stand at the farm and either get it back or be buried on it."

Deni's cavalier attitude bothered me. She never showed any suicidal or imbecilic tendencies before. As we came closer to the town of Nombre de Dios, I began to worry about the upcoming meeting. We were going to try and negotiate a withdrawal from our land with a cartel chieftain named El Cholo Rodriguez.

ALBERTO ARCIA

We had nothing of real value to offer, except another smaller parcel. One without direct river access. Certainly there had to be another plan in place. This one was totally useless. *Why are we going into the viper's burrow with nothing?*

"Deni, surely you don't expect El Cholo to agree to dismantle his lab and move the operations to someplace else without having any leverage?"

"Alex, we're going to see if the brute will even listen to our demands and consider the offer. If not, we will kick the ball and regroup."

"Why don't we sweeten the pot?"

"What do you have in mind, Alex?"

"What do the cartel need more than anything else?"

"Speak, brother. Blurt it out."

The answer is anonymity. Why don't we explore the possibilities of a deal that would allow us to maintain our sovereignty over the land?"

"Alex," said Ronson. "Please explain yourself."

She shot him a stern look. "No one died and made you king, Ronson."

"Denise, if he's willing to fight for your cause, you owe him the right to speak his mind. So, let me explain my thoughts: I figured these guys would not want a scuffle or a public media battle; those things are always bad for business. Don Jimenez put El Cholo in charge because he's smart. Bringing his cartel publicity is bad for business. It will force the government to intervene. I believe he will negotiate, providing the deal is appealing. Let's try asking for a piece of the land for our own use, plus a monthly payment from them for their usage, instead of demanding

116

they evacuate the land and move the lab. They have plenty of money. The deal may suit him."

"Alex, you want me to ask him to share our land?"

"That's not a bad idea for a conversation starter," said Ronson.

"Mind your own beeswax, *Suizo*."

"Sis, can you at least think about it?"

"Alex, we are not going to this meeting to achieve any other goal than to force the cartel to move the lab to another farm, one smaller than the one they occupy and not as lucrative. As long as the cartel operates that drug lab, our land is in jeopardy. There are individuals in power that would love to own it."

"I thought we were going to talk without expectations? And the word lucrative makes me laugh. This farms we own are west of Sabanita. There's never been anything of value there."

"Listen, Big Brother. From our land a road can be built to San Blas. We could connect the Indian reservation, avoiding the necessity of having to fly there."

The next question would tell me everything I needed to know. "Do you think the local authorities have been bribed to look the other way? Are we alone in this quarrel?"

She laughed. "Bro, everyone that could help us has been paid off or intimidated. We're on our own. Are you getting cold feet?"

"No, I just don't like to get into a situation without an exit plan."

"Alex, the exit plan here is to see God."

Ronson interjected. "I don't want to be the rat that ruins the party, but I don't intend to die in Panama, so I'm with Alex. We need an exit plan."

Finally, someone besides me has sense. "Thank you, Ronson. Anyone here able to fly an airplane?"

When no one raised his hand, Ronson came up with a plan of escape. "If we need to run, we can travel by riverboat. I looked at the map, and there are several rivers in the Santa Isabel district where most of the farms in question are located. We could use any of them as a way out or in, if the roads are watched."

"Which rivers?" I wanted to know.

"The Juan de Dios, Saino, María Concepción, and Nombre de Dios rivers."

Deni's eyes sparkled. "Well, it seems we have found our operations manager. Two of them pass through our land."

I was about to object, when Deni cut me short. "Since you have not taken the time to study anything, I'm putting Ronson in charge of our operation with me second in command."

Not knowing what to say, I kept my mouth shut.

"It's settled then. Alex, you will be the face and voice of the team. I will ultimately make or approve the decisions, and Lor will provide the muscle."

We passed the town limit sign and drove towards *El Hotel Colonial*, our meeting place. Lor dropped us off and left to park the car. Two rough looking characters with automatic weapons were waiting for us at the entrance to the lobby. These guys must have felt safe, we were not searched going into the lobby.

"Adonde está el Cholo?" I asked one of them.

The man pointed, *"En el salón Tucan."*

One thug led the way with the other taking the rear. Amateurs. They have allowed Lor to gain their backs. The lead man knocked four times and opened the door.

"Only the Pérezes can go in. You," he pointed at Ronson, "you stay here."

We walked inside while he and the other guy stayed outside.

Waiting for us were three men, one on each flank, standing and armed. In the middle was Cholo. He was sitting behind a table with a plate of food in front of him.

"Señorita Pérez, espero que no me venga a joder la paciencia. Qué diablo quiere conmigo?"

I tried to speak, but he cut me short. *"Cállate, cabrón. Voy a hablar con ella."*

So much for me being the face and voice.

"Cholo, the land you're using for your illegal drug operation belongs to me. I want you to leave."

"Eso es todo? Quiere que empaquemos todo el equipo y que cerremos la operación y nos mudemos? De verdad?"

"Yes, pretty much that's it. Except that I'm willing to rent you a smaller piece of land at a different site. You can set up your lab there. The one you're on I need."

He seemed amused. I was expecting a more violent demeanor. These are *macho* guys who dislike impertinent women. He spent a moment scanning Deni's face and body posture. Then he looked my way.

"Quién diablos eres tú? El marido?"

"No, I'm her *pinche* brother."

ALBERTO ARCIA

He cleaned his teeth with a finger, then wiped it on his pants. I waited for some sort of an outburst but nothing came. Instead he asked an unexpected question.

"Adonde está el otro terreno?"

Stupefied, I looked at Deni. She stuck her hand in her pocket and brought out a piece of paper. I glanced at it and recognized it to be a land survey. She moved closer and gave it to him. Pointing at an area.

"Farm number one thousand-eight hundred and seventy-four. One full hectare on the outside of the town of Cativá. For six-hundred dollars per month, you and your people can stay and work there."

Two thumping sounds came from outside the room. Before anyone could react, the door flew open and Lor and Ronson entered. They were holding pistols. Lor shot both bodyguards immediately, and Ronson pointed his gun at Cholo, who remained uncharacteristically calm. The man had balls of steel.

He looked at Sis. *"No me dijo que quería negociar un cambio de ubicación?*

"Yo sí, pero parece que mi novio no es un tipo de palabras."

I looked at her. "I'll say Lor's not a man of words. We came here to negotiate, not murder."

She shot me an angry look. "That train has left the station, Brother."

Lor handed Deni his pistol. "You shoot him or I keel him."

"Don't do it, Sis. He is willing to negotiate."

She looked at me with disdain. "You're dumber than a pile of manure, Bro. He is playing with us. Cholo has no intention of leaving our land. Right now he's planning how to kill us."

"You don't know that."

Ronson's words sealed the deal. "Alex, you know nothing. Didn't you study the history of your people?"

"*Et tú,* Ronson?" I felt the pain of betrayal and glared at him.

"The conquistadores with a few hundred soldiers conquered the empires of the Aztecs and the Incas. They did it by taking away their king. Without a ruler to guide and inspire, the kingdom falls."

Deni grinned. "Ronson is right." Then she shot Cholo in the forehead. The man's head went backwards and his lifeless body slumped to the floor. With this bloodbath on our hands, we started a war we could not possibly win.

Upset, I blurted out. "Neither Cortez nor Pizarro killed the king before they conquered the nation."

Deni kissed Lor on the lips, high fived Ronson, and shot me the finger. She pointed at Cholo. "He was not a king."

I stood there, dazed, not really believing we had just murdered a bunch of Don Pablo Jimenez's men.

"Okay, Alex, snap out of it. Now comes plan B. You and Ronson load the body of Cholo into the car. We will drive to city hall and seek out the mayor. We will tell him we have struck a blow to the cartel and they can either help us or they will be on the receiving end of the cartel's wrath. Ronson will take a photo of you, me, and the mayor holding Cholo's head by the hair. We then put that photo on the internet, forcing his hand.

ALBERTO ARCIA

"That's plan B? Are you out of your mind? You put that on the internet and the cartel will send an army of *pistoleros* here with orders to peel our skin, slowly, and with dull knives."

She laughed. "Bro, you have no stomach for a hard fight."

"Sis, I can't believe you have been reading my mail."

She laughed again. "Well Alex, today the Perez family, with the help of our Swiss friends, have struck a blow that will reverberate throughout the province, if not the republic. We will be hailed as heroes for standing up against these cruel Colombian drug lords."

Oh, God, Deni has gone clear off her rocker.

Chapter Twelve

El Alamo

With plan B done, and the fear-stricken mayor on board, the police chief, having no alternative, cooperated and helped us remove the remaining men working the lab. Ronson was partially correct. Once the rank and file knew that their chieftain and his henchmen were dead, they threw their weapons down and left peacefully.

A deal was worked out with the head cop. He agreed to split the cartel's weapons between us. He knew we were going to need them to fight off the incoming onslaught. Now we and the local cops were better armed.

To complete our challenge, Deni insisted we burn the lab and put the torching on the internet. A nice follow up to the gruesome shot of the dead Cholo.

As you can well imagine, the photo hit the world causing a major stir. No one could believe the Perez family with two foreigners by their side were willing to challenge the drug empire of Don Pablo Jimenez.

This fact annoyed the government, who to this point had remained quiet. They had no love for the cartel. Any blow struck against them (not coming from them) was welcomed. They had long ago lost the taste for fighting these ruthless people.

Not only were these druggies better armed, but they had an intelligence network that told them who planned to oppose them and when. These people were quickly assassinated and their bodies dumped on the street for everyone to see. Don Pablo's payroll included members of the government, as well as ranking officers in the military. When the offer made to them included a paycheck or death, its way easier to play ball.

This last photo shoot caused the uproar intended by Sis, she aroused the sentiment of the populace. The government inactivity became an embarrassment.

Unfortunately, this situation would eventually bring a man back into my life. One I'd rather not have seen again.

Deni managed to recruit a few locals-- individuals who had suffered at the hands of the druggies. Now we numbered an army of eight men and two women. I'm excluding the police support who had been promised by the mayor and the chief, knowing quite well that at the first signs of hostilities, these men would disappear.

Hell, they had no valid reason to sacrifice their lives and endanger their families. We were nothing to them, not anymore. The Perez family had long ago left the province. We were no longer their benefactors.

If anything, these local yokels needed to be feared. The mayor and the chief, in order to save their own skin, could just as easily turn their soldiers' guns on us.

One day, not long after we put the Cartel on notice, a policeman came to our farm. He asked for me and introduced himself as Sargento Rosario Morales.

124

"Señor Pérez," he said. "Coronel Ortiz wants to meet with you at Rosita's Cantina tomorrow afternoon at five. He wants you to come alone. Will you be there?"

I looked at the soldier and found his countenance to be pleasant. A bit nervous but very polite. He had removed his kepi when he entered the house and now stood at attention.

"Sargento, do I have a choice?"

His face stiffened, and his voice cracked a bit. Obviously he was afraid of me. I realized right then that Deni had given us an image of individuals not to be messed with. A better appearance than that of a family of lunatics bent on an early death.

"I beg your forgiveness, sir, and please don't kill the messenger, but the colonel told me to tell you that if you stand him up, he will come here and bend your sister over a table and screw the life out of her."

"Tell Colonel Ortiz that I will be there, but only to keep him from trying to screw a Tasmanian devil."

I was surprised he understood my meaning, at least I thought he did. He smiled, clicked his heels, and left.

A few minutes later, Deni walked in. "Who was the soldier and what did he want?"

"An emissary from Colonel Juju Ortiz. He wanted to ask my permission for something."

She sat at the table and asked me to bring her the bottle of Ron Abuelo, plus two rock glasses. She poured us a drink, drank hers, and then gave me a puzzling look.

"Permission for what?"

"Sis, it appears the colonel wants to have sex with you."

Her demeanor became serious. She placed her arms akimbo. "Quit screwing around, Alex. What did the man want?"

I drank my rum and measured my words. "The colonel wants me to not show up at a meeting tomorrow afternoon at Rosita's so he can get upset, come here, throw you over the table and give you a good butt screwing."

"Get serious, Bro, what did he really want?"

Disappointed, I divulged the fact that the colonel wanted to deal with me, not her.

"Why do you think that is?" she wanted to know.

"Because you're a woman, and this is man's business."

She glared at me, and with a seething tone came at me. "Who in hell does that man think he's dealing with? Besides, you're not in charge here."

"No, I'm not, but sure as hell need to be. Hear me out, Sis. We go to a meeting to negotiate a settlement, end up murdering a bunch of people, and then give the hotel manager cause to quit his job and run and hide. We incriminate an innocent and hapless mayor and also embarrass the government. All this through your leadership. And, if all that is not bad enough, now we have a man in town you will soon regret to meet."

As I prepared to mention his name, I grabbed my hand and rubbed the pinkie stub. "The president has sent Colonel Juju Ortiz to talk to us. He knows me, which is why I've been summoned."

She stared at me. I had caught her attention. The podium was mine. It was my turn to turn my baby blues on her stern face. "This guy is bad news. He's probably working for both sides, so no matter what we do or don't do,

126

one side will come at us. He is known as the enforcer. He's here to clean things up. So, Sis, where do we draw our line? If we're not careful we may end up fighting our own government."

"Well, Big Brother, you're a self-professed Texan, you ought to know about lines drawn. Colonel Travis drew one at the Alamo. We fight to win, but we don't fight the government. Go to this meeting and fix it so we fight Jimenez. It's the only way we can win. *Capiche?*"

"Yeah, I'm hip. But Travis gave Crockett, Dickinson, Bowie, and the others a chance to run. You snared us."

"Wait here," she said and left in a huff, returning to the room with everyone, including the two men guarding the entrance to the farm.

With some fanfare, she opened a sack of processed cocaine and poured a long line on the floor. There was a time when that wastefulness would have hurt, but that was then, and this is now. Today I didn't give a shit she was pouring pure cocaine on the ground.

She crossed to the other side of the line, separating us. *"Atención, amigos.* We are going to be in a hard fight with the cartel, and maybe with the government. A fight my brother does not think we can win, but one I do think we can win. I am giving you an opportunity right now to avoid this unfortunate situation. If you'd rather not fight, please stay where you are. If you want to fight, state your reason and cross over."

The first to cross was Lor. "Deni," he said. 'Yur fight is my fight. I fight wid you."

ALBERTO ARCIA

I looked at Ronson. He seemed uncomfortable. Being the good friend that I am, I knew what to do, give him an honorable way out.

Lor was a Swiss from the Italian side, which explained his craziness. Ronson was a Swiss from the Austrian side. His feet were planted firmly on the ground.

Before I made my move, a man named Roberto spoke. "El Cholo killed my brother-in-law and raped my sister. Like you, I will fight the cartel, but not the government. He crossed the line.

The three remaining locals followed suit, all giving their reasons, but not wanting to fight the government. This was expected. Then my turn came.

"I will fight both sides if need be, but only until all hope of winning is gone. I will have a plan of escape in place."

Deni glared at me. I smiled at her. Then, with a smug expression, I crossed the line.

We all looked at Ronson, the last man standing on the wrong side. He followed my lead, as I knew he would. Ronson did not harbor any suicidal tendencies.

"I am not a coward. I will stand and fight both sides with you, but like Alex, I will leave when I see there is no chance of winning." He crossed the line.

The next morning Deni was out early. She had two of the local men carrying boards and poles.

When I left for my meeting that afternoon, I saw the reason for all the hammering. She had erected a large wooden sign on the entryway to the farm. The sign read, *El Alamo Panameño*.

She insisted we all stand in front of it with our weapons. Then she set the camera on automatic and joined the photo. Afterwards she posted it on the internet. It went viral.

I had to take my hat off to her. She was a marketing genius. This maneuver will recruit foreign fighters by appealing to their adventurous side. I could already see the graves of Colonel Travis, David Crockett, Jim Bowie, Captain Dickinson, and the one-hundred and eighty men begin to stir up.

Besides wanting to recruit more men, Deni wanted to arouse national patriotism, something very hard to do. The people from the interior of the country, especially the proud *Chiricanos*, wanted nothing to do with the people from the two main industrial provinces, Panama and Colon. Ditto for the inhabitants of Bocas. They were too far removed to get caught in problems not of their making.

Deni also wanted the weak government to stay out of the fight. If the populace joins our cause, the soldiers will stay inside the barracks.

As I drove to my appointment, I understood that she was right. She's the one to lead this fight. I'm not that conniving.

In one swift and clever move, Sis declawed the colonel. I couldn't wait until I saw his face. His ace in the hole card could not be played. She had just forced him to either join our side or stay out of the way. And knowing his pockets were lined with Cartel money, Juju's blood pressure had to be soaring.

Chapter Thirteen

Colonel Juju Ortiz

I walked into Rosita's cantina and immediately became surrounded by several of the colonel's military henchmen. They searched and cleared me. One of them escorted me to the colonel's table. My cocky attitude left me as soon as I laid eyes on him. The man still scared me. He motioned for me to sit.

"*Hola, Coronel,* long time no see."

He let out a loud sigh. "*Coño*, Alex, you're like a bad quarter, always turning up. What are you doing here, stirring things up? You didn't like Texas?"

"It's not a bad quarter, Juju, it's a bad penny. If you are going to use English idioms, you have to get them right. I like Texas just fine, but Panama called."

His right cheek started to twitch, then he slammed his hand on the table, tumbling his glass and spilling the drink.

"*Me cago en Judas!* What are you doing back here? Did I not tell you the next time I saw you I was going to hurt you? Do you think I'm not a man of my word?"

I swallowed hard. I needed to handle this situation gingerly. The monster was already rearing its ugly head. As long as the fangs didn't show, I'd be okay.

"I did not intend to come here, *Coronel,* but my kid sister had a problem and needed my help. I was also hoping you were a forgiving man. Our troubles are old. Hopefully forgotten by now. How did you find me so soon?"

He fumed. I could tell the man had control issues.

"Alex," he growled, "your photo is all over the damn country."

He took a deep breath, poured rum into his glass, and drank it down. He wiped his mouth with the sleeve of his uniform. I looked at the glass. He noticed and offered me some. I accepted, and the soldier behind him brought me a glass.

"I know I have said this before, but I need to say it again. How does an imbecile like you get to live this long?"

"Mostly, *Coronel,* because you and your kind have not been able to kill me." I showed him my pinkie stub. "This is as far as you have gotten. One little bitty pinkie."

That was a stupid thing to say. I often wondered how I had managed to live this long too. The old guy, with a swift and unexpected hand action, grabbed my left wrist and pulled me towards him. Instinctively, the drink I was holding on my right hand went into his face. That's when the pain hit my head, and the lights went out.

When I regained consciousness my head hurt something awful. I tried to touch it to alleviate the pain but realized my hands were tied behind me. The place was cold and dark, confusing my sense of orientation. *Where am I?*

A door opened, watering the darkness. I heard the sound of footsteps enter. Footsteps made by boots. *Oh, yeah, now I remember. Juju.* A shadowy man came close and pulled on a cord. When it clicked, light illuminated the area. It took a few seconds for my eyes to adjust. When they did, I noticed a room void of furniture, and a lone bulb hanging down on a wire above my head. *Oh, God, an interrogation room.* I also saw two soldiers. One seemed familiar.

Once he spoke, I placed him. *Sargento* Morales, Juju's messenger. *Is he my torturer?*

"Señor Pérez, let me apologize for the blow to your head."

He let that statement sink in, then he continued. "You are indeed a lucky man."

I tried to answer but he stopped me. "No, no need to reply. I know you know that already, which is why you tossed your drink into Colonel Ortiz's face."

"I don't suppose an apology will sooth the colonel's sense of bitterness?"

He smiled. "The reason I was chosen to go into your farm is because I know your family, at least your brother. We went to La Salle, in Colon City together. I knew you, but not personally. You left during the eighth grade to study with the gringos across the sea in Coco Solo."

I groaned. My head still hurt. "You are friends with Salvador?"

"Somewhat. Maybe not friends as much as classmates. We graduated together."

He hardened up, making me grasp that someone important was fixing to enter the room.

"Sargento Morales. Como está el huevón?"

He stood at attention. *"Ya listo para la interrogación, mi coronel."*

"Váyanse y cierren la puerta."

Both soldiers left and closed the door behind them. This bode well for me. A one-on-one with Juju is just what the doctor ordered. *The man was born straddling a fence. Double-dealing is in his genes.*

"You know, Alex, throwing that drink on me was a stupid thing to do. Why you do it? You enjoy pain?"

I rolled my head. "Not really. It was just a dumb thing to do. I'm not a masochist."

He laughed. "You could have fooled me. How does your head feel?"

"Worse than your face. I'm sorry for the public insult, but I have a tendency to lose my head from time to time."

He gave me a daunting smile. "And body parts too." He opened a box and brought out a jar. With joy clearly on his face, he showed me a pinkie finger. "You recognize it?"

Damn, it's my little finger. "How have you managed to keep it looking so good after all these years?"

He looked at it closely. "Actually, Alex, its gross looking. Formaldehyde is great for preserving things, isn't it?"

I mustered a faint smile. The pain on my face caught his eyes.

"Your hands hurting you? Did the men tie them too tight?"

"Is the discomfort in my face coming across, Juju?"

He smiled and dug his hand back into his pocket, bringing out a black Swiss army knife. He opened a blade and cut the rope, freeing me from the numbing pain. I rubbed my wrists, trying to renew the blood circulation.

I bit my lip. You never thank the torturer, but the relief I felt made me do it. *"Mil gracias, Coronel."*

He acknowledged my courtesy and called for *Sargento* Morales to bring me a glass of water. I drank it down in two gulps, wiping my wet lips with my forearm. I handed the glass back to Morales. He left, closing the door.

133

ALBERTO ARCIA

It was now time to deal with this devil. Maybe a deal could be worked out.

"What do you want from me, Juju?"

He became serious. "Get off the chair and sit on the floor."

"What's the matter, *coronel,* tired of standing?"

"Listen to me, *maricón,* don't mess with me. My life was fine until you showed your ugly head here. What in the world do you and your sadistic, crazy, little sister thinks you can accomplish? Do you think you can challenge Don Pablo Jimenez and win? Are you both that senseless?"

"I'm with you, *Coronel.* It is stupidly suicidal."

He sat on the chair, stared at me, tapping his fingers on his pant leg, indicating I was on the clock.

"Okay, Juju, let me be as clear as I can. Have you ever seen me throw my life away willingly?"

He stared at me without speaking. His fingers stopped tapping but his cheek began to twitch.

"Anything else you want to know, Colonel?"

He was off the chair and on me in one swift move. His right hand grabbed and squeezed my throat, while his left bent my wrist.

He wheezed, as he spoke. "Don't play with me, Alex. I'm in no mood for your weird sense of humor."

Barely squeezing out my words, I explained the statement. "I'm not in charge here. My kid sister is. I need a way out of this mess."

He let go of my throat and sat back on the chair. "What is your sister's plan?"

"Doesn't the Alamo sign make it obvious?"

Again he pounced on me, squeezing my throat harder. "You want to mess with me, asshole? Let's see how this feels."

He called Morales back, and had him hold my hands from behind. Juju tucked his left hand in his pocket and brought out the Swiss army knife. He removed his hand and left me gasping for air.

He opened the knife and grabbed me by the throat again. *Oh great, now what?*

Juju's eyes were on fire. I had messed up. The guy required a thorough explanation for all my comments. Almost like talking to a child. Yet he was a madman.

Colonel Ortiz, breathing hard, placed the knife inside my left nostril and sliced it, bringing forth a gush of blood. The pain and the sight of my blood became too much. I passed out.

I woke up in an infirmary. A man had just finished sewing my nostrils together. I grabbed his hand before he left. "Are you a doctor?"

"Yes, my specialty is sewing up *pendejos* like you."

"Is he gone?"

"If you're talking about the *coronel,* yes he has left the building. But two of his men are here. Want to speak to the one in charge?"

I nodded and he left. A few minutes later *Sargento* Morales walked in. He looked at my nose and grimaced. "Nasty wound there, Alex."

"No shit, Sherlock."

He sat on a stool. "I don't understand you at all. *El coronel es un toro y tú estás moviendo la capa roja. Porque?"*

ALBERTO ARCIA

"The man has always been a pain in my ass, *Sargento*. I can't help waving the red cape at him. I'm glad he's gone."

"Oh, he's not out of your life. He's gone temporarily. *No ha terminado de herirte.* You are still in trouble plenty. My orders are to escort you to a detention cell where you will remain for the rest of the time it takes to resolve this problem with *los drogueros*. If your sister does not surrender her fort to him, he will hand you over to Don Jimenez's enforcers. Do you know what that means?"

My heart dropped to my ankles. "Yes, *Sargento,* I'm screwed."

He laughed, "In more ways than you can imagine. *Esa gente son peores que los animales.*"

I looked at the man. Although he talked the talk, I felt his heart was not entirely in the game. *Maybe he could spare me the mutilation coming at the hands of Jimenez's henchmen.*

"Oye, sargento. Can we make some kind of deal?"

Chapter Fourteen

The Cavalry Arrives

"Lor, have you heard anything about my brother?"

"No, nothing on your *fratello* yet. Ronson left the *fattoria* to go *ricerca* for him. He took Roberto to help with the *linguaggio problema.*"

"How did they managed to leave the farm? The area has been closed by the local authorities. Since our first group of volunteers arrived, they cordoned the area. No one is allowed in out. Did they give them permission?"

"They left by *imbarcazione.*"

"By boat? I'm in charge here. No one should be going out without my permission."

"Deni, you are a *donna*. A *Bella Dona,* but you can't *aspettarti che un uomo to obbedisca. Capito?*"

She bowed up. Placing her arms akimbo. "Listen to me, I'm tired of this machismo attitude. If I give an order, I expect it to be obeyed. You need to…"

"Deni," replied Lor, "you made Ronson boss of *operazioni.*"

She could not argue the point. She did put Ronson in charge of operations. She did not like the heavy handedness of the male culture, but she knew when to stop attacking it. She grabbed the bottle of rum and left to deal with her anger, alone. All her life she had to play second fiddle to men, and why? Because they had a dick between their legs. Their major weakness somehow became their crowning glory. Figure that one out.

An hour later, Deni heard a commotion outside. She grabbed the sawed-off 20 gauge shotgun, told Lor to follow, and together they left the building to investigate the ruckus.

The three-man police team was trying to keep a number of men from entering the ground.

She walked to the gate and asked Emilio, the policeman in charge, what the problem was.

"Señorita Pérez, estos hombres quieren entrar."

"Who are they, and why do they want to come in?"

"Dicen que vienen a ayudar su causa."

"Okay, if they're here to help me with my cause, let them in."

"No puedo. Tengo órdenes de no dejar a nadie más entrar."

"Emilio, who gave you those orders?"

"El Coronel Ortiz."

"Who in hell is he? Yesterday, *Capitán* Ramirez was in charge?"

"Señora, el encardado hoy es Ortiz."

"Deni, what is the problem?" asked Lor

"The police has been taken over by the military. Orders have been given to not let any more men enter. Apparently a new man, a Colonel Ortiz is now in charge."

One of the men trying to get in managed to get past the guard and came forward. He removed his baseball cap. *"Hola,* Deni. Remember me?"

She looked at his face, but could not place him. "Who are you?"

"Well, I'm disappointed. *Soy Miguel Hargoza,* I'm a good friend of Alex. We have met before."

He looked her over and extended his hand. "You didn't have those puppies adorning your chest then."

She glared at him. "You. You're the fresh guy from Arkansas, aren't you? The one who pinched one of my flat nipples?"

"At your service."

She shook his hand. "If you touch them again, I'll break your arm."

"Deni, touching your breasts is the last thing on my mind at the moment, although they are inviting."

Lor stepped up. "Her *seno* is *mio.* You no touch them."

"You got it, *amigo.* I will keep my hands off her breasts."

She glared at Lor, and gave Miguel a mocking smile. Then looked past him. There were three others to deal with. Two of them had cowboy hats.

"Emilio, déjame hablar con estos hombres."

The corporal stepped aside, letting them come up.

"Are you guy's friends of Alex, too?"

One of them tipped his fedora and bowed. *"Yo soy* Francisco Williams, you may call me *Paco.* Yes, I'm also a friend of Alex. These two with me are Thomas and Harry Thurman. We met at the airport in Houston. They do not know your brother, but heard your call to arms. They are also Texans."

She looked at their feet, all of them were wearing cowboy boots. She smiled, and motioned for Lor to come closer. "Sweetie, we need these men, but the corporal will not let them enter. Do something about it."

"Talk for a minute. I will go and come back."

She touched his arm. "That's what I like about you, Lor. You are a man of few words."

"Quieren algo frio de tomar?" she asked Emilio.

"Si, gracias. Hace mucho calor."

She sent word to the kitchen for a jar of cold *tamarindo* and several glasses.

Deni talked to Miguel and Paco, occasionally including the corporal in the conversation. Before Lor returned, another vehicle approached the entrance to the farm.

The corporal ordered his two men to stop the vehicle. The guy in the front passenger seat got out first. He had his hands raised.

She smiled. *"Hola, Salvador,* what took you so long?"

"Hola, Deni. I had to make a stop in David, and then in Balboa Heights."

The driver got out. He was followed by the two rear passengers. Deni couldn't help but laugh. "Brother, I see you brought the family with you."

"I'm not family, thank God," griped the driver.

"Hola, Fausto. Nice to see you. What brings you all this way?"

"Not you, Deni."

She frowned. "I see your disposition has not changed. Thanks for coming anyway."

She opened her arms and hugged her cousins, Dumas and Jámes Perez. *Gracias por venir, primos. Vienen más o son ustedes los únicos?"*

"The family is gathering."

"Gracias a Dios, Dumas. I'm going to need all the help I can get."

Lor finally arrived. He came wearing a long overcoat, and in the company of a woman servant. She carried the tray with the refreshments. He looked at Deni, then pointed at all the men. *"La cavalleria?"*

"Si, mi Amor. The cavalry is here. Let them in."

Lor opened his coat and pulled out an Uzi. He pointed it at the corporal and his men. Then let a burst of gunfire into the air. All three policemen raised their arms. Deni removed their weapons, told them to lower their arms and gave them the cold drinks.

"Señorita," said the corporal, with *kepi* in hand. *Si nos quitan las armas, vamos a tener que comprar otras y cuestan mucho."*

She scolded him. *"Eso no es asunto mío. Váyanse de aquí, antes de que le quite sus uniformes."*

"Deni," said Miguel. "That's not a bad idea. Besides their guns, we could use those uniforms."

She looked at Lor, he caught the meaning and pointed the Uzi at the policemen.

Deni gave the orders. *"Quítense los uniformes. Se pueden quedar con los calzoncillos. Nadie aquí les quiere ver la pinga. Vamos, quítenselo, ahora!"*

The cops dropped their weapons, and with unease, began to unbutton their uniforms.

"Por favor señora. You cannot leave us in this condition. *Si nos encontramos con maricones, nos pueden perjudicar."*

"There are three of you. Cuantos maricones creen que hay en el pueblo? No me jodan la vida y quítense la ropa. "

Everyone had a good laugh at the concern the corporal had of running into queers with only his underwear on.

Deni, sensing an opportunity, asked Salvador to give the policemen a ride to their station. "Alex is missing. He went into town yesterday to meet with a Colonel Ortiz and has not returned. "Go see if you can get info as to what has happened to him."

"You think the Narcos grabbed him?"

"Hope not. If they did, his mutilated body will find its way to our gate. It's more likely the cops are holding him."

"Listen, Denise…"

"Don't call me Denise. Call me Deni."

"Okay, no need to get your dander up. But let me tell you about this Colonel Ortiz. He's the government enforcer. He deals in torture. Alex may be in big trouble."

"Go find out, and don't get yourself arrested. At any moment the Narcos will make their move, and I need all available men here."

"Deni, when I escort these humiliated men into their station wearing nothing but their skivvies, the police will show up at your door."

"Better that rabble, than these Colombians cutthroats. Go quickly and good luck."

Deni went back inside and came face to face with her volunteers. Some were seated, others standing or leaning against the walls. She took center stage, but her discourse was hijacked by Paco. This affront did not sit well. Another

142

male pushing her down. But instead of it being an insult, he paid her homage by addressing her.

"Deni, before we get involved in this war, we need a good layout of the area, the boundaries of the compound, a good assessment of the weapons available, and where our offensive and defensive strengths lie. Also, where is our Achilles heel?"

Deni beamed with appreciation. She had a commander in charge of her fighting force. "Okay, let's have a council of war." She turned towards Lor. "What's the latest headcount?"

"Contando tu fratelli, Ronson, and Roberto, we have sixteen *uomos, e duo donnas.* Not including you"

"English, please," said Harry Thurman. "Not all Texans speak Spanish."

"Actually, Harry, its Italian, but I get your point. Everyone here speaks English, so we will speak it from now on. The total count stands at fifteen men and three women. We have enough weaponry to arm everyone. Unfortunately, they are mostly pistols and Russian made assault rifles. We do have an Uzi, which is Lor's, and we are fortunate to have a machine gun mounted on a Toyota pickup. We also found a half dozen hand grenades, plus two rifle propelled grenade launchers."

Miguel gave out a long, slow, whistle. "Man o' man. Where did you get all the hardware? Impressive to say the least."

"We confiscated it from the Narcos we kicked out."

"The weaponry we are going to face will be heavier. The Narcos will be armed to the teeth," said Thomas Thurman. "It would be nice if we had cannons."

ALBERTO ARCIA

"No shit, Nostradamus."

"Do not insult your volunteers, Deni," said Paco. "He was stating a wish."

"Are we going to have to deal with the local military, as well as the Narcos?" asked Fausto

"That is anyone's guess," replied Deni. "But if they do fire on us, we do not shoot back. Understood? We will lose the support of the nation if we kill our own soldiers."

"What are the chances of our military firing on us?" asked Dumas.

"Your guess is as good as mine, Cousin."

"How are we for fresh water and food?" asked Miguel. "Can we withstand a long siege?"

"Here lies the problem," said Deni. "Our lifeline is also our Achilles heel. There are two rivers that crisscross our land. The Saino, to the east, and the Maria Concepcion, to the west. The rivers will feed and water us, but they will also bring the enemy to our doors."

"We need to improve our river defenses," said Miguel.

"We need to make cannons," said Thomas Thurman.

Deni rolled her eyes. "Listen Thomas, this is not really the Alamo."

Paco took her aside. "Your lack of understanding is appalling. Do not ever say that again. The reason why we are here varies from person to person, but the word Alamo spurred these Texans to come here. Fighting against a tyrant with a superior force is what Texans do. Be appreciative."

Chapter Fifteen

La Sallistas

Salvador brought the hapless Emilio and his men to the police station. He was immediately arrested and placed in a holding tank. Word was sent to Colonel Ortiz that another Perez had been apprehended.

A jailer came in with a visitor. It was someone Salvador knew, a school mate from La Salle High School, in Colon City.

"Hola, Salvador, long time no see."

"Rosario, I did not know you joined the military?"

"The road for some of us is more difficult. I'm a Morales, not a Perez."

"Not so easy for a Perez. Not these days anyway. How are you?"

"I'm fine. Thanks for asking. I have a wife and two daughters."

Sargent Morales asked the jailer to let him inside the cell. When the man left, Morales spoke. "The reason for your family problems is your older brother and little sister. They are creating a storm that will engulf all of us."

ALBERTO ARCIA

"Listen, Rosario, Alex is missing. He came to speak with Juju, and no one has heard from him since. Can you help me?"

"Coronel Ortiz has him. I can't help him, but I can help you."

"Is Alex still alive?"

"Yes, but he will not be for long. Ortiz will soon deliver him to the Narcos."

"Rosario, you know what those assholes are like, don't you?"

"Si, son hijos de puta."

Salvador spat on the cell floor. "Sons of bitches all right. They love to torture people. If they get a hold of Alex, they will kill him. You know I can't allow that to happen."

Rosario laughed. "The attitude of you Perez's has always amazed me. Your family arrogance is mind-boggling. You're in jail. Alex is in the hands of Colonel Ortiz. Neither one can do anything without outside help, yet you speak in terms of being able to do something. Why is that, Salvador?"

"Because we spent a lifetime making friends and creating alliances. I don't know why my brother and sister insist on causing trouble. I don't. I have friends everywhere, including right here, in this cell."

Rosario laughed again. "You astonish me, Salvador. We were good schoolmates and okay friends. Not good enough for me to risk my life, and the welfare of my family for you."

"Listen, Rosario, I would never put a La Sallista in a position where he or his family could be harmed, but I do expect a measure of help from him. Will you help me?"

146

Rosario gave out a loud sigh. "What is it that you think I can do for you? I can't release you without exchanging places, and that I'm not willing to do."

"You can cooperate with my next move."

He looked at me. I could tell he wasn't sure what I meant.

"Rosario, will you cooperate?"

"Salvador, I don't understand what…"

I reached behind and pulled out a small twenty two caliber pistol. He looked more bothered than troubled.

"Did they not search you before they brought you in here?"

"Rosario, you know damn well *Panameños* don't like to touch another man's dick. They searched me all right, but I had it strapped on the inside of my crotch."

He rolled his eyes.

I looked at him. "Rosario, will you cooperate?"

"Yes, of course. We're *La Sallistas*. We stick together when possible. Besides, this way I can do it without incrimination. The gun is a game changer. Also, I don't much care for the *Coronel*. He is a bad man. And I certainly have no love for the *drogueros*. They are scum. So, what is our next move?"

"Call the jailer and tell him to let you out. When he opens the door, I will produce the gun. Then, with the pistol on your neck, you will escort me out. We are going to find Alex."

An hour later, we pulled into the parking lot of the Arosemena Hospital, in a jeep driven by *Sargento* Rosario Morales, We parked and headed for the elevator. Inside, he pushed the button for the fourth floor. The elevator stopped and he inserted a key, opening the door.

"Hola, Sargento," said an overweight man in shabby military uniform. He was sitting in a chair behind the counter. *"Qué necesitas?"*

That was my cue. I pulled the pistol out again and placed it behind Rosario's head. The man saw it, and his eyes bugged out. *"Qué es esto?"*

Salvador spoke to him. *"No haga nada que me pueda perjudicar. Dame la llave del cuarto número ocho."*

The fat man complied and followed us towards room number eight. We entered, and there was my dear brother, tied and slumped on a chair with his nose bandaged. He looked terrible.

"Hola, Alex, you look like shit."

He raised his head and saw me. A faint smile graced his face. "Hola, Salvador, what took you so long?"

Rosario spat on the floor. "You Pérezes astonish me. My family would have abandoned me the minute Ortiz grabbed me. No one ever escapes from the devil."

Alex smiled at him. "I have, several times."

We tied and gagged the fat guy. Then Rosario called in everyone working the floor. Luckily for us, they weren't many. They walked in, one by one, unaware of what lay ahead for them. Once they were all tied and gagged, we walked out of the hospital.

Leaving town, we saw Ronson. He and another man were talking to a person on the street. We stopped, had a quick parley, and left towards the river. There, we found Ronson's boat.

The guy with him was Roberto, the peasant who had joined our movement. He took Alex with him. Ronson came with us. We needed the jeep. We drove to the farm, hoping to get in without having a shootout.

We made the curve and stopped. There was a line of cars ahead of us. It appeared that a company of soldiers blocked the road. They were letting some cars through, and sending others back.

"Listen guys, we can't get in, too many soldiers. Let's double back and get another boat."

"Salvador, why not try and bluff our way into the farm? We need the jeep, and we have him," Ronson pointed at Rosario.

"Too risky. Let's find a boat."

One of the vehicles that were turned back approached us. Salvador waved it down. It had gringos in it.

"Hey, *amigos*, what's the problem down there?"

The driver, with a leery eye on Rosario, spoke. "We came to join the Perez family and fight the drug dealers, but the soldiers won't let us in."

"Where do you guys come from?" asked Salvador.

"I'm from Tennessee," said the driver. "My two companions are from Kentucky."

"Thanks for coming. My name is Salvador Perez, my companion is Sergeant Rosario. If you really want to join me and my family, follow us, we know how to get in."

"I know where we can find a ferry," said Rosario.

"Where, and what kind of a ferry? Is it big enough to carry us and the jeep?"

"A few miles further down the road from where we dropped off Alex. Yes, its big enough, Salvador, but we might have to throw overboard the ferry's load of coconuts."

"We didn't travel all this way to be turned back," said the Tennessean. "We're with you. Please lead the way."

The river landing had a nice dock, it also had a number of buildings and a lot of people waiting to get on a ferry that had yet to arrive. There were a number of motor boats taking people to the other side. The ferry was reserved for those going up or down river, with either vehicles or oxen pulled carts.

Rosario talked to a man in the ticket office. He wanted to know when the next ferry would be docking. He was told the military had delayed the ferries until one of their own docked.

"Shit, what bad luck," said Rosario. "No more ferries today. They are waiting for a military ferry to arrive sometime tonight. It's bringing men and equipment. The government must be getting ready to get involved."

Ronson looked at me. We both smiled. Rosario, seeing the look on our faces, became apprehensive. "You guys are not thinking of stealing it, are you?"

"*Ja,*" said Ronson. "It's big enough for the jeep, and I bet it has weapons inside."

"It also has armed soldiers."

"Rosario, we're not going to fight them," I said, "We're just going to steal their boat and guns."

"And you are going to do this without firing a shot?"

"No, Rosario. We will fire shots, many of them, but we're not going to kill anyone."

"Listen to me, Salvador. All I have is a side arm, and so do you and Ronson. They have many rifles."

"Wait here," I said." Let me talk to the new recruits."

I walked over. "Guys, we're going to steal a big military boat, but we're not going to kill any one. Are you with us?"

"Does a bear like to shit in the woods?" asked the Tennessean.

"Yes he does," replied the Kentuckians.

I smiled. "I love your enthusiasm, guys. What are your names?"

"I'm David Crockett," said the Tennessean, "but you can call me Davy."

"I'm John Smith," said one of the Kentuckians.

"And I'm John Doe," said the other.

When I broke out in laughter, Rosario and Ronson came over.

"What's so funny, Salvador?"

"You're not going to believe me, but Davy Crockett is here, and he has brought us the incognito brothers from Kentucky. They are going to help us take the boat."

A plan was quickly concocted. Unfortunately, it would require Santiago to tip his hand. His actions will brand him a traitor.

Right around eleven that evening, the military ferry made its appearance. It blew the horn as it maneuvered to dock.

I looked at Rosario. "You sure you want to do this, Amigo?"

"Yes, but let me make a phone call first." He stepped away and dialed his cell. *"Hola, Juana, llévate a la familia a Penonomé, y escóndete. Vete, rápido."*

"Okay, Salvador, let's do it. He placed his palm up. La Sallistas forever."

ALBERTO ARCIA

We waited until most of the officers and some of the rank and file had vacated the ferry before we moved in. John Smith stayed behind manning the Jeep. The rental car would remain, abandoned.

Rosario walked in and told a lieutenant that we were engineers going to inspect a spot up river to build a bridge. He believed him, and we boarded. He went up to the bridge and, at gun-point, ordered the captain to put the engine in reverse. Ronson and I pulled our pistols, fired into the air, and immediately began shouting orders to the startled soldiers.

When John Smith heard the engines rev-up, he floored the Jeep and drove it over the ramp and onto the ferry.

"Suelten las sogas," I shouted. *"Ahora!"*

The ropes were unfastened, and the ferry pulled out and headed up river. No one fired at us from the dock in fear of hitting the soldiers standing in the open with their hands up. We disarmed the men and told them to jump over board. All of them did except for two tall ones. Ronson wanted those two to remain on board until they undressed.

In the middle of the night, Dumas entered Deni's room without knocking and woke her up. "Get dressed quickly, and come outside, Jámes and I will take you to the river. Salvador has returned."

"Why did you enter my room without knocking? You have no respect for my privacy? And why do I have to go there? Why don't I just wait here?"

"Because we need to hurry. You need to see what Salvador has brought with him. *Te va a gustar mucho. Vamos a levantar a Alex.*"

152

"No, Alex needs to sleep. He's been banged up bad. Let's go see what it is that I'm going to like a lot. Let me get Lor."

"Not necessary. He is at the river already."

"I can't believe it. He is not supposed to go anywhere without letting me know."

"Deni, you are a woman. Lor, he is doing a man's job. He is making sure there is no danger for you."

She glared at him. *These men and their bullshit is driving me crazy.*

They walked outside where Jámes, already mounted, was holding two horses. When they arrived at the edge of the river Saino, she couldn't believe her eyes. There was Salvador, Ronson, a Panamanian officer, and two gringos. Docked at their rickety berth, was a big ferry with Panamanian Military markings.

"Salvador, please tell me you didn't steal it."

"We stole it," said Ronson with pride. "Isn't she a beauty? We're going to name it the SS Denise,"

"The hell you are. You're not incriminating me by putting my name on it. What you guys are going to do is take it back."

"No can do, Sis. We stole it fair and square. It's loaded with weapons."

At that moment, a Jeep roared off the ferry and onto the ground. It bounced a couple of times and stopped next to Deni. The driver removed his cap, grinned, and introduced himself. "Hello, ma'am, I'm Davy Crockett."

Deni turned towards Salvador. "Who's the nut-case?"

"Why, he's Davy Crockett. Come here all the way from Tennessee."

ALBERTO ARCIA

"Right, ma'am that is the name my father gave me. I'm here to help you defend the Alamo."

She turned to face the officer. "And who are you?"

"He's a *La Sallista,* and that is all you need to know now. Let's empty the ferry of its valuables."

"I'm in charge here, Salvador."

"Yes, you are Sis. So have a rest, and let men do their work."

"Don't be so condescending, brother. Women can do men's work better."

"Roll your sleeves up then. We have to unload this big boat."

Chapter Sixteen

The Gang Grows

I woke up with a throbbing pain in my head, face, ribs, and hands. Hell, my whole body hurt. I couldn't believe I escaped before Juju could turned me over to the Narcos. The thought of how upset and embarrassed he was going to be when he walked in with the thugs and found me gone, gave me a chuckle. A knock on the door reminded me it was time to get out of bed and get dressed. I climbed out and put my clothes on. To my surprise, they had been washed and pressed. When the knock came again, I opened it.

"Hello, Alex. How do you feel?"

"Good, Deni. Thanks for washing and pressing my clothes."

She winced. "I didn't do it. Why should I do it? Is it because I'm a woman. Is that it?"

"What's wrong with you this morning? Find a scorpion in your shoes?"

"Never mind. We're ready for a meeting, and your presence is required."

She walked ahead of me, and I noticed, as I've done a number of times before that she wore baggy pants.

ALBERTO ARCIA

"You know, Deni, your ass would be more attractive if you put on tighter pants."

In a flash, she was on me. "I don't wear my clothes for the appreciation of men. I can get them with my brains, not my ass. Have some respect for your sister. I'm tired of being addressed as a body, not a mind. In case you have forgotten, the building is full of men, and I'm in charge."

"Jeez, Louise, Sis. What has gotten into you?"

"Men, that's my main issue these days. I'm trying hard to lead them into battle, but can't get their respect."

"Sis, you have it all wrong. Men don't follow women into battle, they follow them into bed. Men follow men into battle. How many do we have so far? And, do you have a commander yet?"

She glared at me. "Twenty three, counting me, and two women. Yes, I have a commander. A guy named Paco will lead them into battle. Ronson will man the command post, and Lor will lead a suicide charge, if one is needed."

"What are you going to do, Sis?"

"Screw you, Brother."

"When did Paco arrive? Did he come alone?"

"No. And I'm done talking."

We walked the remaining distance in silence. Deni was right, it's hard to lead men when you don't have their respect. But she does not need their respect for them to fight for her. All men need is a cause, and she has provided one.

You can't imagine how good it pleased me to see friends and relations gathered in the war room. Introductions were made by Deni, she wanted everyone to know who would be fighting by their side.

She began with her commanders. "Paco Williams, front and center, please."

He stood by her side.

"Paco is from Texas, and he will be in charge of field operations. In other words, he will lead you into battle."

"What are his qualifications? Jámes asked.

"Paco, please give him your experiences, but make it brief."

He scanned the crowd, looking for those who might oppose him. He aimed his speech at Jámes and Dumas.

"I've been in the U.S. military with the rank of Captain, and I've been in so many firefights that it's hard to keep an accurate count. But not all of them were while in the military. I quit my job in a detective agency in Houston, Texas, to come here. Finding and rescuing people is my job. I've been in charge of many clandestine operations and have never lost a man."

There were no more questions. Paco resumed his place.

Deni spoke again. "I have assigned the Swiss, Ronson Wickert, to be in charge of logistical operations. He will remain in here, moving pieces to and from the battlefield. Ronson please give your qualifications.

Ronson stood by Deni's side. "I am a former member of the Swiss National Army, Commando operations was my job. I also worked for the same company Paco did, except I don't find people, I provide muscle."

No questions either, so Deni continued. "Lor, front and center."

He came, patted her ass, and stood by her side. This upset Deni and brought on chortles from the group. She glared at him. "Lor will head special operations."

ALBERTO ARCIA

Dumas, with a snicker in his tone, said he couldn't wait to hear what Lor's qualifications were. This brought on more sniggers from the group. Deni glared at Dumas and motioned for Lor to speak.

"I'm Lor, I'm an *assassino*. I keel people. I can *getto* the head of a *formica* at a hundred yards with a rifle and a *mirino.*"

All of the sudden you could hear a pin drop. No one said anything. Deni had to step in. "He said, he is an assassin, and that he can shoot the head of an ant at a hundred yards with a rifle and scope. Too bad we don't have one."

"What is your position, Deni?" asked Miguel.

"I'm the commander in charge. I supervise, concoct, and improvise the plans."

Chuckle, snicker, chortle. She glared at the group.

That afternoon, Deni asked Paco, Ronson, Salvador, Miguel, and me to meet with her. She seemed worried.

"The stealing of the Panamanian military ferry was a stupid thing to do, but nothing we can do about it now. What we can do is fortify our positions so we can withstand an attack from both the government and the Narcos."

She turned to Ronson. If you were coming to attack us, from which direction would you come?"

"From all directions. We are not many. That information must be known already. We can't properly secure our positions."

She frowned. "Can you be more specific?"

"I would send a small land force to threaten the front and another from behind, forcing you to man those two areas. This will weaken your flanks. Then I would send a gunboat up the Saino River and one down the other one. I

158

RUN, ALEX, RUN

would shoot a few shells into our buildings from one of them and land the majority of my men from the other boat."

She turned pale. "We're done then. The cartel alone will beat us. God help us if the government comes at us too. Do we fight or do we surrender?"

"Listen, Deni, what exactly did you think would happen when you killed Cholo and his men?"

She looked at Alex. "I would start a war."

"Well, Sis, we have one. Now how do we win it?"

"We can't win it," said Ronson, but we can put up a fight until someone comes and interferes."

She became upset. "Ronson, you dimwit. No one is going to save us. The government is not going to save us. They are going to be the ones attacking us. Why? Because you stole their ferry."

Paco interjected and again, scolded Deni. "Do not insult men that are willing to die for you. If you want to be a commander you must know how to act like one."

She swallowed hard. "Sorry, Ronson. I didn't mean to insult you. I'm just worried that I have placed all of you in a bad situation."

"Deni is right," said Paco. "We can't win it if we have to fight two enemies. What are the chances the government will actually move against us?"

"To get a better perspective, we need the counsel of Sargento Morales," said Miguel.

"What can a sergeant tell us about what the higher ups will do?" asked Paco.

"You're right. We need another opinion," I said. "Get Fausto here."

"Why Fausto?" Asked Paco. "He's not a military man."

"He's well connected to the government," said Salvador. "He can be a good judge of what they can do or will not do."

They both came and were brought up to speed. They both agreed that stealing the boat was a stupid thing to do, but they didn't think the government would attack us over that.

"They will make a lot of noise but will not attack," said, Fausto.

Sargento Morales stepped in. "The president and the rest of the country is sick of these cutthroats, but they can't act against them. The Narcos are too powerful. They will wait to see what the *drogueros* will do, before they show their hand."

"He is right," said Fausto. "The government will never authorize Coronel Ortiz to make an assault on us. It's the David and Goliath story. It will bring a massive public outcry down on them, forcing their hand. And that is the only way the government will get involved. If they are forced."

We sat there, astounded at Fausto's words of wisdom. He continued. "Ortiz will push for a more acrimonious approach. He will advise the cartel to send in their spies first, then their assassins."

"We don't have any spies here," said Deni."

Fausto gave her a condescending smile. "Not yet, Deni. With the money they have, and with their love for kidnapping relations, and then torturing them, anyone could become a spy."

"I repeat, Fausto. We have no spies here."

He gave her a stern look. "If it comes to my family or you, you're toast."

Chapter Seventeen

An Ace in the Hole

"Señorita Pérez," said one of the women in the group. *"Llegaron dos más por el rio."*

"De adonde son?"

"Dicen que son Venezolanos."

"From Venezuela? Good God, my call is reaching out."

Lor walked in on the conversation. "What's up, Deni?"

She allowed herself a smile. "Lor, the river brought us two more today. They came from Venezuela."

He frowned. "Yesterday, three Panamanians came from Bocas. We need a hostel to put them up. We have little food."

She ignored him and addressed the woman. *"Alma, gracias. Dale algo de comer y consígueles un lugar para dormir."*

"Deni, we have no *posto qui.*"

"Ronson is taking care of that. He will find room and food for them. You need not worry about domestic affairs. You keep an eye out for trouble. How many do we have on point?"

He gave her a puzzled look. "Point?"

"In the front lines. How many armed men do we have by the front gate?"

"Not my job. You ask Ronson or Paco. My job to make gun shoot far."

She placed her arm around his neck. "And how is that coming?"

"I have Russian rifle and American long glasses. I use Italian know-how to attach them, and *viola*, I can see far. But bullet don't go very far. I need to be closer to shoot people."

"Do you have a problem with heights, Lor?"

"No, Lor is a *cecchino*."

"Good, we can use a good sniper. We have many tall coconut trees around. Find one that affords you a measure of concealment, and then you can shoot the drug lord's men. Do not shoot the Panamanian military, *capito?*

"*Si, capito.*"

She went outside and met Alex coming down the path. He had a smile that could rival the Cheshire cat's in the Alice in Wonderland story.

"Why the big grin, Brother?"

"We have cannons, Sis."

"What? How?"

"Thomas and Harry scavenged metal tubes, and now we can shoot *pivas* a long ways."

She frowned. "So, instead of killing the enemy, we're going to launch food at them?"

"You're such a buzz killer, Deni. They are still experimenting with different types of projectiles."

"Good. With any luck they can find something to shoot that will actually hurt the enemy."

163

ALBERTO ARCIA

An explosion by the Saino River caught our attention. When a cheer went up, I grabbed Deni's hand, and we ran to see the reason.

Ronson, Davy, and the Kentuckians, at a narrow bend of the river, partially sunk and anchored the government's ferry. Effectively blocking the river's path.

Ronson saw us and shouted. "Now no boat can hurt us from down river!"

"How about from up river, Ronson? Can they hurt us up river?"

He frowned. "One problem at a time, Deni."

She waved at him and grabbed me by the arm. "Listen, Bro, we need to talk."

That act held my interest. Deni was never much into touching her brothers. "Do you want me to fetch Salvador?"

"No, Sal can't keep it in his pants. It's always hard to know which head he is thinking with. I need to talk to you."

"You are seriously interested in my judgement?"

"Listen, Alex. You have cheated death many times. You can't be that lucky. No one can. There must be something other than Poo bear fluff in your brain. Please follow me."

We found a corner by the river bank and sat. I could tell she was bothered. "What is troubling you, Sis?"

"I'm good with our two commanders, but not sure about the distribution of the fighters on hand or their ability to withstand a volley of gunfire. I also don't understand the reason for sinking the ferry."

I pondered her issues. "Okay, here is my assessment. With the river blockaded by the sunken ferry, no one can come from down river and attack us."

164

"The government has a garrison down river, and it's our understanding that they will not attack us. At least we hope they won't. The cartel will, and they can do it from up river. We could have sunk it up river, or not at all, and used it to move men and cargo down river."

"Theoretically, we could. But realistically, nothing can move up or down river anymore. Now, if the cartel had a battering ram, they could send it to breach and totally sink the ferry. Short of that, they will send a gunboat, anchor it by our dock, and then rain gunfire on us."

"Alex, how do we counter that?"

"If the gunboat can't speed by us, shooting cannon fire, it would have to anchor and then shoot. That gives us a stationary target. Easier for our inexperienced fighters to hit the boat with a rifle propelled grenade."

She agreed but didn't seem convinced. Frankly, neither was I, but that was Ronson's problem. I decided to deal with her other concerns. "Your call to arms has caught the attention of real adventurers. These individuals will fight without running. They will exchange fire with the enemy. We need more of those. Others are here because you have augmented their sense of romanticism. They will take photos, write in their notepads, sing songs, and run after the first volley is fired at them. They will certainly run when blood is spilled. This brings me to the Panamanians present. These are either family or individuals wronged by the cartel. Both groups will flee when the fight gets rough."

Deni took offense. "You have been away from Panama for too long if you actually believe your words. We are not cowards."

165

"Deni, you're not thinking the statement through. Panamanians are not cowards, but they are also not warriors. Think about our culture. Are we fighters or are we lovers?"

Incensed, she came at me. "We are thinkers, Alex. That's who we are."

"Yes, lovers, thinkers, and opportunists. But not warriors. At the very moment we know our cause is lost, we will leave."

She crossed her arms and glared at me. "What do you mean by We?"

"Did you read any Panamanian names in the dead roll of the Alamo?"

"There was no Panama then, that's why."

"Wrong, Deni. There was a Panama. It was not a republic; it was a province of Colombia. But that is not the point."

She became more upset. I had to tread softly, lest I unleashed her pent-up anger. She came right up to me. "What in hell is the point?"

"Panamanians are not suicidal in nature. Neither are Venezuelans. The Gringos, Europeans, and Mexicans are. We put them on the front lines. They will die for an ideal or a cause. They do that all the time. We might die for love."

"I'm not accepting your reasoning as fact, but I will not argue it either. You know more about Europeans, Gringos, and Mexicans. So, you should assign each commander the fighters they need. I will allocate the Panamanians."

"Where do you plan to put them, Sis?"

"In a back-up position, Alex. They will be our reserves."

"And where will you be, Deni?"

166

RUN, ALEX, RUN

"In the rear, keeping an eye out on things."

That was the end of the conversation. Deni was astute enough to know that she had no business leading men into battle or assigning the troops. She had done her job; she had raised a fighting force.

We had another council of war that night. Davy and the Kentuckians proved to be good marksmen. They were assigned to Lor's squad of sharpshooters. Two, high up and in a forward position on each flank.

I was uncomfortable with having an able man like Ronson, remain sequestered at headquarters. He should be in the field, but Deni vetoed that idea. Since she wouldn't relent, so I had to caution her.

"You need to understand that you cannot and must not interfere with Ronson's orders or strategies. I know you think you're in charge, but you really are not. Let him lead the men. Let him be responsible for their death. You stay put."

"Alex, I am in command. So much so, that I'm putting you and Dumas in charge of the front lines. Fausto and Jámes will be on the back lines. Miguel and Santiago are responsible for the defense of the Saino River dock. Salvador and Paco on the María Concepcion River dock. Thomas and Harry are to operate our field artillery, which now consists of six long tubes, shooting river rocks. Three on each dock, in a hidden position."

I was surprised. Even though I suspected this was Ronson's plan. Yet Deni's forcefulness was going to work. The men needed to see her in this light. A commander does not waver. I smiled. The girl had her shit together.

"Alex, with everyone assigned to a post, and if no one runs, and if the government does not attack us, do we have a chance of winning this fight? Be sincere, don't pull any punches."

What could I say? No way in hell we can win, Sis. But you have to give hope to those in need of it. So I did. "With a good wind on our back, and if hell does not freeze over, we might just pull it out."

That evening, Fausto took me aside. He wanted to have a private word with me. We took a walk. His body language annoyed me.

"What's with you, friend? You're entirely too cool for the mess were in. Tell me something I don't know."

"You seem to have an ace in the hole, Alex."

"What in the world are you getting at, Fausto? I'm up to my ass in termites."

"Your cousin, Piero, he is coming to your aid. I just received word he will be here shortly with reinforcements."

I gave him a morose look. "Give me a break, Fausto. All avenues in or out of here, including air space, are off limits to all. The government will not allow anyone else to come help us. They want us to surrender. Quit baiting me."

"Listen to me, asshole. You need to be better composed."

"You want me to be perfectly balanced on unstable ground with broken handrails? Give me a break, Fausto, I can barely keep my footing."

"Piero pulled some strings. He is coming, and he's bringing men and hardware with him."

"No way. Who told you this, anyway? Juju is in charge of the government forces in this area. He hates Piero. He will never authorize him to enter, especially with men and material. Juju is in Don Pablo Jiménez's pocket. He can't be seen as helping us."

"Well, smarty pants, he is coming. He is bringing ex-pat Zonians and a selected group of soldiers. Heard of the Pumas? They are all coming, and with government approval."

"When are they coming?"

"Tonight."

"Fausto, are you bullshitting me?"

"No, Alex. I'm seriously happy. There's relief on the way."

"I can't believe the government is actually going to help us. What brought on the about face?"

"Not sure, Alex, but before you break out in a happy dance. Only two helicopters are coming with men and weapons. This is all the help Piero could get from the government. After that, we're on our own."

"Yes we are, Fausto, but with real soldiers on our side. This is great news."

Fausto gave me a cryptic smile. Then proceeded to rain on my new found sense of joy. "Alex, there's one more thing you need to know."

The way he said it, along with the mysterious smirk he had, told me I wasn't going to like it. "What is it?"

"Piero is bringing a woman that claims to be your wife."

"What are you talking about, Fausto?"

"Alex, your cousin Piero is bringing a woman that says she's your wife. And he is also bringing the man she's been traveling with. Some Mennonite guy named Gonzalez Brynn."

169

ALBERTO ARCIA

María is coming? Oh, shit. "Fausto, what can Piero be thinking? She's pregnant."

"He is bringing her, but will not allow her to remain. My understanding is he hopes she can talk you into leaving with her. The copters will wait here overnight. Hopefully, in the morning, one will leave with Piero, her, and you. The Mennonite guy can remain here if he wants."

I glared at Fausto. "I can't believe you don't know that Mennonites are pacifists. Gonzo will not carry a weapon. And, where in hell did you get all this information? You have been here with us all the time."

"Alex, unlike you, I have friends in high places. And I also have a cell phone. Where is yours?"

"Turned off. I don't want anyone targeting me through my phone. You need to keep your distance from me. I don't want to be around when the missile hits you."

"Get real. We're not fighting American soldiers. Our government or the cartel do not have smart bombs. You're safe with me."

I knew he was right, but I hated to give in. Fausto was a renowned know-it-all. "I don't understand why María is risking the life of our child."

He smiled at me. "Probably not thinking at all. After all, she married you. What number is this one, five?"

"No, asshole, she's number four."

"Well, Alex, when do you tell the group you are leaving us?"

"Leaving? Fausto, do I look like a runner to you?"

"As a matter of fact, yes, you do. You are a runner, Alex. Isn't that the reason why you're still alive? Always one step ahead of the Grim Reaper."

170

RUN, ALEX, RUN

Better one step ahead than inside his bag. I shot him the finger and walked away. *I can't believe he thinks I'm a coward.*

Chapter Eighteen

We Live or Die Together

At two in the morning, the sound of rotors interrupted our slumber. We froze at first, then counted them. There were two choppers in total.

Dumas came running in. He seemed excited. "Alex, we have company."

"Are they friends or foe?" *Like I didn't know.*

"Dos helicópteros del gobierno. They look friendly."

"Okay, go and tell everyone not to shoot at them."

Deni showed up. Salvador and Ronson were with her. Her body posture showed concern. "Do you think it's a ruse?" she asked me.

I wanted to tell her what I knew, but then she'd only get upset and start ranting about the boy's club. Her dislike of male culture kept most men, except her lovers, a good distance from her. *Who needs an irate female for company? Not me.* "If they weren't friendly, they'd be shooting their way in. Let's go see who is inside."

The whirlybirds landed. The doors opened on one of them, and a number of armed soldiers came out, pointing their weapons at us. They were wearing blue berets, signifying commando units.

"Oh, no," said Deni. "We have allowed the devils to land. They caught us."

"Don't sweat it, Sis. They may be devils, but they are not our executioners. They are reinforcements."

She glowered at me. "Did you ask for them without my permission?"

"Did I say they were reinforcements?"

The doors opened on the other one and out stepped another group of armed men. These were not military, but civilians.

Salvador pointed and yelled, "Piero!"

Deni clutched my arm. "What's he doing here? Did you ask him to help us without talking to me?"

"You lost your happy bone, haven't you, Sis? He's our cousin, and he's here to help."

Piero walked over and hugged me and Salvador. He extended his hand to Deni. She hesitated at first, but then shook it.

"Who asked you to come?"

He rolled his eyes. *Me estas jalando la pata,* right?

She became irritated. "No, I'm not pulling your leg, cousin. I want to know who asked you to come to our aid."

"You did. You put out a call for volunteers, did you not?"

She was taken aback by his reply. Not knowing what else to say, she said thank you and welcome. Then she left.

"Coño, Alex, Esa prima es cosa seria."

I had to laugh. "Yes, Piero, she's serious, all right. Way too serious for my taste."

He hugged me and then whispered. *"Te traigo una sorpresa."*

I gave him an uneasy look. "It's not a surprise if I already know what it is, cousin. I kept hoping Fausto was kidding."

Amongst the group of armed civilians two faces stood out. Two I would have rather not seen today. Fausto was right. My pregnant wife, María Contreras was here. So was my good friend, Gonzalez Brynn.

I cringed when they saw me and began to walk my way. I looked up. *What have I done to you to deserve so little affection?*

My wife approached me. She had a disturbed look on her face. I sighed. *Time to pay the piper. What the hell. It was stupid of me to think I could run away from my troubles. They always seem to find me.* I opened my arms. "María, what a surprise."

Sal whispered. "Who is she?"

"My wife."

"She has a bun in her oven?"

"No shit. And all this time I thought she was just fat."

I figured María would jump into my arms, but she didn't. She stopped just short of my opened arms.

"Alex, did you leave me on purpose, or were you kidnapped?"

Ah, a way out. I looked up. *Thank you, God, for not totally forsaking me.* I looked back at my sweet wife. "I was taken away from you by force."

To totally make up to me for all the grief he has given me, God brought Miguel and Paco to the scene. They overhead the conversation and came to my rescue.

"We took him from you, María," said Paco. "I'm sorry."

"His sister needed him, and he didn't want to come," said Miguel. "He did not want to leave you. We had to force him."

"I told you he wouldn't have left you on his own accord," said Gonzo.

I became really paranoid now. A little help from God was justified. He owed me. But all of this help felt ominous. *I bet he has something up his sleeve, and I'm not going to like it.*

She burst into tears and jumped into my arms. *"Te quiero, Alex. No me dejes más."*

I cringed at the sound of those words. *Yep, I was right. God has a plan for me, and I'm not going to like it.* "María, I love you too. And I'll never leave you again, unless I'm forced to do so."

Deni's eyes sparkled when she saw Gonz and heard him speak. Obviously she liked the accent. She came over to him. "Who are you?"

He removed his cap. "Ma'am, I'm Gonzalez Brynn. I'm a good friend of your brother, Alex, and María's traveling companion."

"Do you come from Texas?"

"By way of Texas. María and I, we are from México."

She grabbed Gonzo by the arm and asked him to walk with her."

Before she left, I whispered. "Deni, you're not going to like him. You're a small girl, and he's a big boy."

She glared at me. "I'm only small in stature. Don't be insulting."

ALBERTO ARCIA

I wanted to say she had misunderstood my meaning, but decided to let it go. *If she gets into his pants, she'll know what I meant.*

Piero broke the party atmosphere. "We need a meeting now. There's going to be trouble tomorrow."

There was not a building big enough to hold all of us, so we gathered outside. Piero spoke. "We received intelligence that the cartel will launch an attack tomorrow morning. The soldiers I brought are members of the Pumas brigade. They were hand-picked by me for the task at hand. The government has given us their blessing. They, for reasons I'd rather not go into, will not protect you. At least not at the beginning. We must withstand the initial attack. The rest of the Pumas brigade are hidden in a place not too far from here. They have orders to wait until such time as the battle is going bad for us. They will come and save us. But…," and he walked a distance before continuing. "But they will not come if we fall quickly. We must withstand the assault. If we surrender, they will stay put."

"Piero, how long do we have to hold out?"

"I'm not sure, Alex. Long enough to justify the loss of blood the government is going to give up for the Perez family, and the trouble they are causing."

He walked some more, and then spoke again. "I'm not allowed to remain with you, but my men will stay. I have brought you a dozen Pumas and a dozen ex-pat Zonians from all over the provinces. They will also stay here. But, if anyone is not ready to give up their lives for our family's cause, they need to speak up. I will take you out in my birds. I can carry out up to thirty."

There was silence.

Piero looked at everyone present and spoke again. "The helicopters leave early in the morning. Those wanting a ride out, be ready."

I grabbed Maria's hand. "Let's go for a walk." She held my hand tightly. I could feel her nervousness. "Listen to me, dear wife. You have a child to consider. I do too. You cannot stay. And I cannot go. This is a family affair."

Her eyes began to water. "Don't even think it, Alex. My name now is María, Contreras de Pérez. I am family, and we either live together with our child, or we three die together. For me, there is no other choice."

"Sunshine, I know how you feel, but you must override your love for me and think of our child. If I die, I will live through him. But I'm not going to die, dearest. I'm going to live. You must believe me when I tell you I will see you again."

"Alex, you do not listen well. Wild horses cannot pull me away from you. We go or we stay, but we what has to be done together."

I heard her loud and clear. I was going to have to resort to trickery, but she was not going to stay here. My kid was going to live. "Okay, *nos vamos juntos.*"

She gave me a kiss. *"Gracias, mi Amor,* I love you. You are my man."

I took her inside with the purpose of introducing her to my sister, but she was busy making eyes at Gonz. I realized the Deni was putting him at risk.

"Give me a minute, dear. Let me talk to Deni. I'll bring her over and have you meet her."

I gave Deni a "pst," and she came over. "What's up, Alex?"

177

ALBERTO ARCIA

"Two things. One has to do with Lor. He thinks you belong to him."

She bowed on me. "I belong to no man."

"Pay attention. Lor is a professional assassin. He is crazy, and he is the jealous type. A crazy jealous man who kills for a living and thinks you are his girl will easily kill for love. Leave Gonzo alone. Second, Gonzo has a foot long huge snake in his shorts. I've seen it. You will too if you persist in trying to bed him."

She gave me an indignant look. "I'm not trying to bed him, Alex. I'm not that easily bedded."

"Okay, I believe you. Sorry for the assumption. But if he puts that huge, long, bone inside you, you will scream in pain. You're too little for him. Now, let me introduce you to my fourth wife."

I could tell she was miffed, but was not going to pursue the argument. She was going to think my comment out. She came to Maria and smiled. *"Hola, soy Deni.* How long before you give birth?"

After that inane conversation, I went to talk to Piero. He was sitting with Salvador having a cold drink. The look on both of their faces told me there was a Russian around the corner. "Who's the problem?" I wanted to know.

"Colonel Ortiz," said Sal.

I looked at Piero. He laid it on the line. "Alex, Juju is between a rock and a hard place. He is in charge of the government forces in the area, except the Pumas. Those are mine to command. He is angry over that. He has to play his cards right or he will have Don Pablo Jimenez to deal with. He can't be seen by the cartel to be helping us, and he can't be seen by the government to be going against us. His orders

178

are to stay put. He can't interfere until further notice. But the cartel is squeezing him to help."

"Will he do it, Piero?"

"That asshole is most dangerous when corralled. If he has to decide whether it's his life or his job, he will chose to live. We need to be careful."

I went to find my wife and bed, but found Dumas and Jámes. They had been waiting on me. By their expressions, I knew they were unsure on what to do.

"Hola, primos. You need to be in bed. Tomorrow promises to be a long day."

"Alex," said Dumas. Are we going to die here?"

Before I could answer, Jámes hit me with an unusual question. "Alex, are you going to die here?"

I did a slow burn. *All this is Deni's doing. She should be the one dealing with this.* But it didn't take me long to simmer down. They weren't here for Deni. They came for me. We were all good cousins. Piero too. From very early in our childhood, we liked each other. *What do I tell them?*

"Guys, this is going to be a bad fight. It's Deni's fight. She's mine and Salvador sister. We are committed to see this through. Believe me when I tell you if I could get on that bird, I'd be on it. Sal too. Living is better than dying or being maimed. If you guys want to fly, I'm good with it. No one that leaves is a coward. They have brains. They also have a good grip on reality. The crazy ones, and those that can't leave, will remain."

They looked at each other. "We need to think this out before morning," said Dumas.

"Go find your wife and get some sleep," said Jámes. "Sorry to keep you up. *Buenas noches, primo."*

179

ALBERTO ARCIA

I bid them good night, found my bed, and snuggled María. The notion of getting on that bird in the morning crossed my mind. I was getting tired of all this adventuring. I was also concerned about Juju, he was as unpredictable as he was dangerous. I grabbed my *Virgen de Guadalupe* medal and kissed it, then ran my hand down Maria's thighs to see if my dear wife had gone to bed without her panties. *Damn, she's wearing some. Bummer.* Might as well enjoy a good night's sleep. No telling what tomorrow has to offer.

Chapter Nineteen

War is Hell

At six in the morning, the sounds of the rotors brought a sense of doom to all of us. We envied and cursed those not brave enough to stay. They will live to tell and write our story. Probably profit handsomely from it.

Deni, to her credit, refused to go. The other two women left. So did Roberto and the other local men. Sergeant Rosario Morales also left.

He took Salvador aside. "My wife and family need me more than you do. I hope you understand."

"Si, comprendo. No te preocupes. Go with God, my friend. You're a good *Lasallista."*

The two men from Venezuela plus one of the men from Bocas also left. The others remained. Our fighting force, counting Deni, now numbered forty-two. A far lower number than the one-hundred and eighty-six men that defended the Alamo. But then again, we didn't have to fight five thousand Mexican soldiers.

The night before the exit morning, I had an unpleasant conversation with Gonzo. "Look friend, I know what she wants, and I know of the trouble she has gone through, but she cannot stay. More than likely, most of us will die here. María is pregnant with my child."

ALBERTO ARCIA

"That's precisely the reason why you have to leave with her. You need to help her raise the child. I will stay here. I will take your pace in the line."

"But you are a pacifist. What good are you in a gunfight?"

"Alex, I've been trained as a medic. I can help with the wounded."

"Regardless. I cannot leave, Gonz, and that's final. Either you go with her, or she goes alone."

"She will yell, kick, and bite if I try to get her into that helicopter without you."

"I figured as much. Don't worry, Gonz, I have some ether. We will have to carry her, but she will sleep soundly."

Gonzo's visage said everything. He did not need to speak. He would take her.

I placed my hand on his shoulder. "Gonz, you are a good friend. If I don't make it, please take care of her and my child. But I promise you I will do all I can to not die here. When this is over, I will find my way to you and her. I haven't forgotten that I still need to finish your manifesto."

Morning came, and the helicopters took off. To my surprise and endearment, Dumas and Jámes were not in them. Then, to our horror, two missiles were sighted. One missed its mark, but the other hit its target, blowing up one of the copters. We had to dash for cover in order not to be hit by falling debris.

"Which one blew up? I asked Deni. "Was it the one with my wife and friend in it? Or was it the one with cousin Piero?"

Deni couldn't respond. All she could do was shrug her shoulders. I looked at Salvador. He didn't know either. I sat down. My legs were unable to hold me up. I went through a series of emotions, none pleasant. *Was it her helicopter that got hit? Did I just lose my wife and child?"*

We did not have the opportunity to stay in shock. Shortly after the tragedy, all hell broke loose. The Narcos attacked. They came at us from both rivers at once. The Panamanian military manning the road checkpoints had vanished early that morning. Now there was a cloud of dust coming from that direction. Yet no hostile action came from our rear. That corridor was open, probably for our retreat. *But who held it? The Pumas? Or was it a trap?*

We rushed to get into our positions. An armored gunboat came from up the María Concepcion River. It was trailed by a small ferry loaded with men. These were the assault troops. The gunboat moved in slowly, spraying machine gun fire and cannon shot at our positions. The tube batteries in place were manned by Harry Thurman. He managed to let loose one volley of river rocks at the gunboat. Once they shot, they were exposed to the boat gunners. Soon after, the homemade cannons were silenced. Harry was killed along with his men.

Lor, perched on a high coconut tree, calmly adjusted his homemade scope. He picked out a gunner shooting from behind a steel plate and pulled the trigger. The man dropped to the ground. His mate, frightened, froze. He had no idea where that shot came from. He didn't get a chance to find out. Lor nailed him, too.

The gunboat had one small caliber cannon, shooting from the top and two machine guns on each side, hidden behind a steel plate with a narrow slit so the gunner could see what to shoot at. One of them had been put out of business. The boat was equipped with one machine gun on the front and one on the rear. These were mounted on a swivel, giving the gunner a horizontal and vertical motion. They were also behind a steel plate with the slit in the middle.

Whoever designed these boat weapons never expected to be shot at from up above. Lor and his counterpart, John Doe, the Kentuckian, annihilated the men manning the four machine gun nests quickly. Unfortunately, a low flying, two-propeller plane came and sprayed the coconut grove, trying to expose and eliminate the snipers. Clearly, someone from the gunboat complained about the snipers.

The plane exchanged fire with the snipers, silencing them. One of them fell to the ground. It was the Kentuckian. The plane turned its attention to our ground defenses before moving towards the Saino River.

Our land based fighters were hidden behind a makeshift barricade. They exchanged volleys of gunfire with the boat and also fired at the plane, but they ended up getting the worst of it. Someone fired a rifle-propelled grenade at the plane, but missed. With our forces beaten down, the troop ferry docked and unloaded a horde of rough looking men. They attacked the remaining land defense and quickly overwhelmed the barricade. The fighting became one of short range shooting.

The ferry, after it unloaded the men, followed the cartel gunboat down river. They both made a U-turn. They planned to dock.

While making the turn, they took fire from both sides of the banks. The ferry took a direct hit from an RPG. It caught fire, then an explosion followed. It sank, keeping the gunboat from passing it. The gunboat, with its forward progress momentarily blocked, began to turn in tight circles, spraying machine gun fire at the land based soldiers. The gunners, again, began to drop. Apparently, Lor was still an active shooter.

One intrepid cartel man, ignoring the danger, managed to get to the back machine gun and man it. He pivoted the gun barrel up and targeted Lor. Before he could shoot, a shoulder-fired missile hit the boat, blowing it up. A cheer went up for the Pumas.

The frontal attack by the cartel was only a feint. They shot a few mortar shells into our lines and hunkered down. Once I understood that, I told the commander in charge of the Pumas to go with his men and help secure the exposed river flank. The Narcos were swarming the area, shooting everyone.

The Pumas had come well-armed. They fired mortar rounds back and used a shoulder-fired missile to take out the plane. Another short-lived cheer went up.

I left my post and came into headquarters, carrying cousin Dumas. He had a chest wound. One of the Pumas and two of the Zonians were medics. They immediately began to attend to him. I looked at the men laying on the floor, some still alive, others, dead.

Deni came to me. "How long is all this incessant noise going to continue? It's so loud we can't think straight. Is the government going to help us after we're all dead?"

"Listen, Sis, war is hell. It makes no excuses, and it gives no quarter. And, personally, you need to get out of here. This is a building, and it will be targeted. You don't want to be in it when it's blown up."

I looked around. "Where is Ronson?"

ALBERTO ARCIA

"He left me in charge and took off, telling me he was needed out by the Concepcion River. He said the fight there was going badly."

"Deni, the fight is not going well anywhere. We're outgunned and undermanned. If the government does not come in quickly, we're all going to die."

She took her pistol out of its holster and checked it. "I'm not staying here. The medics can deal with the wounded."

"What do you think you can do out there with that pistol?"

"Alex, I'm a leader of men. This is my fight. I started it, so I'm going to give inspiration to the men still fighting. No one will run if I don't. Where do you think I'm needed most?"

Here comes a lie from the heart. "Go to the front. The men there are thinking of running. I came here to ask for help. You can do some good there."

"Where are you going?"

"I'm going to help Ronson."

Deni looked at me. Her eyes were watering. "So, this is it, then. We say our goodbyes. Maybe for the last time."

"Yes, Deni, this is our last goodbye. *Adios, Hermana.* I love you."

"*Adios,* Brother. You may not believe me, but I do love you very much."

I kissed her on the cheek and left, wondering if her love would hold after she finds out I abandoned the fight. The battle was lost. It was obvious the government forces were waiting until nightfall before coming in, if they would come at all. Yet, we all be dead by then. I was not going to die here. It's not my time. I needed a floating device to go down the Saino River. *I'm going to find out if María was dead or alive. If alive, I will help her raise our child.*

.

As I made my way through the chaos, Ronson saw me coming his way. He stopped me. "How's the fight in the front?"

"The river flanks are caving in, most of the men have left to help there. Only a few remain at the front. Deni is with them."

"Alex, all seems lost."

"Yes, Ronson. We flee, or we die."

"Alex, I don't want to die in Panama. Do you know where the life preservers are stashed?"

"Yes, follow me."

We went into headquarters. The number of wounded had increased. Miguel was there. He took me aside. *"Esto esta malo.* Let's get out before it's too late."

"I hear you. Where are Paco and Salvador?"

"Paco is coming. He's bringing Fausto with him. He has a leg wound."

"Where is Salvador?"

We heard a loud explosion and knew the other gunboat had been destroyed. However, there was not a cheer, which meant few men left.

"That's where he is, Alex. He, Jámes, and Davy Crockett are the last ones standing on that side. John Smith is gone. So is Thomas Thurman."

I did the sign of the cross and left to fetch the life savers, returning with five floating devices. "Is that all we have?" asked Ronson.

Miguel grabbed his, plus another one for Paco. I grabbed mine and handed one to Ronson. There was one left. They looked at me.

"This is your family fight, Alex. You decide. It's either Salvador, Deni, Lor, or Fausto."

"Alex, *ven acá,*" said a voice belonging to Dumas, who was lying down. I knelt. "What's up, Cousin?"

"No quiero morir en Colón. Soy Chiricano, déjame morir allá. Llévame contigo."

"What's the deal, Alex?" asked Ronson.

"He does not want to die here. He wants me to take him back to Chiriquí."

"But we're not going there," he whispered. "We're going to Colon City and from there, we're taking a boat to Bocas, then to Costa Rica."

Paco came in with Fausto. His leg was bleeding. The medic took over. Miguel threw Paco the life preserver. "It's time to leave."

"Hey, where's mine?" asked Fausto.

I was in a pickle. It was hard to decide what to do. I had to play God, and it didn't sit well. All of a sudden, Ronson joined me in the pickle jar. Lor walked in. He had a shoulder wound. I looked at Ronson and gave him a cryptic smile.

He came to me. "What is it with you, Alex? You and I, we have a problem. We have to choose who lives and who dies. There is nothing pleasant about that."

"That was not a smile-smile, Ronson. It was a solemn one. Showing predicament."

Miguel came over. "I know it's tough, but you two better make a decision before Salvador or Deni walks in. There's only one flotation device left."

188

"There's two," I said. They looked at me, dumbfounded.

"I can't leave Dumas behind. He has asked me to save him. I also can't leave Fausto behind. He joined us, even though he is not family."

"You can't take control of both devices, Alex," said Miguel. "Ronson has a stake in it. Lor is his friend."

Dumas called me. "*Alex, ven acá.*"

I approached him. *"Dime, primo.* What's up?"

"If you don't go, I don't go either. *No conozco a tus amigos. No les tengo confianza.* Promise me we stay together."

"Te lo prometo. Juntos hasta el final." I gave him my hand, and then spoke to my friends. "That settles it. Dumas and I are staying. Fausto and Lor have life preservers."

My heart skipped a bit when I saw Salvador walk in, carrying Jámes. He had a nasty wound on his shoulder. The medics quickly took over.

It didn't take long for Salvador to notice the flotation devices. "You guys going somewhere?"

"All is lost here, Sal," said Miguel. "We're getting out of harm's way."

"Unfortunately, there are no more life savers left," said Paco.

Salvador looked at me. "I'm staying," I said.

"Good, I stay too. After all, it's our family fight."

"Thank God, this is settled," said Miguel. Let's get the hell out of here before it's too late. The *drogueros* are roaming the grounds shooting everyone."

"We can't go yet," said Ronson. "We need to do it after dark."

ALBERTO ARCIA

Deni walked in. She was helping one of the Panamanians from Bocas. He had a leg wound.

"Do what? What is the issue here?" She wanted to know.

"We're leaving here before the *drogueros* come in and kill us all," said Paco.

"He's right", said Miguel. "The fight is lost, Deni."

"There is no glory fighting for a lost cause, Sis. We're done. Do you want my life jacket?"

"Hell no, Alex, I don't want your life jacket. I'm not running away."

"I'm m not running away either, Deni, said Lor. "I stay with you."

Miguel rolled his eyes. "For crying out loud. Someone please take the last one. We have to leave."

"She pulled her pistol and aimed it at Miguel. "I'm in charge here. I give the orders. No one leaves without my permission."

Miguel took offense. He was about to speak when she fired a bullet close to his right foot. He jumped back three feet.

"Deni, are you gone loco?" What's with you?"

"I'm in charge here. Not you, Alex, or anyone else. I say who leaves and when. Understand? And no one with a life-threatening wound will leave. I will not give a life vest to someone who may bleed out. None of the wounded will leave, period."

Deni pointed the gun at Miguel's leg and pulled the hammer back. "Since there is only one preserver left, after Alex takes his. Salvador gets the last one. You guys need to leave at five. That's in fifteen minutes."

"Hey, that's the hour they killed Lola," I said.

190

"No it's not," replied Deni. "They killed her at three in the afternoon."

"You're both wrong," said Sal. "She was gunned down at three-thirty."

"Who in hell gives a shit when she was killed!" Fausto yelled. "If you guys don't leave, I want a jacket."

"Lola was a radio soap opera star. A vixen who stole other women's men. And, again," she pointed at Fausto. "No one with a bleeding wound gets one. Stop bitching."

"Up yours, Deni."

"I think Lola was killed at four," said Dumas.

Deni looked at her wrist watch. Its fifteen minutes to five. You guys need to leave.

"That works for me," muttered Miguel. "Let's blow this joint before we die here trying to figure out why it matters that Lola was screwing other men."

"Lola was hot. The men loved her but the women hated her." said Jámes.

"How in hell do you know that? Asked Deni. She was on the radio. For all you know she could have been some fat ugly woman."

"No way," said Dumas.

"Stop it!" yelled Miguel. "It does not matter a flip to anyone if she was hot or ugly. At least it shouldn't matter right now. Can we please leave?"

As we prepared to depart, Deni broke into a laugh. "Wouldn't that be something if the fight is over, the fort stands, and I get to tell the world that my older brothers ran away. I love it. I bet mother would die of shame. Her oldest, the golden boy, he runs away and leaves his little sister behind."

191

ALBERTO ARCIA

"You do know what they say about sticks and stones, don't you, Sis?"

"Screw you, Alex. Get lost."

"Bye, Sis. See you on the other side."

"Not if I see you first, Sal."

Chapter Twenty

The Escape

The fighting continued. The government troops—the ones deployed out of sight—finally made their appearance. They came from the rear and swept into the compound like a swarm of locusts. The pop-pop-pop sounds made by the Russian assault rifles used by the Narcos burst through the air. The agonizing cries of the wounded filled your heart with sorrow. There was nothing anyone could do, the Narcos were showing no mercy. The wounded not able to hide or be evacuated, were being systematically killed.

We slipped out, walking, crouching, and crawling, hoping to avoid getting hit by the bullets whizzing over us. Here and there, we heard the sound of a grenade exploding or a mortar round landing. The burst of extended machine gun fire kept our heads down. We made it to the banks of the river Saino. The fighting there was still hot. We slid into the water and let the slow current take us down river.

"Too bad we have to float down river, when we're so close to the coast," said Salvador. "Miramar is just a few short miles away."

"This is our safest way to safety, Sal. Since we sank the military ferry, effectively blocking the river's path, the

ALBERTO ARCIA

Panamanian soldiers will not expect any hostile action from us. We made them think we were setting up a defensive position."

"That was the purpose, Alex. We sank it so they couldn't attack us," whispered Miguel. "Surely they are not expecting any river trouble from us."

"We float pass the checkpoints until we get to Lake Alajuela," said Ronson. "From there, the map shows several roads to the main highway between Panama city and Colon city."

"We split up there," said Paco. "Miguel and I flew into Tocumen. We will fly out of there."

"I'm staying in Panama City for a while," said Salvador. "Going to see Mother."

"Alex and I will go to Bocas," said Ronson. "From there to San Jose. We fly out of there."

"Why from there?" asked Salvador.

"We have women on the route we would like to see again."

Miguel laughed. "You may have one Ronson, but Alex's women are all in brothels."

With a no-nonsense tone, Ronson killed the conversation. "My girl works in a brothel."

With that said, we floated in silence, hoping not to run across alligators, water snakes, venomous spiders, or end up covered with leeches.

The river scene was scary. It was dark. The water, slow, cold, and murky. There were shadows looming up the trees, making them appear like ghosts with their branches looking like hands, reaching down to grab us.

We saw an alligator resting on the bank, and then sliding into the water. That brought fear into our hearts.

194

RUN, ALEX, RUN

"Oh, no, not an alligator," I said. "I hate gators. I have a phobia about being eaten by one."

We raised our legs, stayed bunched up, and held on to each other. Maybe that way, the gator would not dare attack. He didn't bother us, but the leeches found us.

"God damn," said Miguel. "I hate leeches."

"Just make sure your pecker is covered up, Miguel," said Paco. "You don't want a leech to suck the blood out of your dick."

"Quiet," said Ronson. "Checkpoint up ahead."

We looked at it. It seemed simple enough. A wooden guardhouse on the right bank, set on stilts. A patrol launch anchored on shore. We counted six men total.

They were not expecting trouble. One of them was talking on his cell, probably to his sweetheart. Another was sitting, cleaning his rifle. Three more were playing cards. The one in the guardhouse was doing his job. He kept an eye on the river with his automatic rifle in hand.

We climbed out of the river, using a bunch of low tree branches for cover. Once out, we pulled the nasty, slimy, blood-sucking leeches off our skin.

"Okay, guys, who has an idea on how we do this?" I whispered.

"I'm glad you don't have one, Alex. Your ideas are haired-brained."

"Ssh. Quiet, Miguel." whispered Salvador. "This is no time for quarreling."

"Listen up," said Paco. "They are too far, and we're too water-logged to sneak up on them. We're going to have to shoot them, starting with the guy in the crow's nest."

That's a lame idea," whispered Salvador. "The noise will alert those down river, killing any chances of us floating by them, undetected."

"I have an idea," said Ronson. He unzipped his pack and brought out two rolled-up Panamanian soldiers uniforms.

"Where'd you get those?"

"I got them from two tall soldiers when we hijacked the military ferry. They are big enough for me and Salvador to wear. We will approach them from the bush, they will see our uniforms and not fire. All of them will be looking at us, not at the rest of you. Who can throw a good knife?"

Miguel raised his hand. "Good, when they turn to look at us, you get as close as possible and take the tower guard out. You, Alex, and you, Paco, come out with pistols showing. No one fires a shot. We have surprise on our side. Are we clear on this?"

"Good plan," said Miguel. "Let's do it."

Ronson put mud on his face to dampen his lily-white, skin. They dressed in the uniforms and left to double back and get behind the card players. Miguel covered himself with mud and slithered with a knife clasped between his teeth as close to the watchtower as he dared. Paco and I stood there in silence, waiting for our turn.

I love it when a plan goes smooth. Ronson and Salvador came out of the bush. Salvador raised his hand in a friendly gesture and spoke. *"Hola, compadres."*

The card players, startled, jumped to their feet. The one talking on the cell, put it down. The guy in the nest walked to the back to see what was going on. When he saw Salvador and Ronson raise their pistols, he lifted his rifle, but Miguel's knife found its mark. The guy grunted, stood

196

looking at the knife imbedded in his chest with disbelief, and fell to the ground. In a second, Paco and I were out with our pistols. That was it, the game was over. Unfortunately, a Panamanian soldier was killed. That, we hoped, would not come to bite us in the ass.

We undressed the soldiers, threw the cell into the river, then tied and gagged them. Paco and Ronson removed their shirts. The rest of us dressed in the hapless soldiers' uniforms. We climbed in the launch and took off down river.

The new plan was to have Paco and Ronson raise their hands in apparent surrender whenever any official looking boat came by. Salvador and I stood as guards. Miguel drove.

We continued for a while. A patrol boat came by and slowed down. We did the same. An officer on the boat spoke. *"Que tienen ahí?"*

Salvador replied, *"Dos gringos prisioneros. Los llevamos al cuartel."*

The officer smiled and waved us off. We continued.

"What was that about?" asked Ronson.

"Told them we were taking you guys to headquarters."

We drove until we reached the dock where we stole the ferry. But here, our luck ran out. Trouble was waiting for us. The officer on the patrol boat must have called someone at headquarters with the news of prisoners coming their way. We had a welcoming committee. Four soldiers with an officer were waiting for us. These guys were smiling. They weren't on to us.

"Okay, looks like the jig is up. What do we do now?"

"Don't sweat it, Paco," I said. "Follow my lead. It's late at night, the place is empty of civilians, and only soldiers on duty are present. We will get off, turn the prisoners over, and then we will all walk together. Let Salvador and I do the talking. Keep the pistols handy because we will force a detour on the way. Miguel, you stay with the boat and drive it up and down river, but stay close to our bank. We'll be coming, running fast."

"God dammit, Alex," said Miguek. "This plan better work or I'm leaving you all here to rot in jail. I killed the guard at the post. I can't get caught. Don't be lingering."

"*Buenas noches*," said the officer. "*Quien está encargado aquí?*"

"*Yo,*" said Salvador. "*Tengo dos prisioneros.*"

We disembarked and handed the prisoners over, then followed them. Salvador walked next to the officer. I walked behind him. As soon as we approached a side street, Sal placed his pistol in the officer's ribs.

"Startled, the man spoke. *"Qué es esto?"*

"Nada, si me ases caso. Coja la calle a la izquierda, y siga caminando."

We made a left turn and kept on walking. My position shielded Salvador's gun from the view of the soldiers. They followed along. We made another left turn and walked towards the river bank.

I turned and pointed my gun at the soldiers. None of them resisted. Ronson and Paco removed their guns.

Miguel showed up with the boat. "Get inside quickly. There's a big gunboat coming this way. We need to skedaddle."

Ronson and Paco, using the barrels of the confiscated rifles, knocked out the soldiers. Salvador did the same to the officer. We scrambled on board, Miguel revved the engine, and we took off.

In less than a minute, the big gunboat approached. Salvador, Miguel, and I, dressed in our uniforms, waved. The pilot blew the horn, and those on deck waved.

We had managed to escape. At least we thought so. Ten miles downriver, the engine sputtered and stopped. We were out of gas. Thinking the military would be on us soon, we ditched the boat. They would find it and search the area before resuming their hunt for us.

"Okay, guys, back in the water," said Ronson.

We let the current take the boat, and we, with our flotation devices, drifted towards Lake Alajuela. To our surprise, the military did not pursue us. We couldn't believe it. We could have kept the damn boat.

Lake Alajuela finally appeared. We made it without any further issues. There was a village on the lake shore. We swam towards it, got out, and were able to feed ourselves in a small *comedor* that served one meal. Rice, beans, plantain, and the catch of the day. Not sure what kind of fish it was, but it was tasty. We washed the food down with a warm *Cerveza Balboa.* The owner seemed oblivious to out wet clothes. Probably thought we were fishermen who managed to capsize our boat.

The *comedor* had a battery powered radio. The news coming from it stated that the fight at the Alamo farm was over. The announcer said the government troops pushed back the cartel's men and claimed victory. Not all the Alamo defendants were killed, but the announcer did not give out the names of the survivors. It also did not give out the names of those killed in the blown-up helicopter, but it did state that it was shot down by the Cartel, and that was the main reason the government interfered.

ALBERTO ARCIA

The news made us realize why we were not pursued. We were small fish to the government. Nothing more than cowards leaving the fight. But you would have figured that the killing of the soldier at the checkpoint would have warranted a vigorous pursuit. I imagine that an investigation would come later. To avoid being tagged for the killing, we needed to not get caught. I also wondered about Juju. *Why was there no mention of his name?*

As was the plan, we said our goodbyes and split up. Salvador, Paco, and Miguel caught a ride to Panama City with a couple of Americans that had been there to fish. Ronson and I spent the evening in the village. The owner of the *comedor* told us we could sleep on his hammocks, and in the morning we could ride with him to a small town called Chiliebre on the transisthmian highway. From there we could hitch a ride to Colon City, although he warned us against going there. *"Muchos maleantes."*

I wanted to tell him I was from Colon City, and we weren't afraid of thugs. But prudence made me remain quiet. All that would do is get me in an argument, because he would not believe me. *Been there, done that. Too many times.*

Chapter Twenty One

Colonel Juju Ortiz

Things were not going well for the colonel. When the cartel's men arrived to grab Alex, Ortiz didn't have him. No amount of explanation was good for them. He had him, and lost him. They were incensed.

"*El Don* is not pleased with you, *Coronel*," said Marcos. "I have orders to stay with you until he arrives. He will come here and deal with you. You are getting paid a lot of money to keep things clean. The military is now involved. How did that happened?"

Juju was beginning to perspire. He had to come up with something quick. The possibility existed that, if things went badly for the cartel, and they lost this fight, these animals would kill him. If for some chance, they didn't, they would force him to help them, and that will expose him. The government would know he was their man on the inside, and that would not do. *What to do?*

"You have to understand, Marcos, that I did not authorize the helicopters. I had a no-fly zone in place. Someone high up gave the order to send Major Piero Perez with the two helicopters. Now there are Panamanian soldiers on the inside. Good ones. The Pumas are great fighters. If you are able to kill them, the government will be forced to interfere. And that will not be good for you."

Marcos spat on the ground. *"El gobierno, y el presidente* can suck my dick."

Juju stared at him. *Who do these assholes think they are? If the government is forced, they'll grow balls and destroy them.* "When is the Don scheduled to arrive?"

"No one knows Don Pablo's schedule. He comes when he comes. We wait for him."

"Listen to me, Marcos. If *El Don* wants to keep the government at bay, he must scare them."

Marcos spat on the ground again. "They are already scared. You mean how do we scare them more?"

"Yes. My meaning exactly. Let's blow up the helicopters when they leave. They should be empty except for the crew. No Pumas would be killed. This in-your-face act will shock them, and they will continue to remain quiet."

The cell phone rang. Juju picked it up. "It's from my man on the inside," he said."

After the short conversation, Juju approached Marcos. "We are going to be given a window of opportunity in which to act. The helicopters are leaving in the morning. My man will be in one of them. He gave me a count on how many men were dropped off. Major Piero will not remain on the ground, which is good for me. That man has been a thorn in my side for a long time. I will take him out. We need to shoot both helicopters down."

"I'm sorry, *Coronel Ortiz*, but I can't let you do that without orders from Don Pablo, and he has a strict ban on communications when he's on the move. Besides, is your man not in one of them?"

"His orders were to remain inside. I have to be able to rely on my men. He has betrayed me. He is no longer dependable, therefore not valuable to me."

Juju took his kerchief out from his back pocket and slowly dried the sweat from his face. It was a hot, humid day.

"Marcos, listen to me. We cannot let those two helicopters leave. It will send a bad signal to the government. They will think Don Pablo is getting weak. We have to shoot them down."

Marcos face tightened. "We will not shoot them down unless Don Pablo Jimenez gives us the order, and he has not arrived yet."

Juju removed his baseball cap and stepped aside. A shot rang out, and Marcos body lunged forward. The two men with him turned to see who did the shooting, giving Juju the opportunity to take his pistol out and kill them.

He raised his thumb to the sniper. With these three assholes dead and out of the way, he was going to do his own bidding. *Piero has interfered with my plans for the last time. He dies tomorrow.*

Juju knew he had signed his death warrant by killing these idiots, but he was hoping the destruction of the helicopters would appease the Don enough to spare him. If not, Juju would either kill the Don, or take the butcher to hell with him. The room where they would meet had been rigged with explosives. He could not afford to have this monster of a man kill or torture his family. *If I die, he dies with me.*

The town of Nombre de Dios, throughout history, had always been spared the aggravation of pirate assaults and

203

pandemics. The frantic life that came with economic growth had invaded the neighboring town of Portobelo. But it never reached Nombre de Dios. This good fortune was due to its territorial position. It was a nowhere town located a long ways from Portobelo in the far reaches of the Province of Colon. Its sleepy nature brought it retirees. They loved to fish, sit on their front porch rockers, and live a life of seclusion. It was the lure of its isolation that brought them the cartel. Here the law was weak.

These days bodies appeared on the street on a regular basis. Some were locals who dared object to their presence, but most were the cartel's own. These animals fought amongst themselves for whatever spoils there were to be had.

Most of the residents remained within their homes. It was prudent to do so, as exposure to the *drogueros* only brought them misery. Businesses that could close, did.

The Narcos had arrived in droves, preparing for the expected assault on the Perez farm. Yet today the town was practically empty, most of the thugs had gone to man their positions. This gave Juju to ability to kill the Don's guard dogs without immediate repercussion.

He recruited two of his henchmen to handle the weapons designed to shoot missiles. Although, it must be said that only one of them had actually fired one of these shoulder weapons before. When morning came, the soldiers were in position. Juju was with them.

"Bueno, muchachos, pongan los ojos al aire, que ya no demoran los helicópteros."

The helicopters were sighted. One soldier fired abruptly and missed. The other took his time and brought his target down."

204

Juju was furious. *"Me cágo en Judas!"* he yelled.

The soldier that missed threw his weapon down, and fell to his knees. He pleaded. *"Por favor, Coronel. No me mate."*

"Párate, pendejo. I'm not going to kill you unless Piero lives."

As they were preparing to walk back, the expected motorcade arrived. Juju counted the cars. "Only three," he mumbled. "Hum...maybe this won't be so hard. I can get this guys to fire the last two missiles at the first two cars. Surely Don Pablo is in the middle one. I'll blow the tires of the third one and riddle it with bullets.

"Oye, Juan, y tu Pedro, síganme. Vamos a matar a Don Pablo Jimenez."

The two soldiers looked at each other. They had fear in their faces, but they followed the *coronel.* He developed a need to water a tree and told them to wait.

Juan spoke to Pedro. "I missed my shot on the helicopter. If Piero was on that one, Coronel Ortiz is going to kill me. Now he wants to us kill the Don. He will blame us if things go wrong for him, and then he or they will kill us."

Pedro spat on the ground. "My shot hit the other one. If Don Pablo gets mad over that, the coronel will kill me. I do not want to die."

"Yo tampoco. Que podemos hacer, Pedro?"

"We can kill him, and tell Don Pablo what he was planning."

Colonel Ortiz came out from behind the tree, zipping up his pants. He came face to face with the two soldiers.

They pointed their pistols at him, and before he could react, they shot him, multiple times.

They took the body to Don Pablo. Since his man, nor the coronel were there to greet him, he had remained in his armored car. His men had their weapons out.

The two hapless soldiers came out yelling for them not to shoot. They were dragging the body of the infamous Coronel Juju Ortiz. A man who never expected his life to end this way. Killed by two nothing soldiers.

Chapter Twenty Two

Capitán Gato

We made it to Colón City fairly quickly. A businessman picked us up and drove us to the old Washington Hotel, a grand structure reminiscent of colonial times. It was my favorite place to stay. I had a history with that place.

My grandmother's house was directly across from it. As kids, my siblings and I, with cousin Piero, played inside the grounds. They also had one of the only two swimming pools in town. The other one was at the American Y.M.C.A., where I took useless swimming lessons. Grandmother's house was still there, but it no longer belonged to the family.

We spent two days there, long enough to learn that Cousin Piero was on the helicopter that was blown up. So was Sargento Rosario Morales. María and Gonzalez Brynn were on the other one. They were still in Panama City, guests of the Mexican Consulate. She refused to leave, waiting to see if my name appeared on the dead list.

The news hit me like a ton of bricks. I didn't care much for Rosario, but Piero was a favorite cousin. One I owed my life to. His death was hard to take.

"What are you going to do about María?"

"Not sure, Ronson. Part of me wants to let her know I'm alive, but the other does not trust her to keep quiet about it. If the authorities realize I'm alive, they will want to question me. When they understand how I escaped, they will put me in the vicinity of the dead soldier. This will not bode well for me. The end result could be my loss of freedom. I can't risk that happening."

"You do know, Alex, that all these worries she is having are not good for the baby."

"What are you, Ronson, the counter and carrier of all my guilts?"

"You have too many to count, Alex, and the weight would be too heavy for me to carry."

"And your point is what?"

He let out a loud sigh. "There is no point, Alex. I'm just worried about the baby. That's all."

"Well, don't. After all this mess my unborn kid has been through, he's going to hit the ground running. He will not be a weakling."

"You know, Alex, we have known each other a long time. We have gone through one adventure after another. Yet, I'm still not sure why I like you. You are a despicable man."

"You know what they say about sticks and stones, don't you?"

"You mentioned that to Deni, but did not explain the meaning. I'm Swiss, I don't know what it means. Please tell me."

"Sticks and stones hurt, words do not."

"You are wrong, Alex. Words hurt more, and their effect last longer than the pain of a beating."

He looked at me. By the expression of his eyes, I figured something deep was going to come out of his mouth.

"Alex, if you love your woman, you need to be with her before your baby is born. If that man she is traveling with is with her when she gives birth, you will no longer own her heart. He will be your Winkelmann. She will leave with him."

"Maybe yes, maybe no. I'm willing to take the chance that Gonzo will not rush into a family. He will wait for me to come take her away from him. Gonzo is not a one-woman man."

"For your sake, I hope you are right."

"Okay, enough talk about unpleasant things. Let's close the hotel bar. I have a powerful thirst for rum drinks. Tomorrow we go to the Cristobal Yacht Club and hire us a captain with a fishing boat to take us to the island of Colón. I wonder if Celeste still remembers me."

We had a good night's sleep. In the morning we enjoyed the continental breakfast and took a taxi to the yacht club. The bar was open so we had a couple of screwdrivers to settle the stomach. The bartender told us there was a man on boat slip number ten that took people out on fishing trips.

"Ronson, stay here. I'll check this guy's rig out and see if he is willing to take us into Bocas."

Thirty minutes later I returned, whistling. Ronson smiled. "Alex, you only whistle when you're happy. So, we have a boat ride?"

"Yes we do. I hired a captain."

"Who is he? Can he be trusted?"

ALBERTO ARCIA

"His name is Capitán Gato. He will take us to Isla Colón today for two hundred dollars each. If we want to fish, then it will cost us another fifty each."

Rosnon stared at me. "Alex, I believe the word *gato* means cat. Does he have a real name? Did you ask to see his license?'

"Listen, Ronson. When I asked him what his qualifications were, he told me he could smuggle a whore into the bed of a married man on his honeymoon without the wife noticing."

"And you believed him?"

"Yes, I did. I hired him."

"Alex, the man is a liar."

"Yes, he is, but he's a good one."

Ronson frowned and swallowed his drink in one gulp. "I don't like liars, Alex."

"Then what are you doing hanging round me? I lie like the American president. Besides, lying is the in thing these days. Everyone is doing it. You ought to try it."

He ordered a double and looked at me. "Did I tell you, you are a despicable man?"

"Yes, Ronson, once or thrice. Please give that word a rest. Next time, try calling me dreadful. It'll be refreshing. Now, drink up. We need to hit a few stores and get us some new duds. We look shabby. The hotel clerk almost didn't rent us a room. If it wasn't for my American Express card, we'd be sleeping outside."

"When are we shipping out?"

"At one-thirty. Drink up. We need to go."

We arrived at the boat slip on time. We were greeted by a gorgeous, voluptuous, and wonderful specimen of female flesh. My mouth flew open. I gawked at the babe.

210

"Ronson closed it for me. Try some composure Alex."

I couldn't speak. I was totally mesmerized. Ronson had to step up. "We are the paying customers. Who might you be?"

She giggled. "I'm your deck hand," she said, and curtsied.

My mouth flew opened again. Ronson closed it. "Where is the captain?"

She turned her back to us and slowly bent down, yelling down an opened hatch. "Yoo-hoo, *Gatito, mi amor*. The customers are here."

My mouth would have opened again, except for Ronson's hand. He kept it shut. But he couldn't keep quiet either.

"Alex that is the most *wunderbar* backside I have ever seen."

"Wonderful and equally as beautiful. I can't believe she's our deck hand."

"Alex, stop drooling and think. Our deck hand has painted toes and nails. Who's going to work the boat? Certainly not her."

Capitán Gato came up on deck. He saw the look on our faces and smiled. "Ah, I see you have met my Chiquita. She's going with us."

"Is she going to be our deck hand?" asked Ronson.

"Did you not see that body? No, Chiquita is my personal assistant. You two are the deck hands. This is a working trip. That's why I'm charging you a cheap, no-questions-asked price."

Chapter Twenty Three

End of the Line

Gato's boat was a beauty. A twenty foot, nineteen eighty-nine Giorgetti & Magrini custom cruising ketch. We left Cristobal and headed for open water. Gato was not kidding about this being a working trip. Ronson and I were up to our asses in work.

"Alex, next time you hire a boat, make sure we're not the crew."

"Ronson, you're a Swiss. You guys are not known for being great thinkers. We are going to Bocas, then to San Jose. Both places require money, and we'll need cash in Casa Mendez. I'm saving you whore money. Be grateful."

That evening, Gato cooked a meal of *corvina* in a butter-and-culantro sauce. I was pleased we were not in charge of cooking. The dish was delicious. Chiquita told us she was from Venezuela. We figured probably twenty year's younger than Gato. He told us he was half Panamanian and half Cuban. "I live on this boat and make a living smuggling and chartering cruises."

The weather could not have been better. Chiquita kept filling our glasses with rum, and Gato, on a whim, brought his guitar out. He played several tunes, but when he opened with *Cuándo Salí de Cuba*, he broke out into song. You could tell by looking into that stunning woman's eyes, that Gato made a good living. That girl was into him. She turned out to be a crier too. We hardly slept with all the noise coming from their bedroom.

"I wish she would stop making all that sexual noise, said Ronson. I can't sleep. I prefer quiet women."

"Not me. The loud ones are best. They encourage you and give you a timetable as to where they are in the sexual process. But you're right, all this noise is making me hard, and it's difficult to sleep when John Henry is agitated. I may have to whack off."

"Alex, don't even think of it. That's disgusting. Don't you dare touch your bone, not with me bunking right here. Don't do it."

We were awakened early. Chiquita wanted us to see the beautiful daybreak. The scene was breathtaking. We had arrived at the province of Bocas del Toro. The mouth of the bull. A place full of pirates, smugglers, Banana workers, whores, Rastas, and expat Americans looking to escape the doldrums of living in the States. Ronson swatted a mosquito, killing the buzz. Yes, we had arrived on the Mosquito Coast.

As arranged, we paid the remainder of our fee, said farewell to Capitán Gato and his beautiful assistant, and went in search of a place to stay. We checked in at the Hotel Angela and headed down to the bar for our morning vodka and orange juice drink.

That afternoon, we took a walk through the small town, stopping at the Library club. I was hoping Celeste would be there. No luck. The person working the place would not tell me where she was or whether she would return. Bummed, we walked back to the hotel.

ALBERTO ARCIA

While at the bar, drinking our before-dinner hi-ball, the bartender turned on the television. A news program came on, and to our surprise, my sister Deni was on. To our chagrin, instead of her being lauded as a hero, she had been arrested as a rebel rouser. She was not a happy camper. Her lawyer was next to her. I recognized him immediately. My cousin Ronny. Deni was in good hands with him as her lawyer.

I was happy to learn that Fausto, and my cousins, Jámes and Dumas, survived their wounds. Unfortunately, everyone was fined and sent back to their homes to recuperate. All except Lor, who like Deni, had been arrested. But he had been charged with the murders of El Cholo and his cronies in the town of Nombre de Dios. Ronson and I looked at each other.

"Before you say it, Ronson. Let me remind you that Paco, Miguel, and Salvador are in Panama City. If Deni can't get him off the hook, they will do something."

He sipped his drink. "What if they don't?"

"Listen to me, friend. You and I, we've been through a lot together. Even though you think I'm a schmuck, I like you. You are a dear friend, but I'm done adventuring. I'm done risking my life. I have to believe the guys will help Deni and Lor. I have to believe it because I'm not going back. I'm going to Mexico to find my wife, raise our child, and tend to my avocado trees."

He gave me a look I didn't like. I waited for the insult. "You're a liar Alex."

"What is it that you think I'm lying to you about?"

"Oh, I believe that you are not going to help your sister and Lor. That I can see in your eyes. It's the part about María, the unborn kid, and the farm in Mexico that I have a

214

problem with. I can't see that scene in your eyes at all. That is just an excuse to keep on going. You can't possibly settle down to a farm life. It's not in your genes. You will never change, Alex. All you do is cut and run."

I was about to engage him when Celeste walked into the bar. She swayed those hips my way. "Alex, it's so good to see you again. My boyfriend has gone back to Paris. He will be gone for several months. Can you stay here for a while?"

I did not want to look at Ronson. I felt his eyes burning a hole in my conscience. Instead I looked at Celeste's breasts and smiled. "Yes, baby. I have some time to kill here."

She squealed. "Good, grab your things and come stay with me."

I looked at my bud. He placed his forefinger on his lips. "Go ahead and have a good time. I'll see you around."

I left with Celeste, but with an uneasy feeling in my stomach. Something was telling me I had seen the last of Ronson. But that was a concern for later. Now, I had Celeste to contend with, and the way she moved her body, I knew she was hungry for me and John Henry.

I checked out, threw my stuff into Celeste's small car, and we drove to her bed & breakfast place.

"What do you want to do now, Alex?"

The situation with Ronson had left me hollow. I was not in the mood to play twenty questions, so I grabbed the woman by the short hairs. "Celeste, I'm horny. Can we screw?"

ALBERTO ARCIA

She raised an eyebrow, and with a mocking gesture answered my question. "Alex, does a weasel like to get into the henhouse?"

We walked into her place of business. A man I did not know was working the greeting desk. She checked with him, made sure nothing pressing needed her attention, and led me upstairs.

"I have a powerful hunger for your bone, Alex. I hope you can stay with me."

She went into the bathroom, and I undressed. When she came out, she was naked with her left hand hidden behind her buttocks. My heart skipped a beat. I reached for her but she stopped me. "Not so fast my eager friend. Today we play a game called riding the pony."

Good grief, not that old game. "Okay Celeste. Are you going to ride me, or do I get to ride you?"

She brought out her hidden hand, and in it, she clutched a leather belt. *Oh God, she's going to whip me. Bummer.*

Alex, you are the horse, I'm the rider. I climb on your back and hit your buttocks with this belt. You make horse noises and move around the room, fast. When my fever is high, I throw the whip away, you dump me on the bed, and then you take me from behind. I will make copulating female horse noises. Okay?"

What could I say? She was a gamer, and I loved sex games. "Yes, let's do it, but hold the belt short. If you strike John Henry, the game is over."

I was right about Ronson. The following morning, I took a walk and called on him at the hotel. The girl at the registering desk told me he had checked out.

"Adonde se fué?" I asked.

216

She shrugged her shoulders. *"No sé. No me dijo."*

I felt bad. Maybe he left to see his whore in San Jose, but my gut told me he had gone to Panama City. *Should I follow him*? Before I could decide, I heard the sound of a motor bike horn blow outside the hotel. I walked out and there was Celeste, my ravenous porn star. She was wearing short shorts and a halter top. Her blond hair loose over her shoulders. She revved the bike engine. "Get on back, handsome. We're going to the beach."

I took the intervention as a sign that God wanted me to leave my adventuring life behind. I smiled at her, climbed on the bike, and threw my worries out the proverbial window, so to speak. But I can tell you that at that moment, Bocas felt like the end of the line for me and Ronson. I was right. I never saw him again.

Two months later, I met a man that was sailing his boat to Veracruz. He needed a mate, so I signed up. I kissed Celeste goodbye and left her standing, teary-eyed, but okay. To a woman like her, I'm replaceable goods.

All during the trip I kept hoping that María was still with child. But no matter how I counted, that baby had to have arrived. I wondered if she remained in Panamá, or had gone back to México. No matter, I was going to have fate decide my course of action. If she remained in Panamá, so be it. I would move on to Texas. But if she was in México and would have me, I would gladly take on the role of husband and father.

Chapter Twenty Four

The Gang Gathers

I can't believe you guys are arresting me," complained Deni. "I'm a heroine. I stood up against Don Pablo Jimenez cartel and won."

"Señorita Pérez," said the arraigning officer. "You caused a lot of trouble for the government, and a lot of lives were lost due to your actions. We have no choice but to arrest you. Do you know a good lawyer?"

"What's going to happen to my friend? He is a foreigner. He's from Italy."

"I'm sorry to have to contradict you, *señorita,* but his passport says he is from Switzerland. I hope he didn't lie to you. Everyone wants to be Italian around here. It's the going thing these days."

Two days later, Miguel showed up in the company of Ronny Perez, a cousin, and the family's attorney. They were allowed to see Deni. When they reached her cell, she was hotter than a two-dollar pistol.

"What in thunder took you guys so long to get here?"

Salvador pointed at the attorney. "He was out on a short vacation. He just returned."

Deni calmed down. *"Hola, Primo.* Thanks for coming."

"Hola, Deni. Sorry to see you in this place, but you caused a lot of trouble. It's going to be difficult to get you out of this mess without doing jail time."

"What? Jail time? Are you crazy, Primo?"

"No, Deni. But first things first. Let me see if I can get you out on bail."

"Can you get Lor out on bail too?"

"No chance of that. He is being charged with murder. You have been charged with inciting an insurrection that directly caused the death of many people, including our cousin, Piero Perez. He was a major in the military. The government is highly upset with you."

Salvador approached Deni. "Listen, Sis. How attached are you to Lor?"

"Why?"

"Because he is a foreigner, therefore a high-flight risk. Bail for him will not be possible. But there is another way."

"Bueno, that's it for me. I can't be a part of this conversation," said Ronny. "I will go and try to arrange your bail, *pero te va a costar mucho dinero."*

"Primo, I don't care how much it costs, but it better not be too much. I'm a Perez, not a *pinche campesino."*

"Got it. I will try to haggle for a good price."

"Cousin, if you have to hock my house to meet the requirements, do it."

"Thank you. That may be necessary."

Ronny looked at Salvador and motioned for him to follow. They stopped and Ronny laid it all on the line.

"Wish me luck, Sal. The Perez surname may still have some influence in Colón, and in Chiriquí, but this is Panamá.

Here, the cost of her release would be less if she were a damn peasant."

"I'm still here, assholes. I can hear you."

Ronny rolled his eyes and left. Salvador walked towards Deni and grabbed her hand. She pulled it away quickly. "Don't patronize me. I'm not some silly school girl or one of your brainless girlfriends."

"Listen to me, Sis. I don't know why you are this way, and I don't care. If you are upset and carry a grudge because Alex and I don't ever come to see you…"

"What in hell do you know about me, Bro? Nothing. Keep your opinion to yourself."

"No, I won't. You are incarcerated, and Ronny confided in me that the government is talking about using you as an example so no one else gets any crazy ideas about challenging the cartel. They are fighting Don Jimenez their way."

Deni spat on her jail floor. "Fighting the cartel while counting the money Pablo gives them."

Salvador looked at the spit and then, at her. He frowned. Please listen to me, Sis. Ronny believes they want to teach you a lesson. This means jail time."

Deni's countenance went from aggressive to amenable. "Sal, get me out of here. I don't care the cost. And, where in hell is Alex?"

"He's gone, Deni. Alex and Ronson should be in Bocas by now."

"He's leaving me here? And I thought Ronson and Lor were buds?"

"Sis, what I'm going to say to you will hurt, but it is necessary. Leaving you here is easy for us. We can't hug you. We can't discuss anything with you without quarreling.

You are like Dad—difficult to love. There is a fire burning within you that demands something we can't give you. It's not our fault that we were born boys in a male dominant culture. It's not our fault that you were born a girl. It's not our fault that mother is not fond of you. You remind her of dad. She hated him. You need to drop that chip you carry on your shoulder. It will allow those that love you to have easier access. The way you are now makes you a royal pain-in-the-ass."

Deni smiled. "Well, that was a mouthful."

"Don't say any more. Let's end this *tete a tete* before I change my mind on staying and helping you."

"So, you are going to stay while Alex runs away. I'm impressed."

Salvador entered the cell and opened his arms. Deni stood her ground, but something in his eyes made her go to him. They embraced, and he whispered. "Paco and Miguel are with me. Once you're out, we will see about springing Lor."

She kissed him on the cheek. "Thanks, Sal. But don't get used to this closeness. I'm not that type of woman."

"No. You're not. You're not like Liliana, and that's too bad."

The following day, Deni was let out on a fifty-thousand dollar bail bond. Ronny drove her to El Trapiche restaurant. Waiting for her were Salvador, Paco, Miguel, and to her delight, Ronson.

"Well, the gang is all here," she said. "I'm sorry to see that big brother is missing."

"He's gone to find his wife, Deni," said Ronson. "He wants to settle down and help her raise the unborn child. He sends you his love, and wishes you good fortune."

"Yeah, I bet he does."

A plan was discussed and agreed upon. But they needed Intel from someone on the inside. Until then, Deni would liquidate all her assets, sign over to Liliana the remaining family property, and prepare to leave Panamá forever. She and her gang were going to spring Lor whenever the government's case was done, and he was officially convicted. They had to do this during the move from his jail cell to the prison. They had one shot at it.

Deni convinced Ronny to lobby the Swiss Consul General to get involved in the case and to hire a counselor for Lor. The reason behind his argument was to keep the government from rushing through the process and convicting him without a proper trail. He persuaded the consul that Lor needed his involvement.

"With you watching, the prosecutors can't cut corners. He deserves a fair trial."

The Swiss consul hired Ronny to be his attorney. He kept us abreast of things and passed on general information from us to Lor. But he refused to listen or to be a participant in whatever it was we were planning, and he knew we were planning something. The selling of personal things and property was a dead giveaway.

Ronny worried that Deni was going to get caught, and her bond would be rescinded, landing her back in jail.

As expected, Lor was convicted. Ronny tried to counsel Deni into not being so hasty in her actions. "There is an angle I'm working on. A possibility exists that the government may release Lor quietly and send him home at the consulate's expense. The men he killed were scum bags. Killers that needed to be eliminated."

He reached for her hand, but she pulled it back. He sighed. "Deni, you are a dear cousin. So is Salvador. Please be careful. Don't screw things up. I don't want to have to explain to a judge why I was not aware of the liquidation of assets. You have a For Sale sign on your car, for God's sake. I have a wife and kids and a profession to take care. I'm sorry *Bara Larga* is not here, but that makes it easier for me to stay uninvolved."

She laughed. "I haven't heard anyone call him that in years. How did you tag him with that nickname?"

"When we were kids, Alex was much taller than the rest of us. I had to stop calling him that when Salvador and I shot past him."

"If I remember right, he used to call you, Lulu. Where did that nickname come from?"

"Never mind about that. Just be careful about being too open selling things. Take that sign off your car window. If my angle does not work and the government decides to keep him, I will let you know when they will move him, but that's all. It's your responsibility to follow the wagon."

She smiled and extended her hand. Ronny shook it. "Thanks, Cousin. When all this is done, I will send you a postcard."

"No, don't do that. I'm going to be watched. Just enjoy your new life. I will know if you are alive or not. The news will tell me. You have achieved notoriety. You have become a sort of Robin Hood amongst the women. Your death will make the newspapers."

223

ALBERTO ARCIA
"Thanks Ronny. A new life without notoriety it will be."

Chapter Twenty Five

Adiós, Panamá

Deni managed to liquidate most of her assets by the time Lor was sentenced. They gave him twelve years. Can't say it was unexpected. The plan in place was to wait for Ronny to call and give Deni the date and time he would be moved from his jail cell to prison. They were going to hijack the prison van, and then steal a plane and fly it to Bocas. There they would look for Alex. Maybe he was still around. If not, a boat would be hired to get them to Costa Rica. From there, they would fly to Houston. The exception being Salvador. He will go to Miami.

Paco and Miguel needed to report back to work. Kermit had already phoned and wanted them back. They had work to do. The issue would be what to do with Deni, although she had enough dough to last her and Lor a while. Maybe Lor could get work at Kermit's office too. He'd be a good hired gun.

In the middle of fine tuning the plan, a call came from Ronny, and the whole thing changed. The plan was turned upside down. The government decided to release Lor to the Swiss Consul General, with the condition he would place him on the next flight for Zurich.

"What are we going to do about this turn of events?" asked Salvador.

"We can't rescue him form the consul," said Miguel. "He needs to count his blessings and fly home."

They looked at Deni. She seemed lost in thought.

"Deni, we're not going to risk our asses for a man that will be released," said Paco. "You and Ronson can fly to Switzerland on the next plane and meet up with him. Miguel and I need to go to Texas."

Deni frowned. "I can't leave the country while I'm out on bond, and Lor can't return here."

"Good, then its settled," said Ronson. "You two fly back to Houston. Deni and I will go to Bocas, check on Alex, and then go to San Jose. I will remain there for a while. Deni can go wherever she wants. Maybe to Zurich, or even to Houston. There she can meet up with you guys. Maybe she can get a job with Kermit's firm. The old sleuth does not require a work visa."

"Hey," said Miguel. "You've been reading our mail."

They had a good laugh, and then looked at Deni again. "What are you going to do?" asked Ronson. "I can give you Lor's family address in the Ticino area. They will know where he is staying. He moves around a lot."

With a sad tone, she replied. "One thing I know for sure, and that is I can't stay here and risk losing my freedom. If you will have me, Ronson, I'd rather go to Bocas and then to Houston. As much as I hate to do it, I will say adiós to my beautiful Panamá."

Understanding she couldn't call Ronny, she took a cab to his house. He wasn't home. She left a sealed note telling him to tell Lor that she'd be waiting for him, if he wanted to see her again, in Houston. And that was it. Once they knew Lor had gone, they went their separate ways.

Ronson and Deni decided against flying, and took an overnight bus to David, Chiriquí, and called on Dumas and Jámes. The guys were recovering well from their wounds. From David they rode a bus to Bocas. This is a ride not recommended to those with a faint heart. The bus chug-chugged up the mountain, then no brakes applied down it. Ronson came out of the bus looking pale. He couldn't believe he had to pay to risk his life.

They made it to the dock on time, caught the ferry going to the island of Colón, and checked to see if Alex was still around. He wasn't. They rented a boat and moved on to Costa Rica. The government never suspected anything.

On the way, Deni asked Ronson a question that bothered her. "The boys told me you have a special woman that works in a brothel. If she's a whore, what makes her special?"

"Deni, don't call her a whore."

Piqued, she came back at him. "If she works in a brothel, Ronson, she's a whore. So, what do you want me to call her, a *puta*?"

"Her name is Mariana."

"Okay, Mariana it is. So, Ronson, tell me why a man as handsome as you thinks a woman like her is special? And I don't need to hear about her sexual expertise."

He grimaced. "My reasons are my own. I just like her. She is good for me."

Deni knew not to push it, at least for now. They remained quiet the rest of the way.

Crossing customs was a piece of cake, and soon they found themselves riding in another bus. They rode in silence for a while, then Ronson broached the Mariana subject.

"Deni, your brother told me that I cannot take Mariana away from her work without either paying the woman in charge for her, or stealing her away. Was he right?"

She laughed. "Whorehouse customs are not my specialty, but if you want to take her away, ask her if she's a slave. If she tells you yes, then ask the Madame how much it will cost you to free her. If she says no, then go ask the Madame how much it will cost you to take her with you. I suppose there is a different in cost."

"How much do you think it will cost me to free her?"

"If she speaks more than one language, is well mannered, and not too young or old, she may be unaffordable. The brothel gets girls that wander in off the street or those sold to them by parents who can't afford to feed them. Management spends money and resources on their welfare and education. Those that show promise, are tutored in social graces. Manners are important to highbrow male customers."

Ronson stared at her. "I thought you said you didn't know much about these things? You know more than Alex."

She laughed again. "I read books on the subject. Alex just pays and plops his pants on the bedposts."

"Deni, she is beautiful, tall, and well mannered. She also speaks English."

Deni, enjoying this very much, decided to have fun with Ronson. She opened her left palm and spread her fingers. Then, with the forefinger of the right one, she began to touch the fingers on the open palm. This finger is for beauty. That cost money. This one is for education. More money. This other one is for being tall. Money. This one is for being bilingual. Money." She stopped counting and looked at Ronson. "Is she good in bed?"

228

"Yes, very good."

"Okay, then," and she opened her other palm, "And this one is for sexual prowess. More money. That's six good things in total. It will probably cost you two-thousand per skill. Plus another two for her upkeep and clothes."

Ronson swallowed hard. "Fourteen thousand dollars? Are you serious?"

She touched his hand to console him. "I would say that to free a high class prostitute, you should be prepared to spend up to twenty grand. Give or take a few thousand."

Greif stricken, he blurted out. "I can't afford that. Not right here and now. I have money invested in Switzerland, and some in a special account. Also in Houston, but it will take me some time to get it."

She turned serious. "Ronson, I can't believe you. Alex told me you were his best mate. He said you plucked him out of trouble many times. I had so much confidence in you, I put you in charge of my Alamo. I have the money, if you want a loan, but a man like you shouldn't have to worry about paying for the woman he wants. You need to take her away, and dare anyone to stop you."

"That idea has crossed my mind, and I spoke to Alex about it. He counseled me against it, telling me these houses have a lot of influence with people in the police and government. He said if I took her, I had to get her out of the country, and away from the long arm of the law. He also said if I took her, a man-hunter would be sent after us. Was he right?"

"Alex worries about everything. Me, not so much. How about you, Ronson?"

The mischievous look in her eyes caught his attention. "Deni, what are you suggesting?"

"Let's steal her."

They arrived at Casa Mendez, and checked in for two nights. Ronson ordered Mariana, and Deni ordered Alex's whore for two nights too, with the morning blow job included.

Maribel, the Madame raised her eyebrows. "I have men available too."

"No, men I can get at will. I've never bedded down a girl before. I'm dying to see how it's done and how it feels. Fix me up."

As per the plan, Ronson asked Mariana if she would be willing to leave with him. She batted her long eyelashes at him and asked the dreaded question. "Are you going to marry me before or after you take me? I need to know now."

Ronson's heart dropped. "Mariana, I don't want to marry you now. I figured we live together for a time, and then we can marry."

"What guarantees do I have that you won't use me and then leave me someplace far away from home? Besides, you have to settle accounts with Maribel. You have to pay her for my education and upkeep. Then you have to pay money to my parents because I will not be sending them any work money."

"Can't we just leave?"

She gave him the arms akimbo stance. More talk was needed, otherwise she would not go away easily.

"Mariana, I don't understand. You work in a sex house. I want to free you from this work. Why don't you want to come?"

230

"You know nothing about what we do here. You think we are here only to satisfy men."

"Well, yes. That is what you do, and you do it for money."

She became upset. "So, you want me to do it for free? Do you think I have no respect? I am here to get an education and to find a husband."

He stared at her. He was at a loss for words. Alex was the one with the magic tongue.

She continued to berate him. "You say you want to marry me, okay I'll do it, but first you must pay Maribel, and then pay my father. You can't steal me, I'm not that kind of a woman. After you settle accounts, we can marry here or someplace else."

That evening, Ronson had dinner with Deni. She seemed elated at finding the love of a woman. "They are better in bed than a man."

Ronson gave her a peculiar look. "Deni I don't know how you can do it without a man thing, but I'm not going to worry about it. I have a problem, and it's not a good one."

"Let me guess. By the puppy dog eyes, your woman will not leave with you unless you pay a lot of money. Am I right?"

"Yes, not only does she want me to marry her, but she wants more money than I want to pay. I'm afraid she will have to stay here. "Let's go to Houston."

"Now? You want to leave now? I'm discovering things I never knew existed. I want to stay here longer?"

"Well, you can stay for as long as your money lasts, but I'm done with Mariana. I'll fly out tomorrow. I'll send

ALBERTO ARCIA

you a postcard from Houston. It will have Alex's address. I
will stay there until he shows back up."

Chapter Twenty Six

A Welcoming

I said goodbye to the boat captain, and climbed on a bus going to Ciudad Victoria. So much had happened that I no longer feared the authorities. My appearance had changed. Today, I was sporting a full beard and a thick moustache.

The bus arrived at the main terminal, and from there I took another one to the town of Nuevo Padilla. I wanted to pay a visit to Doctor Hankamon Switzer. He would tell me if María had returned from Panama, and if my child was a boy or girl.

The ride was long, hot, and dusty. The bus had no air conditioning. We traveled through dirt roads with the windows opened. During the bumpy, uncomfortable ride, my memory kept going through all that had happened since I was last in these parts. The near death experience when the plane went down into Lake Victoria. The stupid robbery of the farmer's pants, horse and plantains. My incarceration in the town of La Esperanza, screwing a nun, and my relationship with Gonzo and María. Then came that ill-fated rescued that took me to Panamá, and the fight against the cartel at the family farm. All of that happened in one year. It felt like I had aged five.

ALBERTO ARCIA

I walked from the bus stop to the hospital. There were things to sort out. *What if Ronson was right, and María hooked up with Gonz? What would I do then?*

Cautiously, I walked into the hospital, hoping for the best. And there, right in front of my eyes, stood María. My wife. I opened my arms to her.

"Well, look at what the *gato* dragged in today. My inconsiderate, lying, no good husband."

Some welcome. I kept my arms opened. *"Hola, mi amor.* Your husband is home."

Doctor Switzer walked in. He took one good look at me, and told María to take the day off. "Take him home and give him a good scrubbing."

I smelled my armpits, no stink there. *What's his deal?*

He approached me and extended his hand. *"Hola,* Alex. Welcome back."

I had to admit it, the guy had class. I shook his hand. *"Gracias,* Hankamon. It's good to be back."

"When you get sanitized and have rested, come back and see me. We need to discuss something."

Shit, he's going to admonish me for vacillating with the promised manifesto. "Sure, Doc. Will do."

Maria changed clothes, and we walked to the bus station. I tried to hold her hand but she wouldn't let me. On the way, I asked the dreaded question. "Do we have a boy or a girl?"

"We have a beautiful baby girl. No thanks to you."

"Sweetheart, don't be like that. You know I love you, and you know why I had to stay. Sorry for putting ether on your nose. I know it wasn't pleasant. Please forgive me."

"I understand you wanting me and Briana out of the way, but you could have come back with me. Your sister did not need you. She told me you were nothing but a *pendejo.*"

"Briana? You named my little girl Briana? Why?"

She gave me a smirk. "Why do you think?"

"So, it was not my child after all. It was Gonzo Brynn's kid. I knew it."

"Alex, you are a *pendejo.* I had no idea if I would ever see you again. I still do not believe you really love me. Yes, it is your child, but I named her after Gonzo. He was here, and he helped me with the child birth. Gonzo is a stand up man. He will be around to help me and Briana deal with things. I don't know how long you will remain with us. Frankly, Alex. I don't know who you are anymore."

"Where is my beautiful daughter?"

"Briana is with the baby sitter."

"What? You left my daughter in the hands of a stranger?"

"Alex, you're the only stranger in her life."

The bus to the town of *La Esperanza* was late, so we sat on a bench and waited and talked.

"Listen to me, sweetheart. I came a long way here. I did it in spite of not knowing whether you would be here. That should count for something."

She gave me a look of disbelief. "Quit being an imbecile, Alex. Where else would I go? I was traveling with Gonzo. I have a home in *La Esperanza*, and a job at the hospital in *Nuevo Padilla*. This area is our home."

No matter what I said, María wasn't buying it. She refused to believe that I actually did love her. Explaining to

235

me, in great detail my past actions. And concluding that my behavior was not from a man who professes to love his wife.

Our ride finally arrived. Much to my chagrin, we climbed on another rickety bus for another hot and dusty trip. She said little, and I kept bombarding her with reasons why she should give me another chance. All I received for my pleading was silence. My best words fell on deaf ears.

The bumpy ride and a headstrong woman who did not want to speak to me made me examine my own reasons for being here. I didn't much care for the area. Backwoods were not for city dwellers. I needed a night life, and here that meant counting fireflies with your sweetie while drinking a cold beer. *What am I going to do when my desire to bounce the mattress at night with her subsides? Go to the nunnery?*

While enduring this ride on a motorized aberration, the realization of what I had to do, hit me. In order to convince her, my attitude needed to change. It required me to show, not tell. I needed to love everything about this place. *Yeah, right. Stuck in the middle of nowhere. That's a hard sell. Can I do it? Yes, I can.*

We made it to the station, and walked home. An old woman came out holding a baby. María paid her and took custody of the kid. After showering Briana with kisses, she handed her to me.

"Here, Alex, meet your daughter."

At first, I was super nervous. I did not know how fragile the baby was, which made me uncomfortable. When the baby had her nap, I took pen and pencil and decided to write the damn manifesto I had promised Hankamon and Gonzo. It didn't take me long, only three rewrites. I knew what he wanted to do, and I went for it.

That evening, after super, Gonzo arrived. He came in his two oxen chariot. He was glad to see me and vice versa. I really liked him. All three of us chatted, and when the baby began to cry and fuss, Gonzo brought out his guitar and sang her a lullaby. Quieting the kid.

After a while, María left with the baby, and Gonzo and I had a moment to ourselves. I needed to make sure he hadn't helped himself to my wife's charms.

We poured a small portion of tequila into our glasses. We toasted to each other and I dove right in. "Listen, Gonz, How much damage did I cause myself by sending her out of the fighting zone with you?"

He sipped his tequila. "She was upset when you remained, but understood your reason for getting her and the baby out of harm's way. But Maria is not a stupid woman, Alex. She knows men better than you think. She has been courted by many, and only a few were successful in enjoying her in a private way."

"Did you enjoy her that way?"

He finished his tequila and asked for more. "You know I did, Alex. I already told you. If you're asking me if I took advantage of her state of mind, and enjoyed her sexual charms again, the answer is no. I'm not that kind of guy. I don't bed married women."

"Bullshit, Gonz. You bed nuns, and they are married to God."

"Not the same thing."

He took another sip and place his cup down. Then he buried his eyes on mine. "But let me tell you this, friend. If you leave María again, I'll be on her before she has a chance to miss you. She is a good woman, and the baby girl is adorable. I have become fond of both of them. I will step up if you step out. *Me entiendes?"*

"*Sí, Gonz. Comprendo muy bien.* You're finally ready for a family of your own."

"Yes I am. But understand I'm not coveting your wife."

"Yes, that is obvious. It's my daughter you're after."

"I'm her Godfather, Alex. I know what is expected of me if you're not around."

I gave him my hand, and he took it. Gonz and I were good with each other. I appreciated his sincerity. As long as I was screwing María, he would attend to Briana's needs. That worked for me. I believed in the old adage that states 'it takes a village to raise a child.

Chapter Twenty Seven

The Manifesto

Eight months later, life had taken me in a different direction. I actually enjoyed being a father, and grasped the notion that counting and chasing fireflies could be fun. I broke through my wife's defenses and bedded her. I knew she hadn't forgotten Johnny boy's abilities. Our love life had taken a turn for the better. The woman let me screw her regularly. She loved me.

One day, Gonzo showed up for dinner driving his two-ox cart. I greeted him at the door with a mischievous grin.

He scanned my face. "I've never seen that look on you, and frankly, it worries me. What's up, Alex?"

Before he climbed off his slow moving chariot, I handed him a large manila envelope. He looked at it, and then at me, showing confusion.

"What's in it, money?"

"No Gonz, I'm not the type of guy who gives money to other men. It's your manifesto. It took me a long time to write it. I had to put a lot of thought into it. I hope you will accept it, because I'm done with it."

He frowned. "Alex, you were supposed to let me read it, so I could approve it."

ALBERTO ARCIA

"Sorry about that, Gonz, but this piece is the best that I can do. It's a take it or leave deal. I'm done. Feel free to change whatever you do not like. My debt to you and Hankamon is paid."

With that said, I walked back inside. He remained seated, opened the envelope and read it.

When he came in, his face was flushed. I never asked him why, and he never mentioned the manifesto. We had a quiet dinner, made small talk, and he went home.

A week later, there was a buzz going round town. I was at the hospital, picking María up to take her to lunch when Ana, the lady from the bread store walked in. She seemed agitated.

"María, take a look at this. The work of the devil."

She handed her what looked like my manifesto. "It's from Gonzalez Brynn. I don't know what has gotten into him. You are not going to like what you read. It's all over town."

Dr. Switzer came by, and María handed the paper to him. He read it out loud. Friends, ex-colleagues, and parishioners. Please clear your minds of ancient things and hear me out. Nothing old should survive the passage of time, unless it has been modified to fit in modern life. Progressive adaptability is something we must all do, lest we fall further behind our stodgy peers, and watch them reap the fruits of our labor.

I am Gonzalez Brynn, your Mennonite neighbor, and I write this article to lambast the Catholic Church, not praise it. Specifically, their outdated stance on women. It's a position as old as the mountains, devised and supported by men whose intent was and still is, to control them. By demeaning woman, they rob them of their pride. This tragedy cannot stand. I will not allow it.

María stood there, motionless. She looked at me, "Is Gonzo attacking the church?"

"It appears so, but please listen and don't interrupt."

Hankamon continued. The priestly attack on women started with the story of Jesus' mother, Mary. She was relegated to being just that, his mother. A grand thing on its own, but not to them. Mary's written history deprives her of other majestic achievements, making the birth of her son, Jesus, her sole important role. Let me say to you, my brethren, that I'm not here to discuss the ridiculous notion of Mary's 'Immaculate Conception.' Something so absurd that only those without a sense of reason accept it. I can hear her now, as everyone surely did then, speaking to Joseph. "Oh, dear husband, you're not going to believe what has happened to me! An Angel came down from heaven and impregnated me. He told me we're going to have God's son, and he will be named Jesus." The simplicity of Joseph's mind, allowed Mary's guile to succeed. Yet, that is an argument for other times. Today, I write to you about my calling, obsession, or quest. Call it what you may, but I will dedicate my life to a cause long in coming. To raise the consciousness of woman in the Catholic Church, a bastion of archaic, male indifference.

María and Ana crossed themselves. "Dios mío, the devil must have gotten a hold of Gonzo. This is a terrible *sacrilegio,* " said Ana.

"Please stop interrupting," I said. "Let the doctor finish reading the paper."

Dr. Switzer continued. Ask yourself, why was Mary chosen to be the mother of God's earthly son? Was it because her husband was a simple minded man. Or, was it because Mary was an astute woman, worthy of carrying the child. We have all been told by priests, during their Sunday sermons that angels are a spirit. So, how did Mary come to be with child? Did she have a secret lover? If so, who was he? An ecclesiastic man? Of course it was. Immaculate Conception indeed. Who else but a cleric could come up with such a fantastic scheme? This is not blasphemy, it's an attack on ignorance. The truth in never wicked. You don't have to like this revelation, but you do have to admit it was one hell of a clever ruse. One perpetrated by a woman and a cleric. Yet, she was portrayed as being innocent and godly, instead of what she was, an astute and worldly female.

Ana crossed herself again. "María, I cannot listen to this anymore. It a sin to hear these words."

I became angry. "Ana, if you can't listen, then leave! I'm interested in hearing it."

She looked at my wife. If she was expecting a reaction or some sort of support, she didn't get it. She left in a huff.

María looked at me. "Did Gonzo just insult our sacred virgin?"

"No sweetheart. All he is saying is that she was no virgin, and Joseph was a simple minded idiot."

She crossed herself again. "Dios mío, I can't hear this anymore. My ears are burning with the sound of sacrilege."

I placed my arms akimbo. "For God's sake, woman. If you can't hear it, leave."

My sweet wife gave me the finger and left the room. I looked at Hankamon, he showed no emotion, yet he did ask me on the quiet. "Did you really write this?"

I smiled. And beaming with pride, I whispered. "Yes, every word. Gonzo has not change a thing. Please Doctor Switzer, continue reading."

For those of you who read my words, and are appalled at their meaning. For the sake of argument, hear me out. Let's discuss Mary's role as the beneficiary of that ludicrous concept sold to us, by the church. So, let's say that due to her piety she was chosen, and then definitely impregnated by a holy spirit. Instead of raising her persona, she is portrayed as a non-miracle maker, just Jesus' mother. This is a travesty. The writers of the Holy Bible were commissioned by rulers with a mandate. I'm sure part of the directive was to ignore Mary's carnal weakness, and keep her reverence down. It is woman's sexuality that is important here. Without it, the population of earth would not be so fruitful.

They were given two important tasks: One was to reproduce, the other to raise the children into adulthood. Finally, let me say that it's time to deal with an issue that's been giving us concern, and dogging the clerics. I'm talking about perversion. They are abusing our children. A woman in charge of a congregation will not mistreat the child in her care, she will protect him. Everyone, from the Pope on down to the local priest is complicit in this vile behavior. You need to stand with me, and together we can eliminate a system that has outlived its time. A system that is as depraved now as it was then. I will come to you soon, and will speak to you, in the same manner as Jesus spoke to his followers on Mount Sanai. If you come to believe in me, together we will force the church to appoint women into their ecclesiastical ranks. And don't you dare tell me that the Nuns are a testimony to their inclusion. Their orders were created to serve the priests. It's time for these nuns to unshackle themselves, and rise to a level of independence from the avaricious, and perverted males. The time has come to make women bishops! This is the first issue of my manifesto. I will write more to you later.

Dr. Switzer looked at me, and a slight smile graced his face. I took that for approval.

María, who obviously was eavesdropping, came back in. She crossed herself one more time. *"Hijole,* Gonzo is going to go to hell."

The paper caused a lot of commotion. None good. Gonzalez Brynn suffered the degradation of having rotten vegetable thrown to his face. No one would buy his goods anymore. He was called a heretic, and much more. The poor man stopped coming into town.

All I can say about his downfall is, beware of what you wish for. He wanted to start a religious revolution inside a country dominated by the church. Instead of supporting him, the community was attacking him. On hind sight, it was an ill-conceived idea.

No one knew I had written the vile paper, except for Hankamon, and he told no one. No blame fell on me.

Chapter Twenty Eight

The Grim Reaper

I thought loving a farmer's life would not be possible. Yet I was wrong. I can't say what turned things around for me, maybe it was Briana, but I became a better man.

When trouble found me, I was reminded of the folly of remaining in one place for too long.

I remember the weather. It's amazing what you recollect when your life comes to an end. It's nothing like drowning. Done that already. Other than a franticness at the beginning while water sips into your lungs that feeling of desperation soon turns into a pleasant affair. I saw myself floating, heard what I consider to be celestial music. It was a pleasant and calm feeling. The final occurrence came with a visual of a film going backwards, just like a movie roll.

I actually saw my life go before me. I was seventeen at the time, and after thinking the scenario out, recognized what that visual fast track of my life meant. The eyes are the lens, and the brain cells is the film. It's a prerequisite for Judgment Day. All your sins and good deeds are recorded.

You can't believe the hogwash the priests tell you about, if you confess your sins, they will be forgiven. I saw my sins fly by me, and I had spent a lot of time in many a confessional booth. I couldn't believe I had to say all those Hail Mary's and Our Fathers for nothing. What a rip-off.

Once you are aware that you're in the grasp of death, there is no resistance or regret. You're actually good with it. Like a relief. But I didn't die, a Gringo friend named Jack Clark pulled me out of Gatun Lake before the film roll ended.

A blinding flash of light hit me, and I felt sick. I threw up for a while, and lay on the floor of the flat bottom boat we were riding in until I could get up. I never went to a hospital.

This time it was different. Right before death took me, I went through three dissimilar stages. First came the realization that the Grim Reaper had found me. This was quickly followed by a panic to do with not being ready to show your report card to God.

There was no ride down memory lane this time, which was good. No need to bring up all the sins I had committed up to this point. There was a flash of light followed by voices in the background, making you wonder where you where, and who was talking to you.

Today I didn't expect to die. The moment made me appreciate the wind. It had a feel of spring to it. The scent of my Gardenia bush graced my nostrils. The smell of death, for me, was going to be sweet.

That day I came home as usual, and immediately realized something was amiss. After living with the same woman and doing the same things every day, you know when something is wrong. Our dog, lying dead in the front yard was a barnburner. The front door left wide opened was also an ominous sign.

247

ALBERTO ARCIA

I touched the dog, the body was still warm. I froze. This had just happened. I quickly regained my senses and looked around. *Do I have one, two, or more men to deal with?* I looked for a vehicle, but there were none around. That meant it was not the cartel seeking revenge. I breathed a measure of relief. The danger was coming from another source. *But who? Is this a random act or pre-planned? Probably random. Maybe thieves or criminals escaping from a jail or prison. That's why they are on foot, which means they are desperate. That scared me. They probably raped my wife by now, or were in the process. But there were no screams from her or Briana. That told me there was no violence. How do I handle this?*

Being the man that I am, my paranoia had propelled me to hide a weapon outside the house as well as one on the inside. The problem with the outside weapon was that it was not a gun, it was a hand grenade. I had stolen one from the cartel's armory at Deni's farm in Panama.

I walked into the small barn and pulled it out from under a loose floor board. As I walked out, I heard the sound of a much too familiar vehicle. Gonzalez Brynn had arrived in his two ox cart. He had a load of sugar cane in the back. I had ordered it to make rum.

I wanted to yell at him, to warn him, but couldn't. I didn't want to expose my position.

I hoped Gonz would spot the dead dog and realize there was danger. He did see the dog, and immediately went over to it. I guess he noticed the bullet holes because he bolted into the house. Two shots rang out, and he stumbled out, falling on the ground.

He moved so I knew he was not dead, yet. I ran towards the back of the house, trying to stay out of sight.

The cement block house had two front windows, and one in the back. It had no side windows, but it did have a back door. I sneaked a peek from one of the windows and saw the enemy. One man. The hairs on back of my neck stood up. It was none other than Captain Luther Franklyn. He had walked out and was standing over Gonz. I looked for María. Her body and legs were tied to a chair, keeping her hands free to hold on to Briana. *Great. They are both safe. No rape had occurred.* If I would have had a gun I could have flanked the captain and shot him, but the back door was locked and my pistol was in the bedroom, inside the nightstand drawer.

I knew the asshole was going to finish Gonzo off unless I moved fast, so I ran towards the side of the house and yelled, "Hey, captain, fancy seeing you here? The federales couldn't hold on to you, uh?"

He turned my way, pointed his gun and smiled. "Well, well, the moment I have been waiting for has lastly arrived."

I glanced at Gonz, he was bleeding but his body moved. *Good, he's still breathing.* I had to conclude this meeting before he bled out. I knew, based upon the weapon in my hand that I would die today. Soon, as a matter of fact. I just had to figure out how to get the bastard away from my house, my wounded friend, and family.

"Captain, there is no longer a monetary reward for my capture. Blanton paid it to an old, fat, Norwegian man-hunter named Kermit Laarssen. But you know that already. So, if you're after physical satisfaction, I have an offer for you."

As soon as I said it, I brought my left hand out from my back. He noticed the hand grenade and lost his grin.

ALBERTO ARCIA

"What do you think you're going to do with that thing, Alex, blow your family up?"

"Only if I have to."

He must have recognized the seriousness of my voice. Maybe the look in my eyes made him understand I would do it.

"What do you propose, Alex?"

"I do not have a knife. You have a Bowie strapped to your side, and Gonz has a nice one in his boot. I'll remove his, and we can walk out to the middle of the yard. You can put your gun on the ground next to my grenade. Then we can fight to the death. Deal?"

He looked at me. I could tell he was wondering whether I would place the grenade down first, or insist he put his pistol down first. I helped him make the decision.

"Captain, you can't shoot me without the gun, and I can't detonate the grenade without killing me. You need to go first."

He grinned, showing his gold front tooth. "You think a peckerwood like you can take me in a knife fight?"

"Yes, I can." I lied.

He threw his pistol down and unsheathed his Bowie knife. I couldn't believe he actually thought I would fight him. He'd carve me out in six seconds.

When I removed the pin and threw it next to his weapon, he stopped grinning. I walked towards him, holding the grenade, his eyes were showing fear.

He started walking back. *Good boy, just a few more steps.* I needed to move him away from the house.

"Alex, what are you doing? We had a deal."

I gave him an enigmatic smile. "It's not what I'm doing, Captain. It's what you are doing."

250

He gave me a puzzled look. Then his eyes grew big when I dropped the grenade between us.

"Your death will get me a lifetime ticket into the Pearly Gates Brothel and Rum Bar."

With the quickness of a cat, he threw the knife at me, imbedding it into my chest, then he jumped on the grenade. I saw him trying to put the pin in it. He didn't succeed. I saw and heard the blast.

Chapter Twenty Nine

Afterlife

I found myself in front of the now familiar crossroad pole. It still had only two signs. One pointed to Nowhere. The other to the Pearly Gates Brothel and Rum Bar. *I'm home. Thank you, God.*

Before leaving for the whorehouse, I saw something else familiar coming my way. By the manner in which he walked, I recognized him to be Alex, my namesake and a most unpleasant fellow. I waited for him.

He arrived, and looked at me. "Well, hello, Alex. It's so good to see you again. Actually, I'm surprised to see you here. I was told to pick up a soul in need of companionship. But the name I have is not yours. What are you doing here?"

"Good to see you too, Alex. I'm not here for you. I have finally earned a ticket into the brothel. Have you been there lately? And if you have, is Inspector Claude Potignon still there?"

"Yes, I go to the whorehouse on their Open House days. Damien has a wonderful time there."

I smiled and grabbed my crouch. "Yes, John Henry and I will be delighted to be accepted. All the rum I can drink, and all the love action he can handle. Can't wait to get in. How about Claude, is he still there?"

252

"Can't say about him. You better ask the gatekeeper."

"Okay, will do. Say, Alex, who are you waiting for?"

"The name I have is that of a Captain Luther Franklyn. He's been a rather bad man. He's destined to walk the long road with me."

I had to laugh. *Been there done that too.* "Well, I hope he enjoys going to Nowhere with you."

He waved at me, and I at him. Then I picked up the pace, hoping that Cassandra, a voluptuous blonde, and Becky, my ravenous redhead, were still around.

I reached the whorehouse. The stucco walls still looked good, and the neon sign was working. The gate loomed ahead. I saw the guard house and slowed down, wondering whether the querulous Englishman or the obstinate Hungarian would be manning the main gate today.

I knocked on the door. To my surprise, it was a Mexican man. He looked at me with contempt. *"Que carajo quieres aquí?"*

I can't believe my luck. A Mexican huevón manning the gate. "Do you speak English?" I said

"Yes, I do. Do you speak Spanish?"

"Yes, I do."

"So," he leaned my way. "What is the problem here?"

"No hay problema, amigo. I just want to get inside."

"Do you have an invitation?"

Oh God, why is it that you put assholes in charge of venues? Things are supposed to be better here. "What is your name?"

He smiled and removed his *sombrero. "Yo soy Napo Martínez, y tú quién eres?"*

ALBERTO ARCIA

"I'm Alejandro Perez, but you can call me Alex. I died so someone could keep his life. Actually I died so several people could keep their lives. One was a baby girl. I should get a ticket to the Virgin's room."

He leaned my way again. "How you know so much about this place. Been here before?"

I smiled. "More times than I care to admit. *Puedo entrar?*"

"He opened his book and looked in it. "Hum, *amigo*, I don't find you in here."

"How can that be? I saw the explosion before the pain hit me, and the lights went out. Please look again."

"Mister, I don't see your name on the entry list. "You sure the persons you saved were saved?"

"Me cago en Judas!"

"Hey, no cursing here. This job is hard enough without having to put up with people like you. Everyone wants to get in here, but not everyone qualifies. Sorry *amigo*, but you can't get in."

I crossed my arms on my chest and stared at him. He, in turn, looked me up and own.

"Your clothes are scruffy, Alex. If you do get in, you won't get past the door man. This is a high class place. You look shabby."

"Oye, Napo. You have a pending file?"

"Pending for what?"

"A file for people who may not be ready to get in, but will be shortly. I bet you I'm there."

"Who did you say you saved?"

"I saved a man named Gonzalez Brynn."

"Hum. Hey, here you are. But there is a footnote."

Oh, bite me. "What does it say?"

254

"It says that Gonzalez Brynn is struggling to keep his life. He may not make it. You cannot enter if he dies. You must wait until the officer in charge of updates, updates the pending file."

I can't believe this shit.

Oye, amigo, how about the woman and child I saved?"

"It says here that a woman named María Pérez and a baby girl named Briana Pérez were too far from the blast to be killed. Since they were not in real danger, you can't use them to qualify. Sorry, but you can't enter unless this Brynn guy lives for sure."

"Jeez Louise, I got to get past this guy."

"Oye, amigo. You know that even though Gonzalez Brynn was shot twice in the chest and bled badly, Maria was close by and she is a nurse. They had a fast cart nearby, and they were very close to the hospital. He is going to live. She will make sure of that. I can bet my life on it. You should let me pass."

He became upset. "You think I'm a stupid man because I'm a Mexican? Is that it? You don't have a life to bet. And if I let you in before your time, what's in it for me, besides possibly getting fired?"

Okay, here is my chance. The guy looked tired. "Napo, how long a shift do you have to work?"

"Ay, Chihuahua, I'm pulling a double, and I have just started."

"Okay, here is my proposition. You let me in, but not right away. You go take a nap, and I man your post until your shift is over. When you return to meet your relief, Brynn will have been saved, and I will be in the book. You can then officially let me in before anyone finds out I'm standing in for you."

Hey, amigo, you're not as much of a *pendejo* as I thought. You got a deal. He placed his sombrero back on his head, buttoned his *charro* vest and explained the book. "This file here has the names of those that can get in. This one here is for those that qualify for the Virgins room. And this one you already know about. It's for the pending ones."

He smiled, shook my hand, and left. "See you in sixteen hours, amigo. Thanks for helping me out."

I made myself look official, but worried that Napo could get drunk and forget to get back in time. The relief guy might not appreciate me being here. I also worried about my clothes. I did look untidy.

An hour passed. I was eager for my first applicant. Soon I saw a man looking all around. *Yep, here comes the first one.* I closed the door and waited for the knock.

When it came, I opened it. "Hello," I said. "Who are you, and what do you want?"

"My name is Rogelio Cuevas, I'm from Colombia, and I want inside."

A Colombian, what an opportunity. I'm not letting him inside. "I don't seem to have your name on the ledger. You sure you're dead?"

"Yes, I'm dead. That's why I'm here."

"You have a certificate that says you're dead?"

"A certificate? A certificate! *Qué huévason es esta?* I don't have no *pinche* certificate."

"You need to watch your temper and your tongue. I'm the decider here, and I say you can't get in without one. No cursing is allowed here either. This is heaven."

256

The man broke down and started to cry. After a minute he regained his composure. "Please, mister gatekeeper, I have to get in. I took a bullet for a friend and was told this was my level of heaven."

That's more like it. "Listen, Rogelio, I can probably let you in although you're not on the register. Do you have any money?"

He removed his hat and threw it on the ground. *"La MORDIDA? Aquí en el cielo? Qué mariconada es esta?"*

"Listen Rogelio, if I let you in without your name being in the register and someone finds out, then I could be fired. I can't take that risk for nothing."

He picked up his hat, cleaned it and placed it back on his head. Then he stared at me. Probably looking for some good words to give me. He soon found some.

"Mister Gatekeeper, I don't have any money. No one told me I needed some. Please let me inside."

I looked at his hat. It seemed to be a nice one. "What about your hat? Where did you get it?"

He brightened up and quickly removed it. He showed it to me. "I bought it in Baranquilla from Casa Ramirez. It's made from the best palm leaves. The weave is tight. It cost me a small fortune. If I give it to you, will you let me in?"

"Sure. I'll take your hat, and you can have mine. I showed him my worn fedora. "I bought it from Sina Hatters, in Houston. It's made in the USA."

We swapped hats and I pushed the button, opening the gate. He waved and walked in. I looked at my new hat. *Yep, it's a good one.*

ALBERTO ARCIA

A half hour later, another guy came in looking all around. I checked his footwear, Cowboy boots. *I wonder if they are my size.* I closed the door and waited for the knock.

I opened it and smiled. "Howdy, partner. Who are you, and what can I do for you?"

He pointed in the direction of the gate. "Colt McCain. I want in."

I went through the motion of looking in the book. "Sorry, but your name is not on the list."

He looked at me. "Are you a Mexican?"

Oh, give me a break. "Do I look like a Mexican?"

He spat on the ground and grinned. "No, you actually look like an Irishman."

Este huevón me está jalando la pata. "Okay, let's cut to the chase. Your name is not on the list, so you can't get in, unless I let you in."

"Surely you jest."

"You pull my leg. I pull your foot. "That's called a Mexican stand-off. Now, if you tell me your boot size, we can negotiate your entry."

I saw the anguish in his eyes. "I wear size nine." Then with trepidation in his voice, he asked me. "Why the interest in my boot size?"

Yep, a true Texan. I need to up the ante. "You want in, but you're not on the list. You can wait until your name appears, if it does at all, or you can give me your boots. I will give you my hushpuppies. I'm a size nine too. In return, to show my gratefulness, I'll write your name into the book as being qualified for the Virgins room. Deal?"

He removed his cowboy hat and scratched his head. "Is this heaven?"

"It's a level of heaven. I'm presently in charge of admission."

"Is what you're offering me legal?"

"Not really, but if you play along, I can get you in. I have the power of the pen." I waved it at him.

He placed his hat back on and began to scratch his cheek. They guy was not the sharpest tack in the box.

"Listen, Colt McCain, my relief will soon be here, and he'll probably want more than your boots. He may want your hat too. You need to decide."

"You did say the Virgin room, didn't you?"

I smiled. "Yes I did."

He came closer and whispered. "How young are these virgins?"

I was taken aback by the question. *This guy must be a pervert.* I gave him my best scowl. "Why do you ask? How young do you want them to be?"

"Listen, mister gatekeeper, I'm from Texas. The virgins there are very young, barely out of puberty. I'd rather go into a room with more experienced girls."

Hum, I thought the statement over. He makes a good point. I scratched my name out of the virgins room roll. "Okay, I can arrange that. Take off your manly foot wear."

Things were looking up. I loved this job. All I needed now was a good coat. And soon one came my way. A guy wandered in, wearing a nice brown suede sports coat. I closed the door.

The knock came. I opened it. "Hello, state your name please."

"I'm Julius Orange."

ALBERTO ARCIA

Oh, for God's sake. Is this weirdo day or what.
"Really? Shouldn't it be Orange Julius instead?"

He became indignant, gave me a hip sway, and offered a limp hand, which I didn't take. *Never know where that hand has been.*

He looked around with disapproval. "I was told this was to be my final resting place. It does not look like much to me. What kind of establishment in this?"

I smiled and pointed at the flashing neon sign. He looked at it and frowned. "Do they have men in there too?"

Got him. I gave him another smile. "Listen, Julius, this is a brothel and rum bar. The place is loaded with women and rum drinks, but, if you give me your fine sports coat, I'll give you a special pass to the men's room. You'll like it there, they probably serve martinis instead of rum. You will also find a bunch of matadors there with their pants down to their ankles."

He removed his coat quickly and handed it over. I tore a blank page from the book and wrote a note, stipulating he was to be allowed into the Men's room. He wiggled his ass towards the gate. *Jeez, someone sure made a mistake sending him here.* I put the coat on. It fit perfectly.

Since I was now properly attired, I needed to make haste, certainly before someone caught on to my antics. I looked in the book to see if my name finally made it. Yes, it had. Gonzo Brynn did not die.

Elated that my wife and child would be in good hands, I taped a 'closed for lunch' sign on the door, pressed the button, closed the door and walked through the heavenly gates.

Chapter Thirty

A New Employee

The plane touched down in Houston's George Bush International airport. Denise Perez and Ronson Wickert walked out into the terminal and headed to baggage pick-up.

"You sure you can hook me up with a job at Kermit's firm?"

"Not totally sure, Deni, fairly certain is the best I can say. Alex quit, so there should be an opening. If not, you can move into Alex's apartment until such time as you can afford your own."

"Where are you staying?"

"I'm staying there. Alex does not mind me bunking in with him."

She raised an eyebrow. "So, Ronson, you're asking me to move in with you."

"Theoretically, yes. But it's not my apartment."

"Well, I'm inclined to accept the offer since it's my brother's place, but you must promise to keep your eyes and hands to yourself."

"Deal. Now let's rent us a car."

ALBERTO ARCIA

They drove to the Barbary Coast Apartments on San Felipe St.

Upon entering, Deni wrinkled her nose. "Ew, this place stinks."

"Don't be too picky, Deni. It's been closed up for the better part of several months. It's musty. Let's open the windows and let it air out. Tomorrow we go see Kermit and talk about a job."

That evening, after a takeout meal of chicken cacciatore and a bottle of red wine, they bedded down. Deni took Alex's bed, and Ronson slept on the sofa bed situated in the living room. Right around the midnight hour, Ronson heard a shriek. Deni ran into the living room and bounced into his bed.

"What is it?"

"Roaches. Three big ones."

He gave out a silent curse and climbed out of bed. He grabbed a newspaper, rolled it up, and with Deni in tow, went to deal with the bug issue. They skulked into the room. Deni pointed at the roaches who were still on the wall. "There they are, Ronson. Kill them."

"Holy crap. They are huge. Must be tree roaches."

"Ronson, how do you think they managed to get in here?"

"Through the open window. They are fliers."

"No sooner had he said that, when one of the roaches flew straight at them.

He swatted it, but missed. The huge tree roach landed on him. He screamed, "Get off me!" He struck at it wildly with the rolled newspaper.

The bug, looking for a safer place flew at Deni. She screamed, "Kill it! Kill it." In a second she was out of her night clothes.

Ronson jumped on the clothes laying on the floor and started stepping all over them, finally killing the roach.

"Holy crap, Ronson, that thing almost bit me."

"Me too. What a fright."

Deni looked at her crumpled clothes, then at him. "You crushed the roach on my pajamas. I only brought one pair with me."

She saw him stare at her with his mouth open. It was then that she realized all she had on was panties. She covered her breasts. "Close your mouth before you drool, and give me one of your t-shirts."

They both saw the two other roaches move and quickly closed the bedroom door.

"Ronson, I have never seen one that big before. Do you think they eat human flesh?"

"Probably. I wouldn't be surprised. This hellhole they call Houston is covered in bugs. At home, in Switzerland, the bugs all die during winter, so you deal with only young ones. Here, the bugs die of old age."

"So, what do we do now?"

"You can sleep with me on the sofa bed. I will keep my hands to myself."

The following morning they drove to Kermit's office in silence. When they turned on to Richmond Avenue, Deni addressed the uncomfortable subject. "Ronson, don't think that what we did last night is going to be a regular thing between us."

ALBERTO ARCIA

"Of course not, Deni. It was not our fault we screwed. It was due to our bodies being close together all night. It was the tree monsters that caused the love making. The roaches were responsible. We were just victims of circumstances."

"Yes we were. I was scared to death. Tonight we go to the store and buy Flit, and then we spray the whole place down."

They parked the car and whistled as they walked into Private eyes For You, which was Kermit's firm. Ronson introduced Deni to Bernie.

"We already met," she said. "Alex told me she was his sister." She extended her hand, and Deni shook it.

"Where is your brother? Kermit is fit to be tied. He has a job and needs Alex."

"I'm not his keeper."

Ronson walked Deni to Kermit's office, knocked on the door, and walked inside. "Hello, boss. I'm back."

"Humpf. You should have been here days ago. I have a business to run. Where in the devil is Alex?"

"Alex has quit. At least that's what he told me when we last spoke. But I have someone here that can fit right into his shoes." He pointed at Deni, who immediately stood at attention.

"What Alex can do, I can do better."

Kermit looked her over. "Alex was a screw up, but he was lucky. And in this business, luck is important."

She clicked her heels. "Boss, with me, you don't need dumb luck. I am sober, skillful, and a good listener. I can run a field crew for you. That way you can stay here and look at Bernie all day long."

"Humpf. Did she tell you I'm interested in her?"

"No, boss. Alex told me you are screwing her brains out. That is why your wife filed for divorce. And, if you don't mind, I would like to add that you have definitely good taste. I wouldn't mind doing her myself."

Kermit banged his head on the desk, and without looking up, pointed towards the door. "Please leave. You, Ronson. Stay here."

When she left, he looked up. "Who is the cheeky bitch?"

"Her name is Deni. She's Alex's kid sister."

"Is she for real?"

"Yes. Same family tree as Alex. She has his genes. I can vouch for that. You need to hire her."

Chapter Thirty One

Road to Nowhere

I whistled while walking towards the brothel's main door. Couldn't wait to get inside and taste Cassandra's and Becky's sexual charms. I rang the doorbell, and a man dressed in a white suit opened it. He bowed. "Good day," he said.

"Good day to you too. My name is Alex Perez, and I'm ready to indulge in your amenities."

He looked me over. "Nice threads. Where did you get them?"

Oh, no. Someone must have complained about me. What do I do? Think Alex. Think. "If you must know, Napo, the gatekeeper loaned them to me. He said I needed to upgrade my clothes. I hope no company rules were broken by accepting them."

He brought his hand to his chin and began to massage it. "Wait here," he said.

I waited until he disappeared through a glass door. No need to wait. The end result would not be favorable. As I made a move to leave, a man appeared behind me. A big man. *Looks like the bouncer. Shit. Now what?*

I tried to get past him, but no luck. Every time I moved, he did too. He didn't speak, but he smiled a lot. I got the drift. I had to wait there.

The door opened and the guy in the white suit reappeared. "Thank you for waiting. You may take a seat at the rum bar if you like, but please do not go any further. Someone will be coming to speak with you."

I frowned. *So close yet so far.* "Who is coming?"

"A representative of the big guy."

"Are you telling me God has reps?"

"Yes, certainly he does. Many are needed to cover all the different departments. Heaven in a complex system."

I pretended to be disappointed. "Darn, and I wanted to meet him."

"The big guy is a spirit. He does not have a body or face. You will see one of his men in a few minutes. Please go order a drink and put it on his tab."

I thanked the dude and took a seat at the bar. It was a nice long one with a curve at both ends and a nice large mirror. I noticed they carried Ron Abuelo, so I ordered a double. "Straight up," I said.

"Where's your drink card?"

"No one gave me one. The guy in white told me to tell you to put it on the big guy's tab."

"Everyone that orders drinks here has a card. Where is yours?"

I was about to get in his face when a man tapped me on the shoulder. I turned and there stood a sharply dressed man.

"Mister Alex Perez, I presume?"

"Yes, that's me. Who are you?"

ALBERTO ARCIA

"I work for management. The admissions division to be exact."

"Good. Tell this bartender to fix me up with a double rum on the house. And while he's doing it, tell me if my friend, Inspector Claude Potignon, is still here. I would like to see him."

He waved the barkeep away. "The inspector didn't like it here. He applied for a transfer to another department."

"Well, did he get it? And if so, where did he end up?"

"He went to the Celestial winery. He's happy making wine."

"Too bad. I was looking forward to seeing him again."

"Mister Perez. I regret to inform you that your entry here, although legal, has been rejected. No drinks or girls for you today or ever."

"Why? I died so someone else could live. Hell, mister whoever-you-are. I have been trying to die for years so I could get my membership. Who rejected my entry pass?"

He pointed up. "The big guy did it."

"God? No way."

"The big guy has been keeping an eye on you. You have been trying to manipulate the system for quite some time. You being in here is a testament to your success. But your lack of sincerity, plus your penchant for blaming everyone for your misdeeds has cost you entry to the brothel. Napo has already been dealt with. He should have never listened to you. The decision is final. Please leave quietly or I'll have the bouncer put you out."

Downhearted I walked back to the gatekeeper's office. The Limey was working the gate. *Hey, maybe he can give me some advice.* I waved at him.

He saw me and quickly closed the door. I banged on it. "Open up bud. I need to ask you a few questions."

"Go away, mate. You're a bloody bad apple. I have been instructed not to speak to you. Go get lost."

With nowhere to go, and with no one to instruct me as to what lay ahead for me, I walked back to the crossroad pole. After an hour or more, the unpleasant fellow came into view. He was coming my way.

I reached for a smoke but didn't have any. *Damn, I wonder if there are cigarette machines in Limbo.*

"Well, hello there again," said Alex. "I thought you had a ticket to get into the brothel. What happened?"

I gave him a loud sigh. "It's a long, unpleasant story. No need to bother you with it."

"If you had a ticket to ride the women and they wouldn't let you in, the big guy must have gotten involved. What did you do?"

"Listen, Alex, I'd rather not talk about it. Let me just say that I'm not sure where to go now or what to do next. You have any ideas?"

He looked at me with his devilish eyes. "If the big guy rejected you, you can do and go wherever you want."

"Can I go back to my old life?"

He smiled. "No, I'm afraid that is not possible. You are dead to the living, but alive in the afterlife."

"Alex, thanks for the revelation. But I thought you were walking the long road with Captain Franklyn. Where is he?"

He gave me a contorted facial frown. "Not much of a conversationalist. A difficult fellow, truly. I passed him over to an assistant."

ALBERTO ARCIA

"You have assistants?"

"Of course. The list of lost and damned souls is a long one."

"Are you hiring?"

He looked me over. "Hum, I could use more help, and you don't have any strings attached, which means no complications. The paperwork should be a snap. But I usually hire from within."

"Listen, Alex. You are me, and I am you. You're nothing more than a reflection of me. You told me that the last time I was here and we walked the long road together. So, why don't you give me a job? I'm stuck in Limbo. Boring place. Wouldn't wish it on my worst enemy. I'd rather walk to Nowhere with those you'd rather not be with. What do you say, Alex, would you give me a job?"

He massaged his long face while staring at me. "Well, I could use someone who is willing to walk with the women that end up here."

My eyes became big. "You have women come here?"

"Yes. Not as many as men, but enough to warrant a female specialist. I believe you qualify. I could use the help with them. I'd rather do the men."

"I don't know how you can be a reflection of me and not like women, Alex, but I'm good with it. I can walk two or three females at the same time. Please hire me."

"Okay. Although it's highly irregular to employ an outsider, I'll do it. Alex, you are hired."

I jumped for joy. "Can I thank God for this?"

"No, this is my realm. You can thank me. I'm the decider here. But to stay employed, you must obey the rules."

Oh, no, he's going to rain on my parade. "And these rules are what, exactly?"

"You must not make their walk a pleasurable one. You must molest them, insult them, make fun of their femaleness, and generally give them a bad time. Make them do things they would rather not do. Give them pain. Can you do that, Alex?"

"Does a bear shit in the woods, Alex?"

He smiled, showing me his ugly, yellow, pointy teeth. Then he gave me his arm. "Come walk with me, Alex."

I skipped a step, and joined him, but did not take his arm. The guy was sweet on me, and I wasn't going there.

As we promenaded down a road that led nowhere, I began to think of a way that I could bed these wayward women without the loving being classified as a good time. *Maybe I can tie them up, or ride them around using a horse whip.*

"Alex," said Alex.

"What?"

"I can read your thoughts."

"Augh!"

"If you are going to be my assistant, you can't break the rules."

Crap. This is not going to be a lovely walk-in-the-park. More like a barefoot stroll down the primrose patch. "Alex, are you the complete boss here, or do you have to answer to the big guy?"

"I am in charge, but the big guy is my boss. He sets the rules and gives me the latitude I need to apply them. I have control over the enforcement."

271

"If that's the case, we ought to be able to modify those rules a bit without suffering any transgression. Is that possible?"

He stared at me. "What do you have in mind, Alex?"

"Explain those rules to me again, in detail please."

"The men that make it to this level of hell are straight, macho, redneck men. They do not like other men to touch them. So, I touch them over and over again. Wherever I please."

"Alex, can you, and do you make love to them?"

"Yes, it's my favorite mode of punishment. They hate that the most."

"What about the women? Talk to me about them."

"They are bad, gay souls. Men haters. Heavy on the butch side. It's going to be part of your job description to make love to them."

Butchy women are ugly and totally sexless. Bummer. "Listen Alex, I have an idea I'd like to bounce off you."

"If it's not going to get me into trouble with the big guy, I'm all ears Alex."

"Since we're going to run the joint, why not add into the daily grind a little pleasure for us? Surely the big guy is busy enough with running his vast, complex, establishment to keep you under constant observation. I'm sure he has a level of trust in you that will allows us to work under the radar. We could bend the rules a little bit."

He looked at me and again began to massage his long face. "Alex, please continue. You have my attention."

"If you are really in charge, which I know you are. Why couldn't we sneak in one gay dude, say for every ten straight ones? The same for the women. Give me one that

272

likes a man. Making love to someone that appreciates it, is a wonderful thing."

"We? Did you say, we?"

"Yes, Alex. You, me, and the mouse in my pocket. Can we do it?"

"Keep talking. I'm liking what you are proposing."

"Good. Now, if nothing happens to us, then maybe we can add two good ones for every ten bad ones. Wouldn't it be great if you got to love two gay guys instead of the ornery straight ones?"

"Yes, it would be nice. I would love that very much."

"Good, then its settled. Please arrange it. I want two horny girls added to my list of men haters."

He smiled, showing me those ugly pointed teeth again. "Alex, I have the feeling this is going to be the beginning of a wonderful relationship. I'm going to like having you here."

"Likewise, Alex. You and me, we're gonna be tight."

"Ooh, Alex, I like that. Holding you tight will please me very much."

"Keep your hands to yourself. I'm not that type of guy."

Chapter Thirty Two

An Unprecedented Decision

In the far corner of the main administration building, a meeting was taking place between the Big Guy, his main man, and the person in charge of supervising the souls.

Saint Joseph was sitting, and Saint Christopher was standing next to the audio apparatus. God was speaking to them. "I can't believe that neither one of you is aware of the goings-on on the long walk of hell. *El diablo* has found a friend, and together, those two are abusing the rules of intention.

Joseph looked at Chris. He in turn had to speak. "Mister Big Guy, I am to blame here, and for my lack of supervision, I take full responsibility. But, I never expected anyone to befriend the unpleasant fellow. He is a nasty, ornery, and slimy spirit. And I'm not going to mention his hideous affection for perversion."

"That is precisely the issue here. We are sending bad souls there. Souls in need of suffering, yet there seems to be very little of that going on. What is going on is a lot of whistling."

"Did you say whistling?"

"Yes, Joseph, whistling. They are having a good time in hell, and why is that?"

Silence.

"Somebody better speak or I'm reassigning both of you."

Saint Christopher spoke. "A request came from Satan, through the proper channels for a new assistant. I brought it to Joseph and he approved it."

"Who is the new hire?"

"A soul stuck in Limbo by the name of Alejandro Perez."

"Are we talking about Alex? The one who tried to sneak into my brothel?"

"Well, he arrived with the proper papers. He actually had the right to enter the brothel. You had him removed."

"I had my reasons. How did he end up in Limbo?"

"I couldn't send him straight to hell. He had earned the right to join us in the seventh level of heaven. So, I let him wander into Limbo. Hoping he would find a place. Not sure how he befriended the unpleasant fellow."

."Who is the rep in charge of doing the actual soul visits on the long road?"

Saint Joseph cleared his throat. "That person is my nephew."

"You hired your nephew? You brought nepotism into heaven?"

Yes, I did, and for that I apologize, but we're a big family here so I didn't think anything of it."

"I want this situation fixed. I will deal with Satan personally. You, Joseph, you deal with *el diablo*'s friend and with your nephew. Remove both of them from their position.

I'm disappointed in you, Joseph. You are my main spirit. How could you fail me in this manner?"

Joseph again cleared his throat. "I'm going to wear a hair shirt tonight and every day from here on."

"That will not be necessary. Just get rid of those two; punish them for their wrongdoings."

"What do you have in mind?"

"I'm thinking banishment. Get rid of the bad apple in hell, and send your nephew with him back to the land of the living. Good riddance to both."

"God."

"Yes Joseph."

"They both cleared the portal into the afterlife."

"I'm giving you the key to reverse the process. Do it."

"Your wish is my command."

"It better be. If I have to speak to you again, you will be replaced."

Before Joseph could say anything more, the audio went blank. Both of them were left speechless. They looked at each other. Joe spoke.

"Chris, go and fetch me Jacob. He has messed up for the last time."

Saint Christopher left the office and found the young man. He was playing chess with Saint Luke.

"Jacob, Saint Joseph wants to see you in his office, now."

The look in Christopher's eyes made him uneasy. "Am I in trouble, sir?"

"I'm afraid so."

With trepidation in his heart, Jacob knocked on the door.

"Come in."

276

He opened the door and there stood Saint Joseph. Without speaking, the gruff old man pointed to a chair.

"What's up, Uncle?"

"Don't call me uncle. Call me sir."

"Yes, sir. Sorry, sir. What can I do for you, sir?" By the look on Saint Joe's face, Jacob knew he was in trouble. "What's this all about, sir?"

"Let me cut to the chase. The big guy is upset with you."

"Me? He's upset with me? I didn't realized he knew I existed. What's the problem?"

"You are the angel who is supposed to be in charge of the dark division, are you not?"

"Yes, I am. Is there a problem I'm not aware of?"

"Jacob, let me put it bluntly. Have you ever associated whistling with pain and torture?"

"I don't believe that is possible."

"It pains me to say that your supervisory skills are the pits. A blind man can see more than you. I can't believe you are family. Your job is to keep an eye on things there, and you have been neglectful. Therefore, I have been instructed to remove you from the position."

He knew it was best to keep his mouth shut, at least until the whole mystery revealed itself.

"The rules of enforcement there have been abused, broken, manipulated, and heavens know what else. God is upset."

Jacob, with a nervous countenance, stared at Saint Joseph.

"I have been instructed to kick one of the resident assistants out. A soul named Alex Perez will be sent back to

Earth. God wants him out of here, and you will be going with him."

"To Earth? The big guy is sending me to Earth. Why?"

"It's your punishment for not doing your job. Sorry, nephew, but it's a done deal. You will be in charge of keeping Alex Perez from losing his life and ending up here again. Prepare to leave immediately."

"But this has never been done before. No one is allowed to go back after they crossed the blinding portal into the afterlife."

"You are dumber than a turkey, Jacob. No one ever questions God. This is his realm. But you're correct. This is an unprecedented decision."

"Yes sir. Thank you."

"Don't thank me, nephew, this is a punishment. You are being banished from heaven to spend time in the company of a very unpleasant fellow. It's called a lousy assignment. Go now and visit with Chris. He will let you know how to remove him from here, and what you need to do when back with the living. I will speak with my sister."

Jacob left his uncle's office and entered Christopher's office. "I was told to report to you, sir."

"Have a seat, and please take notes. You are being sent on a most unusual assignment. Frankly, and no insult intended, you have been nothing but a screw up since you arrived here. This task at the outset may appear to be easy, but in reality it's probably more than your lame brain and lazy attitude can handle."

"Thank you, sir."

"Don't thank me, Jacob. I'm insulting you."

"But you said you didn't mean to."

278

"Yes, right. Okay, hear me out. The big guy wants you to keep Alex Perez from dying. He has become a *persona non grata* here. Go and prepare for the new mission."

"Will I have any of my angel powers?"

"Yes, those will be necessary, especially with an errand such as Alex."

"Sir, may I make an observation?"

"If you must, Jacob, please do."

"Will the ability to not die not embolden the man?"

"There lies the nut of your job. You must do it in a fashion where he maintains his feet well grounded. He can't know he can't die. Understood?"

"Sir. Will I ever be allowed back here?"

"If you can keep that scoundrel from showing up back at the brothel gate, we will, at some point in the future, send a replacement."

"Thank you. Sir."

"Stop thanking me. I'm banishing you."

"Alex, you have gotten me into a lot of trouble!"

"No way could that be possible. What happened?"

"The big guy not only dressed me down, but he has slapped a number of harsh restrictions on me."

"Are you telling me somebody snitched, and we're losing our hard-earned privileges?"

"Yes and more."

"Why?"

"Why do you think? You made me abuse the rules. That's why. And now we're being punished."

"Did you say we?"

279

"Oh, yes. You are being sent back to the land of the living."

"What? No way?"

"Yes way, Alex. You are being kicked out of the afterlife."

"How can I be sent back? I have been dead a long time. My body is decomposed by now. Are you telling me I'm going to be given a new one? Can I pick it?"

"No, Alex. Please listen to me. Time here is ephemeral. It's different from Earth time. Here, it may appear to you that you been here a long time, but in actuality, you have just recently died. Your body is still warm."

"But a grenade blew me to pieces."

"A few nasty cuts here and there. The blade stuck in your chest will leave a ghastly scar, but you're a resilient man."

Alex placed his arms akimbo. "How did we screw up?"

"I listened to you! Now I'm being punished. This misfortune is all your fault, Alex."

"You can't hang this totally on me, Alex."

"Yes I can, and I will. I told the big guy you're to blame."

"I can't believe you. One little shortfall, and you throw me under the bus. Some friend you have turned out to be. I made things better for us"

"Better for you! I was doing fine without you."

Oh, bite me.

"I told you I can read your thoughts."

"Sorry. Who is taking me back, you?"

"No, I've been grounded. Someone else has that assignment. Get ready to leave, and let me say that I'm sorry to have allowed myself to get involved in your schemes. You are a bad influence. Good riddance, Alex."

Miffed, I waited for my traveling companion to appear. While killing time, I began to contemplate my recent calamities. *First I can't get into the damn brothel, even though I have a valid pass to enter. Then I'm stuck in Limbo. Nothing going on there, so I make a move up and go to work with the overseer of hell. And, just when things were going good for me, a whistleblower ruins it.*

My new cohort finally showed up. He introduced himself. "Hello, Alex, I'm Jacob. Let's walk to the crossroad pole. I'll explain the rules of passage on the way."

"Who picked you to be my escort?"

"My uncle, and for reasons that I'd rather not disclose, so don't press me."

"What am I to expect?"

"When we get to the pole, you will begin to hear words coming from afar. Then you will wake up in a hospital operating room with people around you. Your body has been mangled up a bit, but with proper care, exercise, and a plastic surgeon, you will soon be your old self again."

"Am I going to remember any of this? And what will happen to you?"

"You will remember nothing. God has been trying to make you realize the error of your ways, which is why he allowed you to keep your mind. But he's seen the error of his ways. You are an incorrigible fellow. You will no longer remember the brothel, me, or anything else. You are being exiled, and me with you. But you will not remember me."

ALBERTO ARCIA

We arrived at the time travel pole. I stood there, and just as he said, words began to float into my mind. I could hear a woman crying. It was my wife, María.

"Alex, please hang on. I love you. Don't die on me."

A blinding flash of light hit me. Then I opened my eyes and saw Doctor Hankamon Switzer. He was standing by me. Next to him was a woman I did not recognize. She was hovering over me. Her cleavage caught my attention.

Those puppies were almost in my face. The image of Nurse Miriam's enchanting and luscious tits came to mind. These were not as big, and they were not covered in freckles either, but they appeared tasty enough. I licked my dry lips and threw caution to the wind.

With my wife in the room, I buried my nose in those breasts, and gave them a wet tongue kiss.

"*Bastardo*," she yelled, and slapped me.

Maria jumped on the brazen woman, knocking her to the floor. A fight ensued. As I saw the hair pulling, cursing, scratching, kicking and biting, the notion that I didn't die worried me. Yet I could tell my sweet wife still loved me. She was making mincemeat out of the woman's whose breast I boldly tasted.

I looked to see if Gonzo was around. Did not see him. I started to come out of my anesthesia, my stomach began to worry me.

Soon someone came to me with a bucket." Mister Perez, please vomit here. I don't want to mop the floor."

What a cheeky fellow. "Who are you?"

"I'm the new maintenance man. My name is Jacob."

The End

282

Other Works by Alberto Arcia

2009 – **Cut and Run** – The Misadventures of Alex Pérez

2012 – **In Search of High Ground** – The Amorous Antics of Alex Pérez

2013 – **An Ill Wind that Blows no Good** – Alex Pérez Mexican Adventures

2013 – **Marika and the Dragon & Other Fantasy Tales**

2016 – **Jana of Barkom** – Vol. 1 Adventures of the Danube Sisters

2016 – **Alexis Aragon of Fern** – Vol. 2 Adventures of the Danube Sisters

2016 – **Chasing the Moolah** – Alex Pérez goes to Afghanistan

2016 – **Stories Long and Short**

2017– **Korina, Queen of Fern** – Vol. 3 Adventures of the Danube Sisters

2017 – **Isla Grande** – Alex Pérez goes to Panamá

2018 – **View from a Pedestal** – Liberty Enlightening the World – written with Paul A. Bussard

2018 – **For the Love of Lust** – The Seduction of Leopoldo

About the Author

Alberto Arcia is a citizen of the Republic of Panama, and a legal resident of Texas. He is a former member of The Woodlands Writers Guild, and a multi-genre writer. His specialty is bawdy humor. He lives in Plantersville, with his wife, Betsy.

ALBERTO ARCIA

Made in the USA
Monee, IL
15 November 2020